THE GREEN BANANAS

To Adam,

Carpe vinum!,

[signature]

THE GREEN BANANAS

JAMIE ZECCOLA

To Srebrina,
and the fire in your belly!

*"What has become perfect, everything
ripe—wants to die!
...But everything unripe wants to live:
alas!"*
- Nietzsche

*T*he house, the house, the house is on fire!

We are driving too fast down a narrow country road, on our way to a funeral, in the tiny village of *Stoil Voivoda*. Our so-called summer *vague-action* (that's what my wife called it) to Bulgaria was supposed to be a break from everything that troubled us back in New York: the fat cats, dirty rats, smelly taxi cabs, nasty deli clerks, and all the dog shit. We wanted to forget about that stuff, because it made our lives seem so small and senseless. What can I say, I wanted to relax, so I couldn't wait to get to the Black Sea.

Death, they say, is nothing to *joke* about. Some may differ on the subject, like *me*, and say that it is *all* to be joked about–especially, the unbearable *heaviness* of being.

I used to love Milan Kundera, but now, I can't stand the man! All the political bullshit in his books, about *love, unknown consequences,* and *the breathless soul of man*, is just too much to swallow. Don't get me wrong, *The Unbearable Lightness of Being* is a fantastic novel, I've read it many times before, but this *time*, on this trip, I had no desire to read it.

My dealer, Alabaster, knows all about the politics of the art world–I do not! I should stop pandering to the mob, to the man–in–the–street, he says, which is a permanent liability for a painter, like me, who is in need of new collectors. What I really need is a pair *new* eyes, unspoiled *eyes*, that can see clearly into my paintings. A painter is a *slave* to a vision, but his dealer, well, he is the *master* of it. I better shut up, I always talk too much, I don't want to spill the beans, if you know what I mean.

The only way up is down, the only way over is across, and the only why is when, I told myself, as the car brakes began to squeal. Everything is in slow motion: I see a white light, shooting stars, a black hole. I can barely remember anything, so most of the trip is a blur to me.

I am lying on the back seat of a black Audi, which is being driven by my wife's brother, Yanko. We are on our way to their grandmother's funeral. Bulgaria is the *perfect* place for a funeral, I thought, as I looked out the window. But I had imagined a green and pristine land, not this filthy road littered with broken glass and piles of trash. *Don't be sad, your grandmother lived a long and happy life*, I told my wife. She didn't say a word, she ignored me like I wasn't even there. It was really hot, it must have been 100 degrees inside the car, so maybe the heat was getting to her. Before we left, we made up a plan: fly into Sofia, spend one night there, go to the village for the funeral, then drive to the Black Sea. That was our so-called *plan*, but plans can change, so I was ready for anything. Well, it wasn't exactly a funeral, my wife called it a *Sbogom*. It is when the soul–after forty days of being trapped inside of a dead body–is finally free of its mortal coil. Her soul will be *set free*, my wife told me, only *after* the forty days. Then, after her soul is set free, we would drive to the coastal town of Primorsko to meet up with Yanko's wife and kids. That was our original *plan*, but like most original plans, they change pretty fast. When we finally arrived at the Sofia Airport, my wife's parents were waiting for us at the gate. Of course, they had bells and whistles on, and they wouldn't stop talking. Let me tell you, there is nothing worst than a family reunion in a foreign airport. There are too many hugs, too many kisses, too many tears, and too many questions about America. I was dead tired, I got no sleep on the plane, I didn't want to talk, so I kept my mouth shut. After we piled into their car, a tiny white Lada, we finally got onto the highway. I've heard so many horrible stories about this Russian-made car, but I have to say, to ride in one was a real treat. It might be the worst car ever made, that's what some people say, but I didn't care, I had a blast while I was in it. I had so much fun, it was like being on a rollercoaster with no seat belts and no brakes. As we rumbled through the outskirts of Sofia, the engine wouldn't stop smoking, so the exhaust fumes started to make me feel nauseous. The jet lag had suddenly hit me, I felt sick, I wanted to vomit, but I couldn't. I tried to ignore my symptoms, so I rolled down the window to get some air. Then I grabbed a book from my bag; I always bring books on my vacation, but I never actually *read* any of them. They usually stay in my bag, or they fade in the sun. I couldn't stop laughing at my wife's parents, who were now screaming at each other in Bulgarian (which I barely speak). Like most in-laws, they were hilarious, so they made me laugh. I should read a book this time, I thought, it might do me some good. I had *The Unbearable Lightness of Being* (*TULOB*) in my hand, but I was too tired to open it, so I closed my eyes. As soon as I did, I started to see the characters from the novel, one by one, in my mind. I can't forget them, because they have been burnt into my brain. What can I say, if the eternity of return is infinite, like Kundera says, then I was *Tomas*. Of course, my wife is *Tereza*. And her father must be *Franz*; but her mother didn't seem like *Sabina* to me, she was too reserved. I will have to find a Sabina for my story, I told myself, to finish the circle. The ride to Yanko's apartment was treacherous, as the car got filled with smoke, the air got thinner by the minute. When we finally got to his apartment, it was two in the morning, we were exhausted, and we were ready to sleep. After a glass of wine and some chit chat, we went straight to bed. Her parents drove back home, and they would meet us later, at the funeral. I was in some deep sleep, before I woke up in a fright.

Now, I was wide awake, so I walked over to the window and I looked out. I couldn't believe it, there was a pack of wild dogs playing by the railroad tracks. Yes, that's right, *a pack of wild dogs*. I know Kundera would never use a pack of wild dogs in a novel, but I'm not Kundera, so deal with it. And these dogs looked mad, they were ragged, beaten down, as they ran around in circles. Most dogs bark, but these dogs didn't make a sound, they were completely silent. They were mangy, nothing but skin and bones, and their silence made me nervous. Something about them didn't seem right, so I closed the window and I went back to bed. I didn't want to think about dogs, I wanted to sleep and count sheep, but I couldn't, so I just stared at the ceiling. I didn't move a muscle, I felt like a spider waiting for his dinner. We were staying in Yanko's bedroom, and sleeping in his bed, which made me a little uncomfortable. We were made to sleep in his bed, he insisted, and he wouldn't take *no* for an answer, so I had no other choice. Yanko spoke in broken English, mixed with Bulgarian slang, it was really hard to understand him. Most of his words got lost in the translation, but after a while, I got used to him. He seemed mad, he kept pointing at his bed, telling me: *Leka nosht, leka nosht, leka nosht!* He was pissed off, he wouldn't shut up, it was ridiculous. It was an old Bulgarian tradition of some kind, he said, so I just went along with it, I was too tired to fight with him. His wife and kids were already at the Black Sea, *they couldn't wait any longer*, Yanko said with a smile, *so they left!* As I sat on his bed, I was thinking the same thing, but I couldn't leave, I was trapped here. I don't know about you, but I hate sleeping in someone else's bed, it's a torture beyond belief. It's so cruel the way the mattress curves to the exact contours of the bed owner's body, and not to yours. I wanted to sleep, but I couldn't sleep, I was wide awake. My wife was sleeping like a baby, so I got back up and I looked out the window again. I couldn't believe my eyes, the dogs were gone, but now, there was a bloody mess. One of the dogs had been run over, and it was sliced completely in half. There was no more *middle*, it was gone, only the top and bottom remained. The middle part of the dog had vanished into thin air. *Where did it go?* I don't know where it went, but there was blood and guts everywhere. The sound of death has an eerie silence, you can hear it, and I heard it blowing in the wind. The street was desolate, the other dogs were nowhere to be seen, they had disappeared into the night. The pack will come back, I thought, when the coast is clear, so I stood there for a long time, waiting for them, but the pack never came back. After I closed the window, I went back to bed. As my sleep turned into dream, I was out, and I slept like a baby. I had the same dream that I always have: I'm standing in New York City, with my wife by my side, and the streets are deserted, with no people, and only the animals are left. In my dream, we are being chased through the city, by a white rabbit, who keeps begging us to have tea with him. After we oblige the rabbit, we sit down in a cafe and we have tea with him. I don't know why, but I always wake up at the same exact moment in my dream: just when the tea touches my tongue. What can I say, it sounds silly, but I never get *beyond* the rabbit, so I don't know what comes *after* the rabbit. And that's when I woke up again. As soon as I stood up, I went back over to the window again. The sun had just broken over the horizon, it was shining bright yellow, and I had to squint my eyes to see. As I shielded the glare of the sun with my hand, I could see a little better, so my view got better. I couldn't believe my eyes, the dead dog was gone. Yes, both halves, the top and bottom, were no longer there. Maybe the pack did come back, while I was sleeping, and they took their comrade away. Or, maybe, in the middle of the night, a street sweeper had come by and cleaned up the mess. But, then again, who would take the time to do such a thing? I had no clue, it was a mystery, and it would stay a mystery, because I didn't have the time to waste. Some mysteries are like unripe fruit, they linger on the vine for years, without an answer, they're unable to drop. Then, one day, the mystery is finally solved, when the ripe fruit falls to the ground. It's like a bad joke, that's told over and over again, you know the punchline, but you still laugh at it. The biggest mysteries usually turn out to be the most funny. They're beyond funny, I mean, they're totally absurd! All funerals are absurd, but not all of them are funny. At some moment during the ceremony, an absurd thing will usually happen, then the laughter will erupt. Sometimes, you have to wait for the *funny* to happen, because funny takes its own sweet time. A funeral is a comedy of errors, mixed with a bunch of nuts, and filled with sweet sorrow. A funeral will never let me down, I always have a fun time, and I always learn something new. A funeral is like a bad play, it's too good to be true, but you can't wait until it's over. I adore bad theater, because it makes me feel so alive. When the play begins, I sit in my seat like a good boy, as I wait for the fun to wash over me. Let me tell you, there's nothing better than a shitty play. I don't know why I like them so much, it's a guilty pleasure, it's like being in heaven and hell at the same time. The last bad play that I had the pleasure to see is also one of the shittiest ones ever. Yes, you got it, *Chicago* is a big pile of shit! I swear, the smell of it has never left my nostrils. But I loved every minute of it, I swear, I had the time of my life. When I see a really great play, I usually forget about it, but when I see a shitty one, it sticks in my brain like glue. I can remember every last detail of *Chicago*, I still think about that night, it was raining, my sister was with me, and Alabaster was there, too! Every dance routine from that piece of shit was a disaster: the dancers were bored and worn out, so they were always one step behind the music. My sister loved the play, and she wanted me to love it, too, but I hated it, so I played along with the charade. Yes, I told her that I loved the play, but she didn't believe me, she knew me well, I was her brother, so I couldn't hide the truth. I have a love-hate relationship with *Chicago*, I love to hate it, and it hates to love me. While I was sitting in the back seat of the car, I could hear my wife's conversation with her brother. They were speaking in a familiar slang that only a sister and brother can speak; they weren't talking to each other, they were dissecting each other. Most siblings wage a never-ending war with their own family, and my wife and Yanko were no different, they were fighting like dogs. Every family discussion is a song and dance number, and they always have some strings attached. Yes, I am my mother's son, my father's son, my sister's brother, my brother's brother. Everyday is a battle, a war, and a little blood is always expected. I've heard this slang before, with the weeping *p*'s, the rolling *r*'s, and the stinging *s*'s, so their conversation had an unmistakable ring to it. They used acute adjectives to nullify the nouns, and the polished prepositions rolled off their tongues like bullets from a gun. They had the right amount of irony for good measure, but not enough resentment for real pleasure. I didn't want to listen to them, but what could I do, I was trapped in the car. I can't forget *Chicago,* I still remember every last detail about that night. We sat in overpriced balcony seats, with a great view, that my sister had bought, but the big brother in me wanted to scold her for paying so much for them. She's a big spender, so she likes to get the very best seats in the house. I can't blame her, but I still can't believe how much money she spent, it was ridiculous! As I sat in my seat, giggling to myself, I watched the performers deliver a stale bag of tricks. I was in tears, I couldn't stop laughing, and I had a silly grin on my face

7

for the entire play. It was really bad, I wanted to jump off the balcony, to end it all right there, in front of my sister and Alabaster, but I didn't. *Chicago* is a real mess of a musical, the story is thin, and the dancing is lame. When I saw it, I jumped right in, so I had a swell time. Yes, I really wanted to jump, but I hate heights, so I froze. I didn't know what to do, I felt confused and lost. A great play will never cause such a desperate feeling in me, only a shitty one can make me freeze like this. But before I could jump, Alabaster beat me to it, he fell first. Either, I was too slow, or, Alabaster was too fast. Well, you can say, a sneeze changed everything; in a middle of the play, Alabaster suddenly sneezed. In a split second, the momentum of his body jerked him forward and he fell over the balcony railing. He flipped through the air like a pufferfish looking for water. It didn't take him long to reach the lower level, when he hit the ground he made a loud thump as he belly-flopped onto the floor. Luckily, he landed in the aisle, on the carpet, and not on top of anyone. The audience gasped all at once, then the house lights came back on and the music stopped. Even the actors on stage were in complete shock. As Alabaster lay motionless, nobody knew what to do, so he was on his own. He was down for only a few seconds, then he jumped back up to his feet; he seemed a little stunned, but he didn't appear to be that hurt. As he brushed himself off, he looked right at me, then said: *The show must go on!* The audience let out a communal sigh of relief; when the usher ran over to help, he waved him away. *Don't worry, I'm fine*, Alabaster declared, *I can find my way back.* Then he slowly walked up the stairs and he found his seat. When he finally sat down, he waved to the audience, and he gave us a big smile. Some people started clapping for him, even a few of the actors gave him the thumbs up, which made me lose my shit. I was in tears, it was too funny, I couldn't stop laughing at him. But my sister was not happy, she was embarrassed and appalled by Alabaster's *stupid* stunt. I was used to his stupid tricks, but my sister wasn't, so she was out of her element. Let me tell, Alabaster loves to be in the *thick* of things, in the *middle* of it all, if you know what I mean. *I'm a yeasayer*, he likes to say, *so I know no other way.* After the unexpected delay, the house lights when back off and then they finished the play. I should have jumped, but I didn't, so I had to sit through the rest of *Chicago*. Yes, it was a slow and cheesy torture, but I loved every minute of it, because a bad play is a great night out. I was tired of being in the back seat, I needed a break, so I was pretty happy when we pulled up to the cemetery gate. Their grandmother's ceremony would begin in an hour, which gave me some time to relax. As I stood there in the blazing sun, I thought about Alabaster's advice to me: *Whatever you do, never hold anything back.* So, in that vein, I won't! What can I say, most art dealers are futurists, who live in a distant past. Most of them (the ones that I know) are sloppy shopkeepers, messy managers, with a running line of credit. But not Alabaster, he keeps a very clean house, and he thinks only of the present moment. In this world, there's only a few dealers that are worth dealing with, and Alabaster is one of them. Most dealers are pencil pushers, with a knack for small talk and the gift of gab. Alabaster is a different breed, his word is his word, so I take comfort in his integrity. He's beyond book smart, he reads everything, he's a self-confessed *bibliophile*. He has one of the biggest libraries that I know of, and I made a deal with him a long time ago: I supply him with paintings, he supplies me with books. I have all access to his library, day or night, I can run wild through his huge collection of books. Alabaster is a *collector* by trade, so he loves to collect the rarest books. He has all the so-called *classics*, and most of the non-classics, too! Yes, he knows a good book when he reads one, so he has thousands of them. I'm lucky to have a key to this library, because I can read almost anything. Let me tell you, a great novel can linger in your mind for years. But today was different, I thought, I didn't want to think about *TULOB*, so I didn't. The ceremony started right on time, and my wife's mother was the first one to speak. She began by reciting a poem about her own mother. Her voice had a very high pitch to it, so she squealed like a wounded bird. Her poem was about a young girl and her mother, but I could barely understand her, because she was crying so much. To hear one mother, speak about another mother, in such a tender way, was quite emotional, so it brought tears to my eyes. It wasn't a long poem, but it was long enough to get her *point* across. Unlike so many other poems, which beat around the bush, this one was *in* the bush. After she finished, another woman got up to speak, but before she could get a word out, my wife leaned over to me and she said: *It's my cousin Vera, she's a witch!* A witch? I didn't care if she was a witch, I was too tired to care, so I let her talk. I must admit, when Vera began her soliloquy, she did cast a spell over me. I don't know what it was about her, but I was mesmerized by the tone of her voice. What kind of witch is she, I thought, a good witch or a bad witch? Her story was full of good and evil, so I think she was a little bit of both. She was a good storyteller, but she used far too many metaphors, and I got lost in the words. A witch is a witch is a witch, I guess, so Vera was a witch. But *TULOB* doesn't have a witch in it, so why would I want to read it again? It didn't make much sense to me. What if I wrote *Vera* into the novel? She could be a nurse–or, another doctor, and she could even work in the same hospital as Tomas. But I can't change *TULOB*, not now, and it's not my novel to change, I thought. I could reread it, I told myself, if I had enough time, but I don't, so I won't! Yes, it would be fun to have a Vera to play with, especially a *witch*, but Kundera's plot would have to change too much, and that wouldn't be fair to him. It's out of the question, I said, and I don't have the heart for it. Why should I care about *TULOB*? It's been nothing but a thorn in my side, and I'm tired of it. Kundera has seduced me for the last time, I thought, *I'm done with him*, I mumbled to myself. Let me tell you, I won't get fooled again, I swear, his words won't have any control over me. Vera spoke in a sleepy monotone, so she sounded like a hypnotist. She was beating around the bush, but I didn't care, the more she talked, the more I listened. Her story was silly, but her words were not. As her lips moved, I listened intently, I couldn't take my eyes off of them. The witch was working her magic, it was all hocus pocus, I had no chance. To understand her story was beyond my reach, but I was stuck in this graveyard, so I was here for the long haul. After Vera told the story about her grandmother, she started to tell one about her grandfather, who had died a few years ago. He was a Lieutenant in the Bulgarian Army and a Cold War veteran; I'd seen his old uniform back in their Sofia apartment. My wife wanted to take a few of her grandmother's things back home with her, for keeps sake, she said, so we had stopped by her grandparent's apartment on our way out of town. They had been part of the Sofia elite, so their apartment was very opulent. I could imagine it back in the day, when it was filled with the movers and shakers of the city. But now, the place was a total mess, and it needed a good cleaning. As we sifted through their cluttered apartment, for something of value, we searched stacks of picture books, piles of clothes, and empty suitcases. My wife wanted to find anything that had a special meaning, but she was having a hard time finding *it*. It only took ten minutes in the apartment until my wife lost it, and she burst out crying. *My grandmother died right here in this apartment*, my wife said. Their apartment was dark and dingy, it smelled like moth balls and rose oil; every dusty corner was another reminder of the future dustiness to come, it was a depressing place. My wife's grandparents had taken a ton of pictures, hundreds of them, thousands, so the walls were covered with nothing but photographs. But there was something strange about them all, in every photo, they were in the same exact pose. Every country, every city, every beach, I guess, was worth that same stupid pose. If every picture tells a story, as they say, then these pictures told the same story. People experience what they want to experience, their stories change, but their memory stays the same. Once they see it in their mind, it's over, they'll never see it any other way. Yes, the pictures on the wall were proof that they had been to these places, it was all documented, but what did they do there? Their apartment was one big scrapbook; they had been to every continent and too many countries to name. *Look at them in Greece, in Spain, in Italy, in France, in Japan,* my wife gushed. These photographs meant nothing, I thought, only that they were there in the flesh. People visit foreign countries all the time, but most of them can't even remember a single thing about the place. They have tons of pictures to show you, but they have no real memories. Out of all their photographs that I looked at, only one of them really stood out. It was an old black and white polaroid: they are standing on a beach, with stone ruins in the background. A picture can be worth a thousand words, but this one was worth a million. I couldn't stop staring at them, pure love was captured in that moment, so I couldn't look away. As they pose, they cling to each other like magnets, unable to let go. I couldn't figure out what country they were in, and there are so many ruins in the world, they could have been almost anywhere on earth. It took my wife a little while to quit crying, but eventually, her tears turned to giggles, then to laughter. An old photograph can do this to you: it can make you cry or it can make you laugh. I asked her if she knew where the picture had been taken, but she didn't have a clue. I studied the picture up close, like a painter, and I found no clues. I even took it off of the wall, to see if anything was written on the back of it. For some reason, I became obsessed with this photograph, I couldn't put it down. I *want* this photo, I *need* this photo, I told myself, I must *have* this photo! Once this thought got into my head, I couldn't think about anything else, so when my wife left the room, I took it. When I slid the polaroid into my back pocket, I felt a weird sense of relief. *It's done, it's too late now,* I said, *I can't put it back.* I don't know why I wanted it so bad, I just had an urge to steal it, so I stole it. I never know why I want something, I just want it, and that's enough for me. I felt a little guilty when I left their apartment, but I had no other choice, I had to take it, it was *there* for the taking, if you know what I mean. Standing in this old Bulgarian graveyard, listening to Vera tell her story, made me think of Andrei Tarkovsky. I felt like I was in one of his movies, but I didn't know which one. All of them are amazing films, but his last one, *The Sacrifice,* is my personal favorite. Vera talked about her grandparents like they were still living, and standing right there next to her. As I listened to her story, I started to think about my own grandmother's funeral. It was a nice farewell to her, and, by all accounts, a peaceful goodbye. Well, I hope it was a nice funeral, I didn't go; I don't know why I didn't go, I just didn't go. Her death had been expected, but I was relieved to finally hear the news. She had suffered too long, she was almost blind and deaf, and only a shell of herself at the very end. She was ready to go, it was *her* time, she told me, but I still have regrets. Of course, I had my *reasons* why her funeral was out of the question: I was too sad, I was going to Europe, I was getting married. I can't remember *my* final reason, but I came up with some lame excuse why I couldn't be there. To this day, I still don't know why I missed her funeral, it's a mystery to me. I try not to think about it, but Vera and this graveyard was making me think about it. There is a wonderful scene at the end of *The Sacrifice*, which I can't seem to get out of my mind. On the morning of his birthday, Alexander (the main character in the film) wakes up with an unusual urge: to light his house on fire. He realizes that he must keep his vow that he made to God, and he *must* set his house on fire. He will give up everything that he loves, his family, his home, his life, in order to stop the oncoming nuclear apocalypse. It was *his* bargain with God, so he must do it, he thinks, to save the world. After he lures his family away from the house, he tries to light it on fire. When he strikes a match, a brisk wind blows, and the flame flickers out. Then he strikes another match, which stays lit, as the corner of the white curtain slowly catches on fire. When I first saw the movie, I didn't understand what was happening, and it made no sense to me. But when I got home, it made a lot more sense, then I really began to understand it. Was it all a dream? Or, was it reality? When the house goes up in flames, the camera lingers from afar, as you watch the fire burn in real time. While the house burns, Alexander starts to go crazy, and he runs around in circles like a madman. He keeps screaming at himself, in wild gibberish, as his family comes running across the muddy field to help him. They have to save him from himself, it's their duty as family members. When the house is finally engulfed in flames, the camera slowly pans away to the right side; you can still hear the fire crackling, you just can't see it. When the phone, inside the house, starts ringing, I always lose my shit. Who is calling him? God? Destiny? Fate? As soon as Alexander hears it, he starts to run towards the fire. What an ingenious thing for Tarkovsky to do, I thought, to let the phone ring at that exact moment in the film. Yes, it's all smoke and mirrors, I know, but it's filled with so much poetry. Let me tell you, Tarkovsky knows exactly what he's doing, he's a real master of disguise. Whenever Alexander tries to hug his family, he keeps falling down, but he keeps getting back up. He tries to hug them, he falls back down, he hugs them, he falls down. It's a wonderful ballet of chaos, well choreographed, and it's all captured by Tarkovsky's roving camera. Alexander's family tries to corral him, to capture him, but he keeps running away from them. Then Maria, the maid, the so-called *good* witch, comes into the picture. She tries to talk to him, to caress him, to kiss him, but to no avail. When he finally recognizes her, so he begins to follow her, but his family keeps pulling him away. I swear, you have to see this madcap scene to believe it. After a few minutes of this, they finally catch Alexander. Then an ambulance suddenly appears out of nowhere; the two attendants are here to help him, but every time they try to put him into the ambulance, he escapes and runs away. It's a real comic farce, with mixed nuts, and a lot of sugar on top. After some mild corralling, Alexander is finally put into the back of the ambulance. As they depart, they do a few circles in the mud, as if to tease him, then they drive him away. Maria is now desperate, so she jumps on her bicycle and chases after the ambulance. As she rides solo down the road, she peddles as fast as she can, but to no avail, she cannot keep up with them. It's a heartbreaking scene, about madness, and one that I will never forget. Nobody makes movies like Tarkovsky, he's one of the best. The last shot in the movie is of Alexander's son, who is named Little Man. As he carries two buckets of water to a tree, a single camera shoots him from behind. With the horizon in the distance, and the sun shining brightly in the sky, the ambulance, with his father in it, drives right past him. Then Maria arrives on her bicycle, she can only watch as they take Alexander away. She lingers for a moment, she's not sure what to do, so she peddles away in the opposite direction. Tarkovsky's reveal in this scene is perfectly shot, nothing is wasted, so your eyes go straight to Little Man. As he waters the tree, he smiles to himself, then he lies down underneath it. He is ready for a nap, so he speaks his only lines in the film: *In the beginning was the word. Why is that, Papa?* Then the camera slowly pans up the trunk of the tree, to where the land touches the water and the Baltic Sea flickers in the background. *The Sacrifice* is a puzzle within a puzzle, it's a riddle within a riddle, and it's a maserpiece!Tarkovsky wanted to name the film *The Eternal Return*, but, at the last minute, he changed his mind. The film is a problem that is waiting to be solved, and the answer is hidden in there somewhere. There are so many riddles in this world, you can't expect me to solve them all. Here's a riddle: *Why do I paint?* Well, my answer is: *I paint, because I paint!* What can I say, I love riddles, but I hate puzzles. Yes, I was once a Cubist, then I quit being a Cubist! After a couple of years of work, it became so vague and coy, so I gave up! Well, back then, we were known as the Neo-Cubists. We were a close-knit club, but like most clubs, we had our fights. It didn't last long, things got dark, the luster wore off, and the shine faded, if you know what I mean. Our time in the spotlight was short and sweet, so it only lasted for a few years. One day we were *here*, then the next day we were *there*. Alabaster will vouch for us, he was around during those years, and he saw our rise and fall. We were always uptown at the very beginning, but then everything went downtown. The rumor is wrong, I was never kicked out of the Neo-Cubists, I left on my own free will. Back then, nobody cared about the downtown scene, it was much different, it was dead, and everything happened uptown. But times change, and I changed–so, I walked away. I got tired of painting the same damn thing every day; it was enough to drive me crazy. I have no hard feelings, and my exit was done without any malice. After I left the club, I finally felt free, and I never looked back. At this point in my life, I had no other choice, I had to learn a new way of painting. Yes, I taught myself a new style, and a new way of seeing, with more action and less thought. Most of my pals have continued their cubist ways, and they will never leave it behind. Even though we went our separate ways, I continue to keep an eye on their careers. Of course, over the last few decades, most of them have moved downtown or to the west side of Chelsea. The Neo-Cubists are still kicking around, and they still think that their style of painting will never die. I don't know about that, but, somehow, they have kept their club alive. They have built an indestructible house, they say, that can withstand anything. I always had my doubts about this way of painting, so I've never doubted my decision to leave the Neo-Cubists. I applaud them for their effort, they're a lost breed. They went to the very ends of the still life, but I never wanted anything to do with a still life, so I got the hell out of there. I didn't want to think about my past lives, but I couldn't help it, *snap out of it*, I told myself, quit thinking about the past. But I had to think about my past, because Alabaster was in the middle a big deal, which involved one of my older paintings. He had found a *new* collector, a set of new *eyes*, so I had to be ready for anything. I've never doubted Alabaster's zeal for a deal, this is where he shines like gold. *The art of art dealing,* he likes to say, *is an art unto itself.* Those are his words, not mine; but he's right, art dealing is a lost art. Alabaster had one of my old paintings on the market, which was still in limbo, so the sale was still in doubt. And this same collector might want one of my new paintings, too, he told me. *One painting is never enough,* Alabaster says, *there's always room for two!* But two is my limit, after that, it gets boring. The Neo-Cubists have never understood this, so they paint the same still life over and over again. For my old comrades, it was always a mechanical action, mixed with a theory about math, that got them in trouble. I don't know how they still do it, but they paint the same damn thing, day after day, no matter what. They can paint the same still life a hundred times in a row, no problem, without blinking an eye. I couldn't do it anymore, so I left the club. In the beginning, I had the best intentions, believe me, I did. But, in the end, it all became impossible for me, so I made my escape and I was gone. Then Vera finally stopped talking. I couldn't believe it, after all this time, I was in heaven. Yes, the wicked witch was done with her story and it was time for someone else to talk. All funerals are sad, but the longer they last, the funnier they become. And this one was no different, it was becoming funnier by the minute. While I stood in the graveyard, the blazing sun had no mercy on me, my skin felt like hot wax. I was thirsty, hungry, sunburned, and I could barely stand up. A large group of locals was now gathered in front of the cemetary; they had come to pay their respect. The old women had baskets of fruit in their hands, and the old men were all smoking cigarettes. I couldn't believe that I was *here*, standing in this ancient graveyard, it was a miracle that I had made it this far. *I can't believe how Vera is dressed*, my wife whispered, *look out that outfit.* I couldn't have cared less what Vera was wearing, but my wife seemed to care a little too much. She had on a black silk skirt, knee-high leather boots, and a shiny gold top. *She should have more respect,* my wife said, *she looks like a prostitute.* Vera was dressed just fine for me, but my wife was really upset about her outfit. The clothes matched her bubbly personality, and she had a certain style that made you want to look at her. Vera had studied classical ballet, so she looked like a dancer. And she had that dancer walk, which most trained dancers have, she walked on her tippy toes. Trained dancers are a dime a dozen, and they come in all shapes and sizes. But all of them are wild animals, and they'll dance anywhere, they don't care where they dance. Whenever they see a dance floor, they go absolutely nuts! Let me tell you, the love of dance is a disease, it's a sickness like no other, and these dancers make me sick. These dancing fools must be high on something, they're out of their minds, and they have no respect for the rest of us. These freaks, geeks, breakers, ravers, clubbers, call them what you will, they're totally insane! Vera was built like a dancer, her body was all muscle, and her legs were like tree trunks. She still lives in Sofia, with her *boy toy*, my wife said, and she dances in a club for money. These dancers love to take over the dance floor, they dance in a trance, and they always bump into me. Things used to be more civilized on the dance floor, back in the day, they respected your personal space. They used to give you enough room to dance, and enough room to roam, but, now, it's a freaking free-for-all. You see these crazy dancers in the streets, in the parks, and even in the subways. New York is full of *trained* dancers, they dance anywhere they want, and you can't stop them. When I see them, I try to ignore them, but I can't, because they're everywhere! Some things you just can't ignore, and they bother you too much, so they stick in your brain. I mean, when I try to ignore *TULOB*, I can't do it, so I always think about Kundera. Yes, I'm a sucker for his style, he moves me with his words. I have a love-hate relationship with him; he knows how to get under my skin. He's a magician with a hat: his characters appear on the page, then they disappear off the page. His sleight of hand is pure pleasure, and his technique is of the highest quality. But his characters are his secret weapon, they're made of the right stuff, so you always remember them. Then, I found *her*! Yes, *she* came to me in a dream, I had found my Sabina, and she was standing right there in front of me. Vera will be my *Sabina*, I told myself, she's perfect for the role. It was only a matter of time before I found her, and I should've known better than to doubt myself. Then Vera started to cry. I couldn't believe it, she was a river of tears, all at once, they came flooding out of her. Of course, my wife was moved by Vera's tears, so she was crying, too. By this time, they were both hysterical, and they were now hugging each other. The bad blood between them has always been there, it started years ago, my wife said, at another funeral. And, of course, it was over some petty thing, that really meant nothing to them now. It was an alleged family offense; you know the *kind*, where something said in jest is never ever forgotten. A family feud is like a funeral, so a little blood is always expected. And an ancient graveyard was the perfect place to settle things, I thought, as the tears started running down my face. But I was thinking about Sabina's tears, not my tears, because she was now on my mind. Yes, she is the wet noodle in *TULOB*, the one who cries on cue, and she is always mad as hell. Why did Kundera make her cry so much? I don't have a clue, but I don't care, because at the end of the day, what we read, we believe. It's true, most people believe every word that they read. Well, at least, I do. I have no choice, when I read *TULOB*, I always go where Kundera tells me to go. He's a control freak, he plays with my heart, but I don't care, I still read him. I don't love Kundera, I hate him, but I love his novel. I don't want to love it, I'm sick and tired of loving it, but I do, so I'm stuck with it. The sun was making me feel dizzy and my mind was racing, and I couldn't concentrate. Kundera was still in my head, so I couldn't think of anyone else. He's always there, lurking in the dark corners, waiting like a spider for his prey to slip up. Why do I have to read *TULOB*? What about the other Kundera novels? I could read any of them, I thought. What about *The Joke*? Or, *Immortality*? And *Life Is Elsewhere*? I'm being real stupid, I told myself, because *TULOB* is just too good of a novel to put down. Kundera is funny; some people are just *funny*, so you have to laugh at them, and he's one of them. And that's when the funny began, when a stray dog came over and peed on their grandmother's grave. I had to laugh, I mean, it was pretty funny, but my wife didn't think so. The headstone got a little urine on it, which made her really upset, but Vera got more upset, she was pissed off, and she was going to do something about it. When she kicked the dog, I was in shock, the poor pooch flew through the air like a soccer ball. As soon as the dog hit the wooden fence, it howled in pain, then it crumbled to the ground. It was hurt, but still alive, and still breathing. After a few wobbly steps, the dog eventually got up, then it stumbled away. Vera had to get her revenge, it was only fair, I guess, but it was still an ugly sight to see. The dog made me laugh, it was funny, the piss was funny, in a Kundera kind of way. I felt bad for the dog, it didn't mean any disrespect, it was just being a dog. A dog is a dog is a dog, I think, but sometimes a dog is just not enough. It wasn't enough for Kundera, so he put a man and a women into his novel. *TULOB* is a love story about one man, two woman, and a dog. The main characters are: *Tomas*, a surgeon; *Tereza*, a photographer; *Sabina*, a painter, and *Karenin*, a dog. I'm sorry if I'm repeating myself, but some things need to be repeated, in oder to remember them. I don't like it when someone tells you that you're repeating yourself. I repeat myself, big deal, so what, we all do it. We say the same words, over and over again, until we believe them. I'm always yapping about some stupid thing: a book, a film, a game, a painting. *TULOB* was becoming a big thorn in my side, but I was trapped, I had to read it, I was addicted. The first time is always the best time, when I read

TULOB in Santa Fe. It was during my *desert years* (that's what Alabaster likes to call these couple of years) in New Mexico. I got lost in the desert, he says, because I was running away from the city. He's right, but I didn't fall off the face of the earth. I went into hibernation, I took a break from the rat race, I found nature again. I have to admit, the first few months I was lost, that was expected, and I needed to adjust to the altitude and climate. What I did during these years is not a mystery, I painted a ton of paintings. I mean, I went there to *paint*, so I painted. I had a huge studio, right by the Plaza, and it was in the heart of downtown Santa Fe. I had big windows, so I had great light, and I had a great view of the mountains. I wanted to get lost, and that's what I did, I got lost in the landscape. The rat race was too fast for me, I needed some solitude, so I went to New Mexico. The very first month that I was there, my brother came out for a visit. He just appeared out of nowhere at my doorstep, and he was with his new girlfriend (Rosa). I couldn't believe it, they drove nonstop from Florida to New Mexico, with no sleep, they said, just gallons of coffee. It was a total surprise, because he never told me that he was coming to Santa Fe. He appeared like a ghost, without warning, suddenly, he was standing *there*. Most people will give you a few days notice before they visit you, not my brother, he just shows up with love in his heart. They arrived with bells and whistles on, and they were jacked up on caffeine and ready to party. They had just escaped from a jail, my brother said, in some little town in Texas. They had been locked up, on some trumped-up drug charge, he told me, and they just had to pay a fine to be free, so they paid it. They drove as fast as they could, so they got here pretty fast, in a matter of hours. It wasn't a joke, all of a sudden, they were standing at my front door. As soon as they walked into my studio, Rosa pulled out a big joint and she asked me if it was *cool* if she *lit it up!* I felt like a joker with a punchline, so I told her: *No!* But I was only joking with her, and she knew it, then she lit the joint. She reminded me of someone, but I couldn't think of who. When she inhaled the smoke, she took a bunch of breaths in, then she slowly exhaled. When she blew the smoke into my face, I didn't care, she just wanted to show off for my brother, so I let her. Rosa was a fast talker, she talked nonstop, but she had a lisp, so her words sounded like baby talk. I couldn't get enough of her voice, it made me laugh, it reminded of a seal. My brother was quiet, he barely said a word to me. We hugged each other, a hug was enough, and nothing else needed to be said. Brothers don't really talk; we fight, we race, we win. Brothers argue over the past, we do, but we live in the present, for now. It was just like him, I thought, to drive all this way and have nothing to say to me. But Rosa, she had plenty to say, and she wouldn't shut up. She was very sweet, but her voice got higher and higher, so she began to sound like a chipmunk on acid. She was still mad at the *freaking cops*, she said, because they were a *bunch of losers.* Then she went on and on about the state of Texas, and how the whole thing was just a scam to get money, and a big *waste of time!* I knew exactly what she meant, because I had been reading *TULOB* for the first time, so I knew all about stolen time. At this point, I was completely lost in Kundera's novel; I was still painting, but *TULOB* took up most of my time. Of course, Kundera made Sabina a painter on purpose. He did it just to punish me, I thought, and it was working. His novel is full of dirty details and splattered with secrets. He also made her an exile in a foreign land, I know, just to rub my nose in it. Sabina is from the East, but she flees to the West. When I realized this, I had to laugh, because it hit too close to home, and here I was doing the same exact thing in Santa Fe. But I wasn't an exile in another country, I was a painter in the

Land of Enchantment. Kundera wrote *TULOB* in Paris, in 1982, on a wing and a prayer. He wrote all day and all night, he didn't sleep, he claims, until the book was finished. I'm sure he took long walks by the Seine, he had hot coffee in the cafes, and he had his dinners in the Latin Quarter. Well, at least, I hope he did all those things, because that's what I would've done if I was there. I got a joke for you. Have you ever heard this one? *Why did Kundera cross the boulevard?* Why? *To get to a bistro on the other side!* Did you laugh? I hope you did. I'm sorry, but a joke is a joke is a joke. *We're lucky*, Rosa squealed, *that the cops were idiots!* They had good karma, she told me, because the drug bust could have been much worse. If the cops would have looked under the back seat, they would have found a pound of weed. Rosa brought a pound with her, she said, because *I wanted to chill on this trip*. She hid it under the back seat as a precaution, just in case they were pulled over by the cops. I didn't believe it, her story didn't make any sense, it sounded fake to me. Were the cops that dumb? The truth was in there somewhere, as fate would have it, they were pulled over in a small town, so luck was on their side. The car was thoroughly searched, they even brought a dog, but the cops still couldn't find anything but a measly roach in the ashtray. Something didn't seem right, how did these cops not see a pound of weed under the back seat? Her story didn't make much sense to me, but most stories don't, they always seem made up and fake. Some things just get overlooked, I guess, or, you just get lucky. Why didn't the police dog smell the weed? Many things can go wrong: clues fall between the cracks, fingerprints get smudged, alibis aren't sufficiently checked out. Shit happens all the time, people are prone to make mistakes, when they get tired, they get sloppy. After we smoked the joint, I showed my brother and Rosa my new paintings. They barely looked at them, they seemed bored and not that impressed.

People don't *look* at paintings, nowadays, they *judge* paintings. It takes too much time to look at them, they don't have the time, or the patience to ponder them, so they judge them. People don't like to look, all they want to do is talk, which is the opposite of what I want to do, so I look. Yes, they talk, talk, talk, they never stop talking. I get tired of listening to them, all they want to do is talk about art, they don't want to look at it. The lookers *look*, I guess, and the talkers *talk*. Unfortunately, Rosa was a talker, so that's all she she did. She wanted to see the *real* Santa Fe, sha said, and she wanted *me* to show it to her. *Show me the real Santa Fe*, she wouldn't shut up, *I want to see the real deal!* The real Santa Fe deal? Well, that was out of the question, I told her, because I had my own list of things that I wanted to show them, and the real Santa Fe wasn't one of them. I wanted to show them the fake Santa Fe, so my list was short and sweet, but Rosa didn't want to hear about it, she only wanted to talk about the real Santa Fe. She wouldn't listen to my ideas, she just talked over me; she wasn't a good listener, but she was good talker. I loved her spunky style, she had her own way of dressing, so she really stuck out in a crowd. She was a ball of fire, dressed in black spandex, red fur, and white lace. She was very positive person, but she had a very abstract way of looking at life. She described time as a place, where the past was the present, and the here was the now. Rosa was a hoot to listen to, I will always remember her voice. As I stood there in the graveyard, I had one thing on my mind, and that was the Black Sea. I couldn't wait to jump into the cold water, it was the only thing that I was thinking about. But my wife was thinking about the warm dirt, so she couldn't take her eyes off of her grandmother's grave. The reality of the situation had finally hit her, and she was going deep within herself. It was a beautiful service; as the mourners came, they brought flowers, some left candy, and the rest of us stood there like zombies. I took two steps forward, I paused for a moment, I took one step back, then I stepped in dog shit. I couldn't help but laugh at the shit on my shoe, I was used to it, I live in New York City, so shit followed me around. All this shit talk was making me think about Alabaster. I could picture him, back in the city, with a fat cigar in his mouth, sitting at his desk, with a big smile on his face. He would have a swell time in Bulgaria, I thought, it's his kind of place. Vera was still talking, she sounded like a broken record. My wife, who was standing right next to me, barely said a word to me, she was giving me the silent treatment. This whole trip had been like a silent movie, it was all action and no dialogue. As I stood there with shit on my shoe, I could only laugh at myself, because it was my fault. I used to be a filmmaker, but that was then and this is now. Believe me, I put my heart and soul into the craft, but nothing serious ever materialized from it. My methods were dubious to begin with, and I never took control of my style, so I got lost in only technique. I tried to make films with some heart and soul, but I was out of touch with reality, and they were never good enough. I studied at one of the best film schools around, and a well-respected one: The Kaufman Institute. Yes, I learned a lot about film, I had great fun, and I had excellent teachers who knew what they were talking about. It was a wonderful opportunity to learn from the so-called *cream* of the crop. The long history of film was explained to me in great detail, and my teachers gave me the freedom to study at my own pace. While I was there, I was able to use all their equipment, so I got to shoot on old vintage cameras, and the editing room was always available to me. I learned so much, I really did, but I only made one feature film. It was a love story, two hours long, and I had a real blast making it. But the film was barely seen by anyone, no one saw it, and the ones who did, hated it! I don't think it's a bad film, but it's not a good one, either. I liked to pan the camera a lot, so it has a lot of wide angle shots, which seem to bore people I used too much split screen, I think, but I couldn't help myself, I got lost in the process, if you know what I mean. Yes, it's true, my one and only movie was a complete dud. Well, at least it was a funny dud. I did my best, but my best just wasn't good enough. After I showed the film, no offers came from it, so I gave up, I quit! I wanted to make another film, a black comedy, but my passion for it faded with time, and that's when I started painting. Now, I would paint with a brush, it was so much easier. A film takes too long to make, it's a slow torture, with no end in sight. I can paint a painting in an hour, a movie takes months. I hated being on a film set, it was so boring, I wanted to die. There's too much standing around, *waiting* for things to happen, that never do happen. What can I say, it's not my cup of tea, it's too *hot* for me, if you know what I mean. I was smart, I made only one movie, I never made another one. After my fall from film grace, I didn't know what to do with myself. I took some time off, I traveled the world, I visited many far off places. I read books, I took up photography, I played chess. When I was done with all that stuff, I went back to the drawing board, and I became a painter. The rest is history. I needed some water, I was going to pass out, but there was no water in sight. I was thirsty, exhausted, and tired of this graveyard. Finally, at last, Vera stopped talking. The witch was tired, which was sweet relief, because I was ready to leave. Luckily, after a couple of prayers, the ceremony ended. When we got back onto the road, I got back into the back seat. We were now officially on our way to the village house. Stoil Voivoda was only a few miles away from the graveyard, so the ride there didn't take too long. There was going to be a small reception, which would be a celebration of their grandmother's life. Let me tell you, receptions are just like funerals: they're filled with the barely alive and the walking dead. My wife had told me many stories about this village house, so I already had a picture of it in my mind. She spent most of her summers here as a child, it was a mystical place and her lost paradise. The house had been in their family for hundreds of years, so it had many stories to tell. My wife had come back here to remember her *past*, she said, and to find her *present*. She has longed for this place for years, like a bird longs for its nest. She had come all the way from America to see this house, so she couldn't wait that much longer. She *was* lost, but, now, she *is* found, I thought. I was burnt, my body ached, and I was dying of thirst. I really needed to get out of this car, I couldn't take it, I was going crazy. I tried to strike up a conversation with Yanko, but he ignored me, like I wasn't even there. When the car finally came to a stop, I was in heaven. *It's about time*, I mumbled to myself. My wife gave me *her* look, then she told me not to embarrass her. I was glad to be back on my own two feet. I was thirsty as hell and desperate for water, but before I could find any water, I still had to meet the rest of my wife's family. I had to meet all of them, one by one, which took too much time, if you ask me. They were all very nice, but only her Uncle Leo made a big impression on me. When I first met him, he was standing in front of the house, smoking a cigarette. Right off the bat, he gave me a big bear hug and a steel-claw handshake. He made me feel right at home. *I come from Russia, I love America*, he grunted, as he blew his smoke into my face. Leo was the so-called *funny* uncle, my wife told me, so we had an instant connection. As soon as I heard his burly voice, I knew that I was in good hands. Leo was a proper gentleman, so I had trust in him to do the right thing. He knows what *is* real, I thought, and what *is not* real. Well, he seemed to know what he was talking about, so he put me at ease. Leo was born in Russia, but he moved to Bulgaria when he was in college, and he never left. The Russians really know how to hug, they are some of the best huggers in the world. They make you feel special, so you open up more, you kiss and tell. Leo spoke broken Russian English, but I understood him. We're cut from the same cloth, we'e on the same wavelength, so words don't matter as much. Leo was the real deal, in every sense of the word, he was a man's man. I was feeling queasy, so I grabbed my wife's arm to hold myself up. She will find me some water, *I know she will*, I thought. Of course, my wife came to my rescue, just in time, when she handed me a bottle of water. But I wasted no time, I chugged it down in one big gulp. *This house is special to me, I have great memories*, my wife said, *why don't you believe me?* I knew that the house was special, but I still didn't believe her. *Why?* Well, because I know my wife, I know how she is, she loves to improvise on the fly, to invent things. And she loves any kind of drama, so the truth always gets lost in the story. I have to really listen for it, which is harder than you think. When I looked at my wife, she he looked like a ball of white light, she was shining as bright as the sun. If I closed my eyes, she turned into *Tereza*. Yes, it was that simple, fiction was fact and fact was fiction. If you read *TULOB*, then you will see what I mean, it's all in the book. Yes, Tereza's dream is to truly *love* someone in her life, she says, and, lo and behold, what do you know, she finds *Tomas*. My wife is just like Tereza, they're so alike, I thought, it's like they're the same person. With my eyes closed, I can't tell them apart. I blame Kundera for this, this is his mess, it's his fault. *TULOB* is an omen, I read it, but it never ends. My wife and Tereza are the doppelganger in full effect, and the mirror is always there for them. Tereza is only a reflection, so any woman that looks like her, will always sees herself in the mirror. Kundera is genius to do this, to make her a stand-in for all women. Yes, he made Tereza into a mirror, on purpose, it was by design. That little devil was devious, he will burn in hell. *It's kill or be killed,* he says, *make the first move,* and, I have to agree with him. I need to be more like Kundera, a cold killer, I thought, with no conscience. Yes, I have to show the collectors that I mean business, that I won't be pushed around. If I don't, believe me, they will murder me in my sleep. Alabaster tells me that I'm not hungry enough, and he might be right, but I don't care, because I have my own way of doing things. I was still thirsty, and that's when Leo pulled out his bottle of vodka and two glasses. Let me tell you, if you ever need a drink, just find a Uncle Leo, and he'll set you straight. Of course, he filled my glass right up to the top, I swallowed it like a camel, and I was ready for the long haul. Leo wasn't playing around, I *needed* another shot, he told me, so he poured me another one. It was gone in a second, then he poured me a third shot. The vodka tasted like sour cherries and bitter lemons, and it was delicious! Leo had *saved* me from a thirsty death, so I was grateful. My thirst was quenched, and my mouth was as wet as a nipple. The Russians are life savers, it's in their blood, they love to save lives. *To Russia with love!* Leo screamed, as he poured me my fouth shot. After this shot, I was a little tipsy, I needed to stop. I was ready for anything, but I was pretty drunk, so I stopped drinking. Of course, Leo wanted to give me my fifth shot, but I declined it, because my wife wanted to show me the guest house. As we made our way around to the backyard, we passed rows and rows of fruit trees that were full of fruit. There were apples, figs, pears, peaches, so much fruit! But I saw a lot of rotten fruit, too, on the ground, under the trees. As I walked along the path, I smashed the dead fruit under my feet, step by step, I made a mushy mess. The ground felt like quicksand, it was hard to walk, my feet were glued to the earth. After a few more feet of this mushiness, I couldn't take it anymore, so I got off the path and I starting walking on the grass. I needed to clean my shoes, but my wife wanted to show me the old family well, where the fresh spring water comes from. When we looked down into the well, it was filled with nasty brown water. My wife said that the water was fine to drink, the color didn't matter, but I didn't believe her, this water looked real dirty. On the patio, next to the well, was a giant picnic table, which was completely covered with black and white bird shit. The square table looked just like a Jackson Pollack painting. It was gross, I thought, but it was a natural masterpiece of selection. Yes, if you look deeply into nature, you will *see* art everywhere. The guest house was hidden behind a wall of trees, so it was very secluded and private. As soon as I saw the huge glass windows, I fell in love with the house. *This would make a great studio*, I said, *I could paint in here!* My wife looked at me like I was crazy, but I'd seen that look before, so I wasn't surprised by her reply. *You don't even live here*, she shouted, *are you out of your mind?* No, I wasn't out of my mind, I just know a good studio when I see one, and this was one of them. When my wife opened the front door, a dank odor came whiffing out. The smell was really pungent. *I used to sleep in here every night, I had so much fun in this house,* my wife said. I didn't believe her, she would never sleep in here, I thought. The inside of the house was very dark, so I couldn't see where the smell was coming from. Then I took another step into the room, it smelled like death, so I walked over to the window and I opened it. When I pushed the curtains aside, the light came flooding in. Now I could see where the smell was coming from. In the corner of the room, stacked high to the ceiling, was a humongous pile of moldy peaches. I had to hold my breath, the stench was almost unbearable. The fruit was just *rotting* away, which made no sense to me, it seemed like such a waste. My wife mumbled something about *no one having the time* to eat it, but I didn't believe her, because they had plenty of time here to eat it. Yes, nature can rot anything, if you give her enough time, but this was ridiculous, I thought. I went to another window, but it wouldn't open, so I tried another window, and that one wouldn't open, either. The smell didn't seem to bother my wife, maybe she was used to it, but I wasn't, so I was feeling sick. When my wife walked over to a cabinet, she was overcome with emotion, then she pulled out a knife, and she started balling her eyes out. *I can't believe I found this,* she cried, *it's my grandfather's knife!* Of course, it was his knife, but I didn't believe her. She had no proof that it was his knife, it could have been anybody's knife. She kept on insisting, so I had to hear her out, it was possible. But after listening to her story, I still wasn't convinced that it was his knife. Her facts didn't add up, but I still had to leave that option open, just in case. I really didn't care about the knife, but my wife seemed to care a lot, which made me care a little bit more. She probably made the whole story up, I thought, on the spot, like she always does. *After all these years, I finally found it,* my wife cried. I didn't believe her. *When I hold my grandfather's knife in my hand, I feel closer to him.* My wife loves to collects souvenirs, she can't get enough of them, but I hate them. Every place that we go, she has to get a souvenir, and this was another one of *her* souvenirs, I thought. Then my wife found a bucket of rusty farm tools in the bottom of the cabinet; they looked more like mangled bones, and most of them were broken. When my wife pulled out one of the old shovels, it had no blade on it. She had a smile on her face, which meant only one thing, that she had another story to tell. *This was my grandfather's favorite shovel, and these are all of his tools.* I wanted to believe her, but I didn't. Then she picked up a large box, that was full of stuffed animals, and she grabbed a furry white rabbit out of it. *I found him, after all these years,* my wife yelled, *I found Simon!* Simon who? I didn't believe a word that she said. *Simon was my pet rabbit, I used to sleep with him, and he used to say funny things to me.* A talking white rabbit? I wasn't buying her Simon story, Simon says it's bullshit! I mean, it could have been her brother's rabbit. *Simon was my best friend, he never left my side, we did everything together.* My wife likes to exaggerate, but this story was getting a bit ridiculous. Exaggeration is an art, and my wife is a master of it, so I had to listen to her. I could smell the scent of sandalwood, when I took a step into the hallway, I heard someone crying. It sounded like a female voice, I wasn't sure. I looked for the light switch along the wall, but I couldn't find it. Then I took a few more steps, and I found it. As soon as I flipped the switch on, the bulb above me flickered on and off, before settling for a dim glow. There was a large painting hanging on the side wall, it was hung crooked at an angle, so I reached out and I straightened it. The painting was a landscape, with a yellow sunset in the background. I studied it for a moment, at all the different angles, I wanted to see *it* for what it was. It was painted in oil, with acrylic, and it was done by a very deft hand, I concluded. I liked it, it had a loose style that went against the grain; it was all reds, yellows, and blues. And it had a wonderful gold leaf frame, that made the painting look even better. Then I heard the crying again, but this time it was even louder. I still couldn't see anyone, I could hear them crying, but I couldn't see them. Well, I think they were crying, I don't know, maybe they were laughing, I wasn't sure, a laugh and a cry can sound the same. It was too dark in the hallway, I couldn't see anything. *In the dark, all bets are off,* Tarkovsky said. Why? Well, because anything can happen in the dark, and it usually does. What sounds big in the dark is usually tiny in the light. Tarkovsky used lots of long takes and wide shots in *The*

Sacrifice, but, for what purpose? To move the story along with an exaggeration of time and space. This film was his homage to Ingmar Bergman, and it was made in Sweden, too, on the island of Gotland. He used some of Bergman's actors, his production designer, and even his great cinematographer, Sven Nykuist. What a weird thing to do, I thought, it sounds like some kind of inside joke, but it isn't. Nykuist was diagnosed with Aphasia, a language disorder, which made him unable to speak, read or write, so he slowly drifted away. What a great way to go: to never see it coming, to meet death in the dark. It just snuck up on him; first, he couldn't read, then he couldn't write, then, he couldn't say anything. Believe it or not, Nykuist was also the cinematographer for the film version of *TULOB*. Yes, even Kundera got into the film business. He needed the money, so he sold the rights, and his soul, to the devil. If you ask me, he's a scoundrel in sheep's clothing, disguised as a lamb. I have to confess, the movie isn't that bad, but it should have been much better. Then the crying stopped, and someone turned on the radio. The music sounded muffled, and distorted, like it was being played underwater. When I took a couple of steps closer, I heard laughter in the dark. Then the music was turned up louder, but it still sounded like a fog horn, so it made me flinch. I couldn't see anything, but when I got to the end of the hallway, I turned the corner and I went into a room. There was a lamp on, but it was too dark to see clearly, but I could see the shape a person. I could hear more laughter, I think, or, was it more crying? The person was sitting on the edge the bed, and they had long black hair. I think it was a woman, but it could have been a man, I wasn't sure. Kundera was still in my head, so he was playing tricks with me, but I didn't care, I was used to his games. He is a crazy fool, who likes all kinds of drama, so he gave Sabina a free spirit and Tereza a captured soul. He wanted *you,* the reader, to have to *choose* sides. Is Sabina *light,* and is Tereza *heavy*? Kundera is a sick fool, and he's full of himself, so he leaves it up to me to decide. Who is the *master,* who is the *slave*? Well, I'm a slave, and Kundera is my master. I can't escape his chains, I can't fight him off. He gave me a life sentence, and *TULOB* is my ball and chain. Most people say that Tereza is the heavy one in the book, so they want her soul to be free; but I think Tereza is the light one, so her body needs to be freed. Of course, Kundera made Sabina a fighter for all women, and Tereza a fighter for only herself. I took one more step closer, then I saw *her,* I couldn't believe it, there she was, it was Vera! Yes, it was the wicked witch of the west, and she was back for more. I don't know how she did it but she got here before we did, and she was already causing trouble. Vera was a trained dancer, so she is fast, sly, quick, and she knows how to get around. Luckily, she wasn't crying, or laughing, anymore; she looked a little sad, but happy at the same time. She wanted to dance, she said, so she turned the music up and she started dancing in a circle. I just stood there, as I watched her dance, I didn't know what else to do, so I didn't do anything. While she twirled like a ballerina, I could hear her breathing hard and heavy. I could tell that Vera loved to dance, because she had a big smile on her face. Yes, Kundera is the king of kitsch, but he's also the queen of cheese, if you know what I mean. He likes the way that his book smells, and it stinks, because he's full of shit! Of course, he gave Tereza a cruel and unloving mother, who teased her nonstop about her body. Kundera did this on purpose, so you would feel sorry for her. Her mother's jokes made the human body seem vulgar and dirty to her; so she sees only the *flesh,* and not the *spirit.* All bodies are the same, her mother said, so she thought only about her soul. Her body did not exist, she ignored it, as she searched for her spirit. Kundera is a snake, he tricks you with his slippery tongue, he lures you in, and his venom is deadly. If he bites you, that's it, now, the music is in you, and there's no going back! When Vera finally saw me, she immediately turned the music off. I didn't know what to say to her, I felt like I was intruding on her privacy, but it was too late, I was already in the room. And that's when my wife walked in, and she had a lot to say: *What are you doing back here? You don't belong in this house, I told you not to come into this room! Why don't you ever listen to me?* Vera looked spooked, like she just saw a ghost, but my wife was no ghost, she was real. *I just wanted to see this house again,* Vera said, *because it always makes me think about my childhood. I have such fond memories about this place, I had the best time of our life here in this house.* As soon as Vera said the word *house,* my wife looked right at me and she said: *I told you so!* She's right, I never do believe her; but, believe me, I have my reasons why I don't. What can I say, I should believe her, but I don't. Well, sometimes *I do,* most times *I don't.* My wife loves to have a little drama in her life, so the truth is always filled with a few white lies. *Do you want to smoke a joint with me?* Vera asked us with a sly smile. It sounded like a peace offering, but my wife still said no. It was too good to be true, I thought, so my answer was a definite *yes!* For whatever reason, my wife didn't want to smoke, but I did, I was ready and able. But Vera didn't light the joint, instead, she held it in her hand while she blabbered away to my wife. I don't know how long I waited to smoke, but it seemed like an eternity. Yes, once again, I had no other choice, I had to *wait* for it, so I just listened to her talk. Kundera loves to talk, too, and he never shuts up. Let me tell you, he knows exactly what he's doing to me, I'm like putty in his hands. Will Tereza find her soul? I don't know. Will Sabina find her home? I hope so. Kundera is just like Danielle Steel, he knows how to hook *you,* the reader, with his bullshit.

To find the answers to his questions, you have to read the entire book. I promise you, it's all in *there*, on the pages, if you read between the lines. Kundera loves to listen to himself talk, so he won't shut up. But I didn't want to listen to Kundera talk, I just wanted to smoke, so I still had to wait, because Vera was still talking. Then, I got lucky, I couldn't believe it, when Vera finally stopped talking. When she lit up the joint, it smelled so good. But, to my surprise, she smoked almost half the joint, before she handed it to me. I took one puff, but before I could take another puff, she grabbed the joint from out of my hand. The weed tasted like burnt coffee, but I didn't care, I needed to relax. Vera wouldn't stop talking, she was making me feel jittery, and the more she smoked, the higher her voice got. *I was so happy here,* she squealed, *so happy there!* I wanted another puff, but Vera wouldn't give the joint back to me. Then again, one puff was enough, I was feeling really high. I could tell that my wife and Vera needed to talk about some things, so I left them alone and I went outside. I was in need of a good nap, I wanted to rest my body, and that's when I found a tall fig tree to sleep under. I got horizontal, when I looked up through the tree branches, the sun blinded me. I saw white spots, I couldn't see straight, so I closed my eyes. Under the fig tree, I was at peace, dozing off, I was in another world. Yes, I was a spinning planet, lost in space, in an unknown galaxy, and I was in my own private universe. In my mind, I felt ancient, ripe, full of hope, bursting, exploding, expanding. When I rolled over in the grass, I could feel something sticking me in my side, so I sat up, then I pulled the object out. It was a fat fig, and it looked pretty ripe. I was hungry, so I ate it. The fruit tasted as sweet as sugarcane, the flesh was like melted butter, it was delicious. When I closed my eyes again, I was adrift in gooey nothingness. All at once, I was a shooting star, a cosmic snowball, a raging volcano. I was ready to dream, but I couldn't, because Tarkovsky was still on my mind. Let me tell you, he can, and will, put a spell on you, just like he put one on me. He's a hypnotist, with a mission, so he waits for the perfect moment to work his magic. When I first saw *Andrei Rublev*, you can say, that I went under, and I never came back. Since then, I have been living on borrowed time, *his* time, and I have been a loyal slave. Yes, Tarkovsky is a master, a master craftsman with a chip on his shoulder. When I saw this film, I couldn't think of anything else; I got really inspired, so I read the great Russian novels. I read them all: Dostoyevsky, Gogol, Tolstoy, Turgenev. The Russians are life savers, I mean, they save lives everyday. Most of them are fortune tellers, so their stories will always speak to the masses. I swallowed every last Russian word, and I'm a better man for it. But Tarkovsky is a Russian fruit cake: he's too sweet and his nuts are hard to crack. *Andrei Rublev* is about a 15th century Russian icon painter, who was considered a prophet and a saint. The film is about the passion of a painter, it's a revelation, and a complete work of art. When I first saw the film, I was speechless, shocked, because I had never seen anything like it. The film is about the freedom of a man, of an artist, in the modern world. It is a story about the meaning of faith, and truth, and the struggle to overcome one's place, through the history of time. Of course, Tarkovsky made Andrei into a martyr, so he must give up the act of painting, then take a vow of silence to prove his faith. He shot the entire movie in black and white; only the epilogue is in color. Andrei is a dreamer, and, just like me, a lost cause. But a painter without a cause, I thought, is like a saint without a sin. I was dreaming about Tarkovsky, but thinking about Kundera, so when the sun hit my face, I was suddenly awake. Then I woke up, I felt liberated, and when I opened my eyes, the world was alive again. The field in front of me was in full bloom, the flowers were at their peak, so they were bursting with the colors of the rainbow. The floral air was mixed with the scent of cow manure, which made my nose a little confused, but I didn't care, because it smelled like paradise to me. I was starting to sound just like Kundera; I didn't want to, but I was under his spell, so I couldn't help myself. I smell just like him, I thought, I smell like a wild beast. Yes, it's true, after you read him, you start to smell like him. While I sat under the tree, I could only think about the present moment, which seemed larger than life. As I gazed into my past, I looked into my future, and they both seemed to come together into this moment. I was seduced by the beauty that was all around me, but with so many old memories still in my head, I was in complete denial. In *TULOB*, it is Tereza who first seduces Sabina, when she stops by her studio. She is there to see her paintings, but after a photo shoot, and a seduction, Sabina is stripped completely nude. Of course, later on, Sabina will seduce Tereza. Or, is it the other way around? Well, it's all fair in love and war, they say, and what goes around comes around. Yes, there are always two sides to every story, and it's all there in black and white. Kundera writes like a maniac, so he sneaks in a dual seduction. Why would he do such a thing? Well, I don't know why, but after that scene, I was hooked, lined, and sunk. Kundera is a bulldozer, he's a wrecking machine, and nothing can stop him. He has style to burn, and he knows it, so he likes to show off. I'll say this, finding your own *style* is not an easy thing to do, it takes years to find it. After I left the Neo-Cubists, I tried every style in the book, I had nothing to lose. I had to find a *new* way of painting. A new style doesn't come over night, it's hard to come by, and almost impossible to keep. But, sooner or later, if you search long enough, you'll find *it*. And, if you're lucky enough, it will find you. My new style appeared out of the blue, in my old Broadway studio.

Yes, it was pure luck, a gift from the gods, when it happened to me. I tripped, I fell, then I found it. I experimented with *time*, I *lost* track of it, if you know what I mean. It was trial by fire, hours of anguish, and a month of joy. Yes, it was waiting for me to pick it up, so I picked it up. I went for it, I didn't have any rules, I got lost in the paint. My style is a smorgasbord of styles, it's a goulash, but it's all mine. Of course, Alabaster saw the promise in my new paintings, so he didn't mind waiting around for them. After my sabbatical in Santa Fe, I finally moved back to New York. I got a gigantic new studio, south of Canal Street, and I got to work. I loved the space, but Alabaster couldn't stand it, it was *too big* and *too old*, he said, whatever that meant. I didn't care, because I was on a roll, in the zone, so I could have painted anywhere. I was in a trance, in a romance, I was dancing with my new muse. Alabaster hated to come downtown, so he barely came to my studio. Most of his business was uptown, and that's where he spent most of his time. But every few weeks he would show up at my door, always unannounced, with a new collector in tow, who was interested in one of my *new* paintings. My time in New Mexico had been fruitful, because I brought back a large cache of paintings, which were *now* for sale. I painted a madman, I painted day and night, with little sleep. I was like a monk in a monastery, I had to follow my vision to the very end. I was finally alone, with my angels and devils, so I had to face both of them. In the studio, there is no place to hide, you can't hide from yourself, it's impossible. *Go west*, they say, so I went west. Santa Fe was the perfect place to go, and it took me in with open arms. When I first got there, I was like a fish out of water, but I loved it. I had only one thing on my mind: *Paint!* Yes, I was hungry, I ate up every style, so I got fat. I swallowed them whole, without a care in the world, I let them guide my hand. But, that was then, now, I know my limits as a painter, so

I never go beyond them. Back then, I didn't know better, and I went way beyond my comfort zone. Of course, some of these paintings were not that good, but I didn't care, because it was all a test. We're nothing more than our doubts, they rule us like a whip, and I have my scars to prove it. In New York, there are limits, but in New Mexico, I had no limits, I felt limitless. I paid my dues with my own blood, sweat and tears. I became a slave to my craft, a vessel to my vision, I lost all control. My imagination was on fire, so my new paintings were on fire. They piled up like firewood in my studio. I was a hot flame, I had to be careful, because everything in my studio was flammable. In the beginning, Alabaster thought my time in Santa Fe was all for nothing, and a big bluster. He had nothing against Santa Fe, he said, he just didn't like me living there. I still remember his one and only visit, which I will never forget it. He showed up in town dressed like cowboy, in a big Stetson hat, with snakeskin boots and leather pants. I had never seen him dressed like this, he usually dressed in silk suits, so it was a real hoot to see him so free. Of course, he stayed at the best hotel in town, and he hired a local to show him the sites. I barely saw him, he had his own agenda, so I left him alone. *I'm here for my Zen back rub*, he told me, which meant: *I want to be left alone*. This wasn't a business trip, it was a pleasure trip, he said. I saw him on his last day in town, when we had dinner together. He showed up at the restaurant looking like a mess; he had cuts all over his body and his legs had burns all over them. The place was called *On Water*, and like most seafood restaurants in the southwest, it didn't smell like the sea, it smelled like mesquite wood. The decor was ultra-modern western, but it had a classical bent, so it looked ridiculous. We didn't have a reservation, but it didn't matter, because Alabaster slipped the hostess a hundred, and we suddenly had one. The only available table was on the patio, whch was not my choice, but there was no other table, so we took it. I hate patio dining with a passion; there are too many flies, the birds shit on you, and the wind always blows everything away. Alabaster looked busted up, like boxer after a hard fight. His hands were wrapped in white gauze, and he had bandages all over his arms. He was in pretty bad shape, but he was in a really good mood. *I really love Santa Fe*, he declared, *I can't wait to come back!* When I asked him where he had been all week, he just smiled at me, and in his heavy New York accent, he said: *It's none of your goddamn business!* He was only joking, but he was right, I thought, I do ask too many questions. But I can't help it, I like to know *who* I'm speaking to, if you know what I mean. *I went fly fishing, river rafting, horse wrangling, and I even did some rock climbing*, he bragged. I was surprised to hear this, because in New York, Alabaster was a lazy dog. I mean, he won't walk more than a couple of blocks, before hailing a taxi. But strange things happen to city slickers when they come out to New Mexico. They go mad, they forget who they are, they lose their minds. They come dressed in jeans and hiking boots, with their long underwear and bandanas, looking for a good time. These fools like to explore nature in high style, so they always bring too much stuff. Went they finally get into town, they go absolutely nuts! Perhaps it's the desert air, or the altitude, or the mountains, or the sky; I don't know what it is, but when city slickers come to Santa Fe, they really know how to raise hell, and they party hard. *My dear boy, you won't believe it, I spent the night at Ghost Ranch*, Alabaster gushed. Ghost Ranch? No way, I didn't believe him. *Yes, I slept where Stieglitz slept, it was incredible, and I really felt Georgia O'Keeffe's spirit in that house.* I didn't believe him, because he didn't like Georgia O'Keeffe, so this seemed a little odd to me. *They rent the place out in the summer, I had a blast there, it was worth every penny! I ran naked under the stars, I mooned the moon, I got baptized in the lake!* Like I said before, this wasn't the Alabaster that I knew back in the city, no, this was the new and improved Alabaster, so he seemed like a totally different person. *I love New Mexico, the stars are so close to me, I can almost touch them!* When the busboy appeared, he poured us some water, but he spilled half of it on the table, then he disappeared into the back. He was real clumsy, I could tell, he didn't give a damn. Most busboys don't give a shit; they might be nice and polite, but they're really rude idiots. They like to play silly games, and the love to laugh in your face. When our waiter finally came up to our table, he announced himself with a: *Hello, I'm James, and I'll be taking care of you tonight.* He was dressed in a turquoise and orange outfit, and he had a little pad in his hand, with a black marker. James had one of those toothy smiles on his face, that all waiters have when they greet you, it was fake as hell. When he started telling us about the daily specials, he got nervous, he started stuttering, so it took him a while to recite them. When he finished, he said some stupid joke about himself, then he stood there like a log. I ignored him, I didn't say a word to him, and I acted like he wasn't even there. When I'm with Alabaster, I never talk to the waiter, I never have to, because he likes to do all the talking. During a business dinner, I always ignore the waiter, and I let him order for me. It's one of the rules, it's in our contract, and I like it when I don't have to talk. I can't order anything–no appetizer, no entree, no dessert–he is in charge of the whole meal. *I know what you like, and what you don't like,* Alabaster tells me, so I believe him. I have total trust in him, I mean, if I didn't, he wouldn't be my dealer. When James came back to take our order, he seemed a bit confused by our way of doing things, but after a while, he got the hang of it. He had the look of desperation on his face that all waiters have, and a smugness that he couldn't hide. He seemed like a nice guy, but there was something weird about him, I couldn't figure him out. Then the busboy brought us our bread and butter, and he was still laughing at me, so I ignored him. The bread was stale, it was as hard as a rock, and there was a hair in the butter. When Alabaster told the busboy about it, he laughed at him like it was all a joke. He eventually brought us some new bread and butter, but he wouldn't stop laughing at us. *I met a couple of collectors at the O'Keeffe place*, Alabaster said, *two cowboys from Texas, and they love modern art.* Yes, it was his business to find new collectors, so anywhere that he went, he would find them. He was always finding new clients, so I wasn't surprised that he found some at Ghost Ranch. *They have a sweet taste for modern art, one guy loves Warhol, the other one loves Motherwell. They both come from Houston families with oil money, and you know what that means, they buy what they love.* Alabaster loves to talk about families, as if all families were the same. One is born into a family, one does not choose your family. From the very first slap on the ass, it's perfect, then, after that, it's no longer perfect. Our seed is sown in the womb, then we mutate into what we become. And Alabaster had become a mess. *How did you get all those cuts and burns on your body?* I asked him. Of course, he ignored my question and kept on talking about the two collectors from Texas. Then James came out and served us our first course. He announced the dish with a wave of his hand, and he gave us a long description about the beet salad, as he ended his soliloquy with: *Please enjoy!* I hate it when the waiter tells me to enjoy my dish. I don't need to hear their two cents, they should just shut up and let me enjoy my food. My water glass was empty, but the busboy ignored it. I wanted some more water, and he knew it, so he was teasing me. It was all a big joke to him, he didn't seem to care about anything, he was just having a good time. I was the punchline to his joke, and he wanted me to know it. He was getting on my nerves, but I were sitting in his section, so I had to deal with it. *I love this beet salad,* and *the walnuts and goat cheese are a perfect match,* Alabaster said. He's a sucker for perfect matches, and his taste buds know what they like, so he is always pairing things together. *My dear boy, Ghost Ranch is a filthy pigsty,* he screamed, *but I love it!* Alabaster had a sparkle in his eye when he said that, he was giddy, like he was ready to tell his tale. *The ranch is filled with nothing but animal bones and clay pots, the rooms are hot as hell, with no air-conditioning, the toilets are horrendous, the food is really bad, and there's no hot water!* Alabaster shouted. *It's still a working ranch, but nothing works, they don't take care of the place, it's a real dump!* I couldn't stop him, he wanted to rant, so I let him rant. *But the sky is beautiful, the sky is amazing!* I couldn't follow his story, he was all over the place, as he went on and on about the sky. I was surprised by this new obsession with the sky, because in New York, he never looked up at the sky. But this was the new and improved Alabaster, so I had to get used this one, which made him seem even more hilarious. *My dear boy, there is nothing more refreshing than a nice swim in a cold lake, I mean, it really makes you feel alive!* What lake? *Did he mean Abiquiu Lake? I don't know what the lake was called,* he told me, *but the water was freezing, and I got baptized in it.* Alabaster was on a roll. *Abiquiu! I love that word! Abiquiu, Abiquiu, Abiquiu! And the folks at Ghost Ranch treated me like a king, their hospitality was unbelievable. I had a big bungalow, with a kiva fireplace, that had a nice view of the mesa. But the sky here is something special, you're so close the stars, you can almost touch them!* Yes, Santa Fe is a paradise, and there is nothing like the southwestern sky, but Alabaster was overdoing it, I thought. The city slickers who crave open space, they will always go crazy in this emptiness. Alabaster talked about the sky like he owned it, like he had just bought a big chunk of it. I couldn't stop laughing at him, because I had never seen him so enraptured with the open sky. *How did you get to Abiquiu Lake?* I asked him. I wanted to know, but he wouldn't answer me. *My dear boy, you're not going to believe it, but I skinny dipped in that freezing lake. I was heaven, it was pure bliss! You know you can't do this shit in New York, and that's why I love it here!* The busboy was ready to clear our plates, so on his first approach, he took Alabaster's, but I was still eating, so he left mine alone. But, in a matter of seconds, he came back for it, and he asked me if I was *finished* with it. I wasn't finished, but before I could say *no*, he snatched my plate like a snake. I couldn't believe it, he was fast, so it was gone in a second. Busboys must be on some kind of speed, because they act like they have nothing to lose. They all have an axe to grind, and they don't care who they hurt, so they laugh in your face. This busboy was hyped up on something, he was out of his mind, and he was about to learn a lesson. *I have never felt so alive in my life, and so free,* Alabaster said, *I really love Santa Fe! In all this empty space, I can run wild, out here, no one cares what I do. Back in the city, I can't get away with anything, and the cops are always looking to bust you for something. I swear, they'll give you a ticket for almost anything, it's a crying shame. New York is dead, it died a long time ago. I mean it, New York is dead!* He was ranting like a madman. *New York used to have it all, but it lost it, and it's not coming back!* What did New York lose? I said. He wouldn't tell me, he was being evasive, he was beating around the bush. Our business dinners always ended like this: after the first bottle of wine, he loses his way. *It was my duty,* he said, *I had to go back to nature, so it is my destiny to jump into that lake!* What on earth was he talking about? I couldn't follow his logic at all, but I still listened to him, and I let him talk. While Alabaster was ranting about Abiquiu Lake, a giant fly was buzzing around his face. It wouldn't go away, and it kept landing on his nose, which made me laugh my ass off. Of course, the fly made me think about Kafka, but when it landed on Alabaster's nose for the third time, Pinocchio suddenly popped into my head. Now, he was acting like a drunk lotto winner: he was being obnoxious, talking nonstop, he wouldn't shut up. I couldn't get a word in, he was losing his cool. *I shouldn't have smoked that grass last night, you know I don't smoke that stuff anymore, I used to, back in the Seventies!* Alabaster loves to talk about the Seventies, it's his favorite decade, in a sentimental way, they were the best years of his life. *Back in the Seventies, anything was possible*, he said, *and the future was bright. But, now, the future is so uncertain, and nobody dreams about anything. My dear boy, last was a night to remember, the old boys from Texas played a trick on me. They said the grass wasn't that strong, but I should have known better. I admit it, I got a little crazy, but when I jumped into Abiquiu Lake, I was in heaven!* Alabaster wouldn't stop talking. *Yes, things got crazy, I even broke my bottle of Cognac.* Alabaster is in love with Cognac, and Cognac is in love with him, so he always has a bottle of it with him. He likes to sip it from a glass goblet, with his pinky finger sticking out. *It's my secret weapon for any occasion*, he says, *because it always gets the conversation going.* His voice was getting louder and louder, but I didn't care, I was used to his timbre. *Ghost Ranch is too tame for me, the place shuts down at midnight, after that, it's lights out!* Alabaster has very strong opinions and he isn't afraid to state them. He is a true professional, he respects everyone, and he is driven by a positive life force. He is oblivious to the passage of time, so he thrives under the pressure. I wish I had an ounce of his will, or some of his stamina, then I would be unstoppable, I thought. Alabaster is like a bull in a china shop; he won't die, he just keeps on kicking, as he breaks everything in sight. When James arrived with our main course, once again, he flashed those white teeth, as he waved his right hand, he told us: *Please enjoy!* The busboy made another lame attempt with the water pitcher, but he missed my glass by a mile, so now the whole table was soaked. When he smiled at me, I gave him a big frown, but he just giggled, as he ran away into the back. I ignored the water, I acted like it wasn't even there, I had to look strong. But I knew the busboy had to come back, so I had something up my sleeve. *I love Ghost Ranch, I had a great night there, but it's a bloody pigsty!* Alabaster has a real knack for words, but he was getting on my nerves, and I was tired of listening to him. This was the last act, I thought, before the fat lady sings. I had seen this scene many times before, so I knew what to do next: I would let him talk himself out of breath. Believe me, after all these years with him, I'm still in the dark. His last aria usually happens during dessert, or, before the cheese, so I still had some time left on the clock. *My dear boy, Stieglitz would be pissed off if he saw the place, you should see it, it's a bloody mess, it's falling apart, and it looks like shit!* Alabaster was singing now. *All these damn tourists make me sick, with their backpacks, fancy hiking boots, they can all go to hell!* I could barely follow him, he was talking so fast. *How did you get to Abiquiu Lake?* I asked him. Alabaster ignored my question, like he never heard it, and he kept on ranting. *They have no damn respect for the rest of us, these crazy freaks, they're idiots! My dear boy, tell me, what is the most essential thing inside of us?* He wouldn't let me answer. *You won't believe it, it's the shape of our backbone. Yes, if you don't stand up straight for yourself, you won't be able to be straight for someone else.* Alabaster likes to ask me questions, then he likes to give me the answers to them. Yes, it's a little game of cat-and-mouse that I play with him, but I'm always the mouse, never the cat. James was circling the table like a cat, waiting for the perfect moment to ask me that eternal question: *Are you enjoying everything?* Let me tell you, these waiters are out of their goddamn minds, I know they're just doing their jobs, but give me a break, they ask stupid questions. *You must jump into Abiquiu Lake before you die. It should be on your bucket list, it will cleanse you, just like it cleansed me.* Alabaster was now singing his heart out. *My dear boy, history waits for no man, when your destiny calls you, you must answer it, you won't regret it!* I couldn't stop staring at his flip-flopped feet, which were covered with some serious wounds. They looked like second-degree burns, maybe third-degree, but he didn't seem to care. Alabaster loves to talk about history, especially, his own history, which is a deep lake that he can jump into at anytime. If *he* jumps into the water, then *I* must jump into the water, those are *our* rules. *You must complete the circle, and jump into the lake,* he told me, *then the world will be all yours!* But the busboy didn't care about history, he was only thinking about the present, so he really wanted my plate. But I was on guard, this time I was keeping my eyes wide open, and I was ready for him. Alabaster was acting like a drunk pirate, he had a goofy look on his face, which I'd seen many times before, so I knew what was coming next. A painter knows his *glazes*–I really do, especially my own *dealer's* glaze; which meant, the Cognac would be arriving soon. It was only a matter of time before things got really sticky, I thought, then the fun would begin. I love to listen to Alabaster's stories, but the meat and potatoes are always missing. *How did you get the cuts and burns on your body?* I said. He was silent for a moment, then he gave me a big smile, as he said: *Life is a clock, I'm the arrow, and you're the number seven. It's a long and complicated story, I don't have the time to explain it to you, but one day, when the time is right, I will!* Alabaster was making no sense at all, so I blocked him out and I let him talk. The busboy couldn't take his eyes off my plate, I tried to ignore him, but he was eyeing me like a tiger. But I was on to him, and I knew his moves, so I was prepared for him. Of course, James was nowhere to be seen, he had vanished into the

49

thin air of the kitchen. He was probably back there laughing his ass off, and counting his tips. Let me tell you, waiters have one thing on their mind: *tips, tips, tips!* Yes, that's all they really think about, they don't care about anything else. Waiters are human percentage machines; before you even sit even down, they already know what you're going to tip them. They read people, they're just like pickpockets, they know a good mark when they see one. *I have no idea how I got these cuts and burns. I woke up this morning and they were there. I must have fallen down, I don't know, last night is still a little foggy to me.* Alabaster was playing dumb. *I had a great time at the lake, but, as your dealer, I must advise you, that last night is off limits to you. I have my personal life and you have yours. What I do on my own dime is my own business, so please respect my privacy.* He was right, I always need to know the *fine* details; they matter to me, without them, I'm lost in the story. Before I could finish my thought, the busboy swooped in and stole my plate from me. I couldn't believe it, I blinked once, and it was gone! I never saw him coming, he lulled me to sleep, and I was suddenly dumbstruck. I was mad at myself, but this battle wasn't over, because I still had the dessert. The last course is the best course for sweet revenge, so I was whipping up something special. Then James reappeared with a bottle Cognac and our desserts, but this time, he seemed less poised, more nervous, and his sappy smile was gone. His priceless panache had deserted him, now, he looked kind of sad, and a little unsure of himself. As soon as he poured the brandy, he slipped away like a seal, then he ran away into the kitchen. *I love Santa Fe, I'll be back here next year,* Alabaster said, *I can't wait to visit you again!* Of course, he never came back again, it was his one and only visit. But he hates to visit a place more than once, he says the second visit is never as good as the first visit. I'm the total opposite, when I really like a place, I go back and I visit it, over and over again. Alabaster has his way, and, I have my way, but, somehow, we come together in the middle, and we make it work. Let me tell you, a good dealer is hard to find, especially one that allows you the space to roam. Since his trip to Santa Fe was a pleasure trip, I never got the full story. I don't know what he did there, he left out all the good parts, so I have no clue what he really did in Santa Fe. Alabaster is a thrill seeker, so he likes to have some dangerous fun every once in a while. Art dealing is a funny business, and it's filled with some funny people, it's a never-ending comedy. I can't help but watch it unfold, because it's divine, and I can't look away, so I laugh. This business is a lowdown and dirty racket, I try to have as much fun as I can, but sometimes I can't. The last course was not that much fun, the dessert was tasteless, and the flies had arrived just in time. My carrot cake was as chewy as leather, I took two bites and I was done with it. I still wanted my revenge on the busboy, but I had to come up with a plan. I needed to surprise him, so my plan was a silly plan, but so what, it could work, I told myself, if everything went as planned. I was ready for him, I had studied his moves, and I was prepared for his tricks. I would have to confront him, face to face, I thought, with my mushy truth. I wanted to teach him a lesson, it was now or never, the time was right, so I needed to make my move. I took the rest of my carrot cake and I doused it with the Cognac, then I smashed it up into a creamy paste. When I smeared it on the bottom of my plate, I had to laugh, I couldn't help it, because I knew it was the perfect plan. It was a simple plan, but a good plan, and I was ready to put it into play. The busboy was a speedy freak, I had to have patience, so I had to wait for him. Sooner or later, he would come for it, and when he did, it was all over. I would get the last laugh, so I couldn't wait to laugh my ass off. I didn't want to hurt him, I mean, I just wanted to scare him a little. Let me tell you, there's nothing sweeter than a delayed revenge, it's pure sugar, with a cherry on top. But I had so much time to think about it, I was getting nervous, and a bit jumpy. I couldn't wait another minute, it had to happen soon, or I was going to go crazy. To lure him in, I closed my eyes for a moment; knowing that he would take the bait, I counted to five, then I opened my eyes again. I couldn't believe it, the busboy tried a frontal attack, he was like a lightning bolt, when he zigzagged in front of me, I held onto my plate. He was now standing right there in front of me, as he grabbed my plate, we made eye contact, it was bliss, when I let go of it. The look on his face was priceless, at that moment, he knew, that there was no going back. He already had my plate in his hand, it was too late, so he had to pick it up. When he turned around, he swooned really fast, and the plate slipped out of his hand. As it sailed through the air, I was full of joy, I finally had my revenge, so I was happy. When the plate hit the floor, it broke into tiny pieces, it sounded like a firecracker going off. A hushed silence came over the restaurant, nobody said a word; there was a moment of silence, then everybody started clapping. They were clapping for the busboy, but I didn't clap, I just laughed. Why do people always clap when something breaks in a restaurant? It happens all the time, I hate it, when something breaks, these fools clap. But the busboy didn't care if he broke a plate, he acted like it happened everyday. I had won, but he was oblivious to my victory, he didn't care. As I sat there in my seat, I was giddy with my win, so I had a big smile on my face, like a king on his throne. The busboy didn't care about my victory, he was still laughing at me, but I didn't care about him, so I ignored him. He disappeared into the kitchen, but then he came back out with a mop in his hand and he cleaned up his mess. *I won*, I told him, *I beat you fair and square!* He didn't say a word to me, he looked like he wanted to punch me, but he knew better, so he left me alone. I had gotten my revenge, it was sweet, but I didn't want to gloat, or embarrass him, it was over and done with. I won, and I beat him at his own game, which made it even sweeter, I thought. I found out later, from a friend of mine, what really had happened to Alabaster. Yes, there was a crazy night at Abiquiu lake, with the two cowboys from Texas, but there was also a huge bonfire, and a vicious dogfight in a truck. It was a reckless and dangerous stunt, but Alabaster is always willing to live with the consequences. He likes to face his problems head on, *in truth*, he says, *with no fear.* How did they get to the lake? Well, a ranch hand lent them his pickup truck and they drove there. Are you lost yet? Can you follow the story? Yes, a reader can get lost in a any story if they're not careful. But bear with me, because the best is yet to come. I mean, give me a break, I just started my story, and I have so much more to tell you. When you get lost in a book, it's a good thing, you should enjoy it. It's such an easy thing to do, to get lost in a book. When I read *TULOB*, I always forget to mark my page, I lose my place, so I have to start all over again. It's a pain in the ass, but I love it, because the novel is that good. I let Kundera do his job, I give him enough time to tell his story, so please do the same for me. Funny is funny, and Alabaster's story is funny. A dog attack, in a pick-up truck, on the open highway, in the middle of the night, is a hard thing to forget. Unbeknownst to Alabaster, or the two Texans, the ranch hand's poodle, Henrietta, was sleeping under the passenger seat. They were already halfway back, I heard, when the pooch unleashed her brutal attack on them. Alabaster hates dogs, so the thought of him trapped with Henrietta, is a pretty terrifying thing. Well, that explained all the wounds on his body, but what about the burns on his legs? When they got to Abiquiu Lake, they decided to build a bonfire on the shore, then, they wanted to jump over it for some reason. And, of course, Alabaster was the first one to fall into the fire. This sounds like a fake story, but it really happened, so you better believe it. Where did they get the wood for the fire? They got it from the bed of the truck; for some reason, the bed was packed with antique furniture, which turned out to be worth thousands of dollars. In the end, Alabaster's bonfire cost him around five thousand dollars. But he didn't care about the money, *it was worth it,* he said, *because you only live one life!* These city slickers are out of their minds, they come up with the craziest ideas, and they live in this void, between the city life and the natural world. You can't stop these crazy fools; every summer they appear in town, with their cowboy boots and cowboy hats. And when the summer ends, they disappear like smoke. Yes, they come to Santa Fe for a fantasy, but they usually find the real thing. Nature always wins in the end; you can fight her, but she eventually burns you out. I kept looking at Alabaster's feet, they looked like burnt chicken wings, but he didn't seem to be in any pain. *My dear boy, it was incredible, one day soon, you must jump into Abiquiu Lake!* He didn't want to talk about the bonfire, he wanted to talk about the lake. *That lake has magic in it, I was blessed, I swear, I feel like a new man. It was cold as hell, but it made me feel warm inside!* Alabaster wouldn't shut up about the lake, so I let him talk. When they got back to the ranch in the morning, the staff had to call an ambulance. Alabaster was in pretty bad shape, and the Texans were in worse shape; they needed medical help, my friend told me, but they all refused it. The inside of the truck looked like a bloody mess. Henrietta had no mercy on them, she was a vicious little thing. Of course, Alabaster spilled his Cognac all over the inside of the truck, so it was a real sticky situation. The paramedics wanted to take them to the local hospital, but they didn't want to go, so they couldn't take them against their will. After they bandaged up their wounds, they just left them there. *What happened to your feet?* I asked him. *I didn't have my morning coffee, and I was in a bad mood, so I didn't go to the hospital. You know me, I need my coffee, it's do or die!* It was just like him, I thought, to refuse to go to the hospital, so he can have his morning coffee. Alabaster drinks more coffee in a day than most people drink in a week. If he doesn't get his coffee in the morning, I promise you, he's of no use to anyone. *My dear boy, I had to choose, so I chose my coffee. Don't worry about me, I feel like a new man, and I had a great time at the lake!* He didn't look great, he looked like a crying shame. That was the last time I saw Alabaster in Santa Fe. After dinner, he went straight to the airport, then he flew back to New York. He has never told me any more details about his trip, it's been *his* little secret for all these years, so the truth will never be known. That's why most stories change over time, truth is slippery, and each time you read it, it becomes a whole *new* story. While I sat under the fig tree, I was daydreaming about my past, but I was thinking about my future. In Santa Fe, I had nothing to lose, so I lost myself in my studio. Yes, I jumped, but it wasn't into a lake, no, I jumped into a new style, Well, I didn't find my new style, my new style found me, if you know what I mean. I still remember the night I found it. I swear, one moment I painted one way, the next moment I painted another way. It's hard to explain why it happened, but my paintings changed over night. One can say, I quit talking and I started painting. I let my painting do the talking for me, so I didn't have to say anything. Now, I talk too much, I know, but in Santa Fe, I didn't say a word, I finally shut up. After a while, the paintings started talking back to me, and they had a lot to say. But I got lucky, because Alabaster loved my new paintings, too, and he really pushed them hard. He had the hungry collectors all lined up, they wanted red meat, so it got real crazy during this time. I can barely remember any of it, it was such a long time ago, the years all blend together. Most of the collectors liked my new paintings, some didn't, but he sold them all. *It's a buyer's market, the sellers just live in it,* Alabaster likes to say. My time in Santa Fe was well spent, and I had the paintings to prove it, so even Alabaster had to admit it. *Your sabbatical in Santa Fe was worth every penny,* he told me, *because I found you some new collectors.* Let me tell you, *new* collectors are hard to come by, they don't come cheap, so we were both pretty happy. I know how to use the tricks of my trade to get what I want; the results are usually mixed, but that doesn't matter, because the real *magic* happens in the studio. By now, Alabaster knows most of my tricks, he has seen them all, so he knows how the magic works. We are a team: he is the hat, I am the rabbit. Painting is trickery; I trick people for a living. I play chess with a blank canvas, my brush is my queen. I always fetch the queen, because she knows how to make my paintings appear. And, if I'm lucky, Alabaster will make them disappear. We made a deal years ago, and the same deal stands today: I paint the paintings, he sells them. After my time in Santa Fe, I came back to New York, but the city was much different, it was a funnier city, so it made me laugh a lot more. I was in pain from laughing so much, but I hurt in all the right places, if you know what I mean. New York is a microphone, you have to hold it close to your mouth in order to be heard. When you live there, you can be *in* the city, but you can't be *above* the city, because the white noise won't let you. Yes, the shit is deep, so once it sucks you in, you are dead on arrival. You can walk in the city, lots of people walk, or, you can run in the city, running is fun. But the one thing that you can't do in the city is *rise* above the city. I try and try to rise above it, but it keeps pulling me back down. When you live in New York, you start to smell just like the city, so I was beginning to stink. I had to get out, so I came to Bulgaria. *First, you plant the seed, then, come the roots, the branches, the leaves, and, finally, the apple appears!* Alabaster sounds like a poet. Yes, I got lost in Santa Fe, but then, I got found, so I came back to New York. I don't know why I came back to the city, but I did, and that was that. New Mexico is a hard place to leave, as you're leaving it, it whispers to you: *Stay with me.* The Land of Enchantment lit a fire in my soul, I could have stayed there forever, but the city called me back. Of course, I missed my wife; she visited me as much as she could, but it just wasn't enough, so I came back to the city. New York is a rotten apple, so every single day, you must take a big bite out of it. It's sweet and sour, it sticks the roof of my mouth, but I can't stop eating it. I was daydreaming the day away, so my mind was filled with fluff. The Greeks were on my mind, and they were calling me. I love the Greeks: Aristotle, Homer, Plato, Sophocles. They really know how to make you laugh. Plato is my favorite, because he practiced what he preached. A type of love is even named after him, which makes no sense at all. What is love? What is friendship? I should read Plato's *Symposium*, I thought, just for the fun of it. But, then again, it takes a lot of time to read a book, so maybe I'll pass on it. I can go on and on about Plato, because I like to talk shit, and shit attracts shit. In ancient Greece, a symposium was a banquet full of food and wine, but it was also a feast for debate and discussion. That sounds like a whole lot of fun, but I know one thing, you'll never catch me at a symposium. The last thing that I want is a room full of talking heads. If you ask me, most people talk too much. A room full of talkers sounds like a nightmare to me. Don't get me wrong, I can enjoy a fine feast, but a bunch of *winos*, talking about the meaning of love, is not my cup of tea. When I read Plato, I swear, I always want to shoot myself. Yes, when I read him, I get very drunk, and the more time that I spend with him, I get dizzier and dizzier. No, no Plato for me, I told myself, I'm taking a break from him, so I don't need him on this trip. I wasn't going to let Plato ruin me, I thought, like Kundera has ruined me. Yes, I'm a slave to *TULOB*, you can say, it my ball and chain. Kundera is a scoundrel, without a heart, and he knows how to write. Why did he make Tereza *heavy* and Sabina *light*? I don't know, only he knows, but the answer is in there, somewhere, if you read between the lines. But I didn't want to think about *TULOB*, I had other things on my mind, so I woke up. The nap under the tree had done me some good, I felt relaxed and at peace. But I was thirsty, so as soon as I opened my eyes, I stood up and I started walking back to the house. *Where's Leo when you need him?* I said with a laugh. I needed him now, and he was nowhere to be found. Let me tell you, if you are ever in need of a drink, always find a Russian, and your thirst will be quenched. Like I said before, the Russians will race to save you, and they will drown you with love. If I really wanted to, I could talk all day about the Russians, but I don't have the time, so I won't, I'll save it for another day.When I finally got back to the house, everyone was in the back yard. They were sitting at a wooden table, which was covered with a real spread of food. Of course, Leo found me before I found him, so I had a drink in my hand in no time. He had a bottle in one hand and two shot glasses in the other hand. He had broken out the *hard stuff* for this special occasion, he said, *because that's how we do it in Russia*. As soon as he poured the shot, I guzzled it down like a pauper. This bottle was only served *after* funerals, he said, because it was so *deadly*. I believed him, my throat was in flames, and my tongue was on fire. I don't know what was in that bottle, but it burned like hell, it was a good burn, it made you feel *alive*, if you know what I mean. Everybody was eating, drinking, and dancing around, it was a party. An old boombox was blaring some polka music, which was making everyone dance like crazy. I couldn't believe it, my wife was dancing with and Vera, I guess they were friends again. Even Yanko was doing a dance, some weird two-step on top of a chair. He kept screaming like a fool: *I love polka, I love polka, I love polka!* I liked the music , it was pure polka, nice and fast, so it made you want to move your feet. Even Leo got into the action, when he started doing the Russian twist, which made me laugh my ass off. I couldn't help myself, the music was too good, so I started dancing with Leo. Polka is so much fun, and anyone can do it. Even Kundera loves polka music, he admits it, and he likes to go to a Paris club called Alice. I've seen pictures of him, in old magazines, all dolled up, dancing his ass off with a pretty model by his side, dressed like a Czech playboy. Let me tell you, once you start doing the polka, you can't stop doing the polka! So I was dancing the polka like there was no tomorrow, and I let the rhythm take a hold of me. The beat was nice and hot, so my feet told the rest of my body what to do. *I love polka, polka, polka!* Yanko screamed. I couldn't stop laughing at him. He was finally coming out of his shell, and it was nice to see. The party lasted for a couple of hours, until the food and drink ran out, but the polka music never stopped. When we were finally saying our goodbyes, Leo got choked up, and he gave me bear hug, then he wished me good luck. *One day, I want to see Chicago,* he said, *I love America!* The Russians don't mince their words, they say what the feel. But I still didn't know, did he mean the city of Chicago, or was he talking about the play? I hope he meant the Windy City, because I wouldn't want him to see the play. Unlike the many critics, who loved the play, I hated it. I disliked it, but in a good way–I mean, it was so bad that it was so good. I won't sugarcoat it, I'll get straight to the point, *Chicago* is a stinky piece of shit! But it was sold out for years, and it got really great reviews, and it still packs them in like sardines. The theater critics run Broadway, so they have the last word on the shows that open and close. They love cheesy song and dance numbers, and they push what they like, so they went nuts for *Chicago*. I mean, if a certain critic writes a good review in a newspaper, then the show is written in gold, and it survives for another season. If you ask me, we should get rid of all these so-called critics. Yes, throw them all into a blender and press *liquefy*, then, watch their tight asses spin out of control. Let them spin like idiots in a fish bowl, because I don't want to listen them anymore. But, I must say, I love to read their reviews, some of them are quite entertaining. The best ones have big balls, and they like to show off their guts. After you turn off the blender, the critics will now be a mushy mess, so drink up! Once you've swallowed them, say a prayer, then stick your middle finger down your throat. Be careful, because they can come back up fast, and it can get real messy. I read their reviews, because if I don't, I might choke on them. The critics see what they want to see, and they write what they want to write. When I saw *Chicago*, I almost threw up, and I couldn't believe my eyes. It was a pretty bad play, but after it was over, all I wanted to do was talk about the play. I hated it and loved it at the same time, which was kind of confusing at the time. The cast members seemed bored, and the bothered looks on their faces made me laugh. I still can't get the smell of that play out of my nose; I smell it in my nostrils, I'd rather not smell it, but a bad play stays up your nose. Unlike a good play, which floats away, a really bad play never leaves you. And *Chicago* is one of them, like a road that never ends, I will never forget it. When we finally got back on the highway, Yanko put his foot to the metal, and we were officially on our way to the Black Sea. As soon as my head hit the leather seat, I fell asleep, I was dreaming again. My wife and

Yanko stayed quiet too, so it was nice to have some silence. I was tired and burnt out from the funeral and reception, and we still had a long ways to go. My body was sleeping, but my mind was awake, and I was thinking about the Black Sea. It's a very special place, I was eager to get there. But then *TULOB* popped into my mind again, and I was back inside it. I didn't want to think about Kundera, but I had no say in the matter, I was brainwashed. It's like a childhood memory, as you slowly remember it, it all comes flooding back into your mind. I wanted to sleep, but Kundera was now talking to me, so he was keeping me up. He never shuts up, I swear, he's always there, talking his shit to me. I could die out here on this Bulgarian highway, I thought, and no one would know that I was dead. It was a relief to think of disappearing in Bulgaria, and I didn't have to say goodbye to anyone. My mind was playing tricks on me, and I couldn't feel my body, but my soul was heavy. Bodies don't choose their souls, souls choose their bodies. *Bodies die,* Kundera said, *but souls live!* Well, I think he said it, at least, it sounds like something that he would say. If I had no body, and I was just a soul, then I would be free, I told myself. But all this soul searching was making me feel silly, so I tried to think of something else. I want to be more present, I thought, but Kundera is a vampire, and he sucks the life out of me. His fangs are like diamonds, when he bites into my neck, I always fall under his spell. I didn't want to think about *TULOB*, not on my vacation, but I couldn't help myself, it was too late not to think. I'm always thinking about it, one way or another, it invades my thoughts. It's all in the *Grand March of Souls*; a chapter devoted to the death of Joseph Stalin's son. First, Kundera sucks my blood, then he laughs right in my face. He writes a joke into the story, so is son, Yakov, dies in a German prison camp. He can't control his bowel movements, and he makes a mess in the latrine, so he's embarrassed and ashamed. Of course, Yakov kills himself in the most violent way, when he jumps into an electric fence. Kundera is a sadist, he loves the gore, and he's a sucker for burning flesh. As his body is still smoking, his soul flies away and it is free. But this isn't good enough for Kundera, it never is, so he brings up the religious problem of shit. Yes, that's right, how holy is shit? *Did Adam shit in the Garden of Eden? What is inside of God, pure shit?* I know Kundera is full of shit, but, come on, this is ridiculous. *Is shit holy?* Did he really write that? Yes, he did! Shit talk is gross, but Kundera won't shut up about it. But there's shit everywhere, I mean, just the other day, I was at an uptown gallery, and you won't believe what I saw hanging on the wall: framed pictures of shit. Yes, some hotshot artist has taken new photographs of human shit. It's been done before, but once is enough, I don't think we need anymore shit pictures. When I first saw them, I almost threw up, I couldn't stop gagging. I still can't look this artist in the eyes without laughing in his face. I couldn't believe my eyes, how was this even possible? Who in the hell wants to hang pictures of shit in their home? Well, believe or not, a lot of people do, because the entire show sold out. Holy shit? But this didn't surprise me, the collectors want what they want, and they wanted anything with shit on it. What's next, pictures of vomit? No, wait, it's too late, it's already been done. Holy vomit? Well, yes, another so-called artist has taken pictures of vomit. And, guess what, this show sold out, too! Some collector from Texas, with a fancy food fetish, bought every last piece. Nowadays, they collect almost anything: shit, vomit, blood, piss. These collectors don't care, they'll buy anything that they can get their hands on. I must admit, my paintings don't sell as fast as the shit and vomit pictures, but they sell at a steady pace, so I do just fine. I don't have to worry about the numbers, because my dealer has my back. Like our deal says: I paint them, Alabaster sells them. I'm lucky to have him, he is a man of his word, so I trust him completely. There are three types of men that need to be observed, Kundera says. The first man is: a man who needs a public of *unknown* eyes. I plead the Fifth on this one. The second man is: a man who needs a group of *familiar* eyes. Like most painters, I need my collectors. The third man is: a man who wants to be *completed* in the eyes of their lover. Yes, I was in love with my wife, and I was still working on her, so the best was yet to come. Then I opened my eyes and I looked out the window. Now, I was really awake, and my eyes were open wide. The highway was almost empty, and the land around it was desolate; there were no houses, no trees, no people, no nothing. It was my kind of landscape, it was flat and barren, so you could see for miles and miles. Alabaster would love Bulgaria, it's his kind of country, I thought. The land here had a vibration all its own, I was in love with its beauty, and captivated by the history of it. My wife was slowly falling back in love with it, I could tell, but it would take some more time for her to really adore it. She needed this vacation much more than I did, she's a workaholic, a self-described *perfectionist*, she never stops, so she wanted to relax. My wife works for the Fony Corporation, which is a world-class operation, and one of the best companies in the world. She is one of their top financial *examiners*, whatever that means, and she examines anything and everything for them. She deals with the numbers, the digits, the highs, the lows, and she works her magic, until she is satisfied with their net worth. She is one of the best in her field, but I still don't know what she does at Fony, it's a mystery to me. She has explained her job to me many times, and I still don't understand what she does for a living. But I know one thing, whatever she does there, it makes her a nervous wreck. She's in the right business, because she can wheel and deal with the best of them, and she never gets tired. She adds and subtracts the totals, she divides the dividends, multiplies the multiples, in order to reach the highest margin. It's complicated stuff, she says, I don't understand it, but she loves her job, because it makes her feel so alive. I could never do her job, no way, and her dedication and determination is inspiring to watch. She is very hardheaded, she commands respect, and she loves to teach people. The upper management noticed her on her first day of work, when she gave them her mission statement. My wife knows how to get noticed, she's whipsmart and independent as hell. When you make a good impression, they notice you, and she got promoted accordingly. She works with the big boys, but she holds her own, and she is a major asset to the company. Fony needs people like my wife, so they do their best to keep her happy. She's very hard on herself, and being such a critical thinker, she likes to overthink things. She loves her job, even though it makes her crazy, she likes to push herself. She is just like Alabaster, she loves a good contest, and she loves to win. Yanko had opera music playing on the car stereo, which fit the mood perfectly. This piece of music sounded familiar, but I couldn't pinpoint the composer. Was it Handel? Verdi? Rossini? Well, I know it wasn't Wagner–I know Wagner, and it wasn't him. Most classical music puts me to sleep, but this music woke me up. The bass kept perfect time, as the brass and strings blended together, the flutes flirted with the cymbals, and the piano floated over the beat, until the drums came in. I loved the music, it really carried me away, but I still couldn't think of the composer. Some people sing for a living, and my wife is one of them. She sings all day, then she comes home and she sings all night. She is like my teacher, and I'm her student, but I have a very closed mind. If life is a dance, then it's a slow waltz with no hands. It is full of twists and turns, hard to master, and with many mistakes along the way. Kundera knows all about this dance, and he loves to write about it, too. If *TULOB* is a dance, then it's a tango in the dark. Of course, Kundera made Tereza dream of a cultured life, filled with books and music. It's the oldest trick in the the book, but he has no shame. She dreams about love, because she wants to be *in love*, so Kundera gives her Tomas. She wants the right kind of man, a man who loves her soul, and not just her body. Kundera loves to play games with his readers, he gets off on it, I know he does. At first sight, Tereza falls in love with Tomas, and their love story begins with a bang. When she first visits him at his hotel, he has Beethoven playing in his room. She's in high heaven, in pure bliss, because it's the sweetest music that she's ever heard. At that moment, she can only imagine her life with Tomas, she dreams of being in his arms, when they are finally together in love. Her future is now *full of promise*, she says, because she will be happy with *him*. They'll live in Prague, a city made for lovers, as they grow old together, their love will blossom. When Tereza meets Tomas, she can't control herself, she is too exited, she is overflowing with love. She has many questions for him, but does he have the answers? She is willing to wait for him, she says, until he sees her as his wife. Love is a question mark, so Kundera makes her fall deeper and deeper in love with him. When you're in love, the answers don't really matter, only the questions matter. Yes, that one silly question about love still remains: *What is love?* Then the composer's name came to me, I suddenly remembered the music. *It's Mozart!* I said. I should have known that it was him, but my mind went blank. It was silly not to know Mozart's music, his sound is all his own, so I should have recognized it. But we live in a world of our own creation, that was his creation, and I had my own, which was being a painter. I always have my tools at the ready: my paint,

JAMIE ZECCOLA

my brush, my canvas. And my wife has her tools: her computer, her phone, her shredder. Our very large apartment has gotten very small over the years, because we have collected so much stuff. Most people can't live like this, it's too messy, too cluttered, too lived in. My wife tolerates my stuff and I tolerate hers, what can I say, it's a match made in heaven. Alabaster loves our apartment, and every time he stops by, he will always knock something over. It's kind of a game for him, he likes to play with me, and he likes to watch me squirm. But his favorite thing to knock over are my books. I have so many of them, so he does it with ease; if he sees a pile of books, watch out, they will fall like dominoes. He gets a weird thrill from it, so he does it whenever he can. My wife loves to see the look on my face when Alabaster shows up at our door, with a bottle of Cognac and that goofy look on his face. Of course, he spills his brandy all over the place, and there is no way to stop the sticky stuff from seeping into the cracks. My books always get the worst of it, especially the paperbacks; the hardcovers hold their own, they protect their inner pages. Spilt Cognac is Alabaster's signature, it's his pride and joy, and he's one of the best *spillers* out there. It doesn't matter where goes, he will spill his Cognac. He comes from a family of doctors; his father, mother, brother and sister have all become doctors. I don't know how, but Alabaster broke the mold and he became an art dealer. *I didn't find the art world*, he says, *the art world found me!* The beginning of his art dealing career is still kind of a mystery, but it involves a trip from London to Paris. He has tried to explain this trip to me, but I never get the full picture, because he always leaves out the important details. Alabaster loves to tease you with his tall tales, so you never get the real story. Key moments in his life are left out, while fleeting moments are fawned over. But one thing is for sure, he does have a favorite painter, and his name is J. M.

W. Turner. All he ever talks about are those damn Turner paintings that he saw in the Tate Gallery. *The paintings were beyond this world*, he said, *they were made for another world, so I became an art dealer!* He sounded like an English poet, so he liked to hear himself talk. He loved to reminisce about this trip, as if it held some deep meaning for him. In London, he met a red-haired Scottish girl named Samantha, who became his accomplice. He first laid his eyes on her in the main gallery, he told me, while she was staring at the one of Turner paintings. She looked just like Aphrodite, *floating on the sea foam,* he said, as she glided through the old gallery. Their love affair started in London, but it ended in Paris. This clandestine trip with Samantha, to the City of Love, was a major bump in their relationship. They went to Paris in order to retrieve a lost Augustus John painting, he claimed, but that made no sense at all, because Alabaster doesn't like Augustus John, so that's where his story falls apart. When I listen to him talk, I have to read *between* the lines, because he will divulge only so much truth. His friends call them the *Cognac Tales,* and they are always the talk of the town. His tales are notoriously packed with white lies and half-truths. Most of us have our own sticky tale to tell, and I have mine, but his rendezvous in Paris is still clouded in mystery and intrigue. I don't know what really happened there, but I do know that Alabaster and Samantha got arrested for trespassing. There was even a story in *Le Monde*, the headline translated to: *American Art Dealer Arrested In Attempted Art Heist!* But Alabaster was overjoyed with his arrest, proud of it; and he still has the newspaper article hanging in his office. He had it framed to look like a doctor's license, in honor of his parents, so it makes him happy when he looks at it. They were caught red-handed with the John painting, inside of some rich Parisian's apartment. I don't know what they were trying to do, but Alabaster claims that the painting wasn't being *stolen*, no, it was being *returned*. They weren't stealing the painting, they were returning the painting. Yes, he admitted to the break-in, and Samantha did too, but they had the painting already in their possession, so they couldn't be charged with anything serious. They had every intent of leaving the painting behind, he said, but they didn't know about the alarm system, and that was their only mistake. The French police were baffled by their *stupide* crime, it didn't make any sense to them, but they had to let them go. Of course, he didn't tell the cops everything; and he never gave them a straight answer as to how they got inside the apartment. After a few days, the police realized that the painting wasn't stolen, it had been *borrowed* from Samantha's father, so they had to give the painting back to her. Yes, she was on vacation in London, with the painting, when she met Alabaster at the Tate Gallery. For some reason, the apartment's owner didn't want to press any charges, and the police let them go. I still laugh when I think about their caper, because the *crime* doesn't fit the *time*, if you know what I mean. Alabaster still brags about his time in jail, he proudly says: *I took it like a man, and I did my time.* Even though there was no crime, he is not shy about talking about a crime. *I was in the wrong place at the right time, so my only crime is love!* Yes, he's right, love is slippery, and time is a thief, I thought. The clock tick tocks as it goes round and round, until it finally stops. But Alabaster has his own clock, and he lives on his own time, so his life has been full of timeless love. He fell in love, with art, late in life, and he has been making up for lost time ever since. He was going to be a doctor, but after his trip to London, and Paris, he became an art dealer. If it wasn't for Samantha, I don't think Alabaster would have become a dealer. In a strange way, *she* made him into what *he* is today. I don't know what she did to him, but he became a so-called *connoisseur* overnight. The romance of art is kissed with many good intentions, and Alabaster got French kissed on this trip, so he was a changed man. He is in love with his job, and like any marriage, it has its ups and downs. But he is one of the best dealers around, I think, so I'm very lucky to be with him. He has always kept me in the loop with what is happening in the market. Yes, I have my unsold paintings, but I have nothing to worry about, because he will sell them sooner or later. There is one painting in particular, it is for sale and on the market, that I'm very curious about. But I was on my vacation, so it was silly to think about it now. Alabaster has one rule as a dealer: *Don't call me, I'll call you.* It makes a lot of sense, because a deal can take forever, so I never call him during this time. He doesn't want to jinx the deal, he says, so he keeps his code of silence, which is fine by me. Some deals take only a day to close, but most deals last a few months, before all the paperwork is signed. The big deals can take years to work out, and those are the hardest to get done. But the art business is a year-round business, it never stops, so Alabaster is always on the make. Before any deal period begins, I try and buy only the bare essentials: food, water, wine, paint. I'm usually prepared for the long haul, so I always have enough rations to last a couple of weeks. We never talk about the deal, not a word is spoken between us, we have zero communication. It's bad luck if we discuss the deal in the *middle* of the deal, he says, so I don't! Plus, so many things can go wrong: a collector can get cold feet and change their mind; the painting can get damaged in transit; or the selling price is to high and it doesn't sell. But once the deal is done, I mean, signed, sealed, and delivered, then, we pop the corks! Alabaster likes to celebrate the end of every deal with a lavish party. His parties are out of this world, they're insane, and they usually end with a riot. I still remember this one party in particular, it was for Duke A. Barnstable, a fellow painter friend of mine. People still talk about this party, it was something special, and surely a night to remember. For one night only, the uptown folks mingled with the downtown folks, and everybody got along just fine. Alabaster's parties always start off very small, but as the night goes on, they always become bigger and bigger. In the beginning, the party is just an *idea* in his head, then, over time, it becomes a living reality. Most of his parties are slow going at first, they groove along at a steady pace, then they catch on fire in the morning. When the sun comes up, a good party turns into a great party, and that's when most of the crazy things happen. Let me tell you, Alabaster really knows how to throw a victory party, he likes to spend money, so it can get kind of ridiculous. And Duke's party is a party that I won't soon forget. It almost turned into a riot, before the cops shut it down. Alabaster had sold out all of Duke's paintings from his show, for the asking price, so he had a hot painter on their hands. The paintings were well-received by the critics, and most of the art magazines gave positive reviews of the show, which was quite surprising, because they never agree on anything. But Duke's party was a shitshow, it was too crowded, they had invited too many people, so it got real crazy real fast. I have to say, Alabaster found a great building for the party, on Greene Street, in SoHo. It was the former home of a fortune cookie company, which made it the perfect space for a victory party. This place was stacked; it had a huge dance floor, an outdoor patio, and a rooftop bar. Let me tell you, this kind of space doesn't pop up on the party scene that often, so Alabaster took full advantage of it. An anonymous collector had given him the place *free of charge*, he said, *with no strings attached!* Duke's party was packed wall to wall with anybody and everybody, it seemed like the whole art world was there that night. Of course, Alabaster was the ringleader of this circus, so he was the life of the party. When I first saw him, he had a Polish sausage in one hand and a glass of Cognac in the other hand. Duke was finally having *his* moment in New York, which was nice to see, and he had the sales to prove it. Duke was happy, so Alabaster was happy, and it showed on their faces. This didn't happen most of the time, it almost never happened, so they were really making the most of the night. Believe it or not, most paintings never sell for the asking price, they're usually bought at a discount. Who buys paintings? Well, the collectors do, but the art world has no rules, the collectors run the show, so they buy them on the cheap. Alabaster lives for this business, he really enjoys it, and he loves the action. We work well together, and I have total trust in his judgement. Every painter needs a dealer like him, so when I finally found him, I kept him. I have one dealer, but he has many other painters that he represents. He has a nice stable of horses in the race, we keep him very busy, but that's the way he likes it. Alabaster is a dealer's dealer, he'll do anything for you, and that feels quite nice. He's one of the best in the business, I think, so I'm lucky to have him. Yes, it was Duke's victory that we were celebrating that night, but it was also Alabaster's. Duke had painted the paintings, and Alabaster did the heavy lifting, he sold them all. He's a hustler by trade, a gambler by choice, and he loves art. He knows how to buy art with the best of them, but selling paintings is almost impossible, it's a lost art, and even harder to do. It takes a special skill to sell a painting, and Alabaster has mastered it. I could never do what he does, I don't have the patience; and he could never do what I do, he doesn't have the time. All painters rise and fall out of fashion, but when it happens, it's reassuring to have a dealer like Alabaster. I got lucky, I met him at the right time, early in my career, so it's been a slow and steady climb so far. But Duke's climb to the top was like a rocket, and his fame came fast, so, back then, he was loving every minute of it. When his show sold out, his star was shining bright, and the paintings were all spoken for, so he had nothing to worry about. Here's a little secret: most paintings don't sell. They're traded away, or, they're stored in the basement, never to be seen again. Out of sight, out of mind, out of the way! Galleries are expensive storage containers, but it's a built-in operating cost, *it comes with the territory*, so *you better get used to it*, Alabaster likes to say. I have never gotten used to it, but what can I do about it, I can't buy my own paintings. But on this night, Duke was a wanted man, because Alabaster sold every painting in the show, so his prices went through the roof. There was now a waiting list for his work, and his future paintings had already sold out, which is always a good sign for a painter. All of a sudden, Duke was a big blip on the art radar, which was strange, because he was more known as a street artist at the time; but after this show, he became a gallery artist. Nothing is off limits to the collectors, and now they wanted Duke's paintings, so he spent most of his time painting them. At the time, Duke was considered a *cross-over* artist, but after he crossed over, he never left the gallery. He had the ability to be popular in a gallery, and he was well respected on the street. His street tag was *DAB*, he had a huge following, but most people didn't know about his paintings. In the gallery, he was Duke A. Barnstable, and on this night, he was the toast of the town. After this party, Duke gave up street art, and he focussed more on his paintings. I have never done any street art, I don't want to, I never have, so I prefer the inside of my studio. The street is no place for me, I thought, the weather is always unpredictable and the cops are always following their orders. Well, I tried it once, when I went out with Duke one night, but I hated it! We painted some clowns on the side of this building, but it took us three hours to do it, so I over it. I must confess, for the first hour, I had some fun, but the last two hours were hell; I got paint in my hair, I cut my hand, and I stepped in dog shit. I was stupid to try it, I got what I deserved, and I learned my lesson. But Duke loved every minute of it, he was in heaven, and he looked so happy on the street. Back then, he loved the streets, and the streets loved him. But, these days, he has pretty much given up the streets. Well, every now and then, *when I get the urge*, he says, he'll go out and do some street art. But he wears a nice suit and a nice pair of shoes, *when I do it*, so nobody suspects him. He still gets a big thrill out of it, but now, *I look more like a banker than a painter*. Duke likes his new *DAB* disguise, because he can walk around and not be bothered by people. His fans still recognize him, but not like they used to, back when he popular, everybody knew his face. I swear, back then, *DAB* was everywhere in the city. He first got known for his pink lions, the smiling cats were hilarious, and they were spray painted on every corner. The lions had quotation bubbles above them, with funny jokes written inside. Everybody was talking about these pink lions, but nobody knew who painted them. Back in the beginning, *DAB* was just a tag, and he was anonymous, so it fed into his street persona. Duke didn't want to be recognized, he just wanted to have fun, so he kept *DAB* under the radar. But his street art was in your face, it was everywhere, so he got noticed right away. Duke tried to hide his identity, but it didn't work, he was eventually found out. New Yorkers love to gossip, so the word got out real fast, it was too late, Duke was *DAB*. After the truth was revealed, it was like a bomb going off, and he was the hottest thing in the city. *DAB*, not Duke, became a bona fide celebrity. And this is when Alabaster came into the picture, when he brought Duke into his gallery. It was the perfect time for them to team up, because Duke was getting tired of his fame, so the time was right for something new. But the public wanted *DAB*, not Duke, and his paintings were nothing like his street art, so his fans deserted him. The critics thought it was all a big joke, and his first gallery shows got mixed reviews. Yes, now, Duke was just another painter in the city, he was no longer *DAB*, so it took him some time to find his footing. He was no longer known by millions, now, only a few collectors knew his name. I have always liked Duke's paintings, they have a lazy style that really appeals to me. But the critics weren't so kind, they treated him like a clown, they wrote absurd things about his style and technique. But Alabaster never wavered, he stood right by Duke, and he kept on pushing his paintings. He was never interested in the *DAB* stuff, so he never got involved with it. *I'm a gallery dealer, not a street dealer,* Alabaster likes to say. Even though Duke's paintings have been seen by a lot of people, his street stuff was seen by millions. Alabaster has very fine taste, he's old school, he collects only oil paintings and bronze sculptures. He prefers one-of-a-kind paintings, and he ignores diptychs and triptychs. Duke was tired of his *DAB* persona, everybody wanted a piece of him, so he was happy to be in Alabaster's gallery. Duke is very aloof, claims to be misunderstood, and he has a penchant for privacy. He is Chaplin, mixed with Houdini and Warhol. Back then, at the height of his fame, he liked the attention that he got from being *DAB*, but now, he can live without it, it makes him nervous, so he longs for a quiet life. People still stare, and his fans want photos, but it isn't like it used to be. *DAB* became a burden to Duke, so he quit being *DAB*. He used to crave the attention, but today, it's a burden to him, and he is happy being himself. On this night, Duke was the toast of the town, and the city came out to show him love. It was a wild and crazy party, and like most victories, in ended with a loss, with the cops at the front door. Alabaster and Duke are made for each other, they're a perfect match, and they really know how to enjoy life. This party must have been the only party in town, because the place was completely packed. Of course, we were late to the party, so by the time we got there, it was at full capacity. You couldn't even see the front door, so there was complete chaos in the street. A mob of people decided to bum-rush the entrance, but they got pushed back by the doormen. The crowd wanted to get in but there was no more room, they didn't care, they just wanted to get in. Duke had invited his friends and Alabaster had invited his, so it was like a zoo in there. Luckily, Alabaster came to our rescue and he snuck us in through the back door. I couldn't believe how many people were crammed inside this building, it was hot and sweaty, the place smelled like sandalwood and sardines. As soon as my wife and I got on the dance floor, we were immediately sucked into a sea of people. When I started dancing, a bunch of talkers came over and they stood right by me. They weren't dancing, no, they were talking, and it was getting me mad. Let me tell you, there's nothing worse than a bunch of talkers, talking on the dance floor, it drives me nuts. I wanted to dance, but I couldn't, because the talkers were talking. I didn't want to talk, I just wanted to dance, but they wouldn't let me, so my wife and I got off the dance floor. When we finally found the bar, Duke was there, and he two victory cocktails in his hands for us. After we did a toast, I said a few words of praise about him, then we had a short talk. He seemed happy enough, he had this goofy smile on his face, and he kept licking his lips. Duke's paintings were hanging on the walls, which was a nice touch, and a proper way to honor him, I thought. But I could barely see the paintings, because there were so many people standing in front of them. Alabaster had hired belly dancers, fortune tellers, and a couple of clowns. Duke was with his new girlfriend, *Bibi*, a young Swedish artist. She had a nice style, she looked super cool, she was wearing a bowler hat, a silk dress, and hippie boots. She looked like a Swedish cream puff, she was very white, with deep blue eyes. I know a Swede when I see Swede, and Bibi was a Swede, if you know what I mean. She had a Swedish smile, she was silly, a little shy, but real sweet. She was an avid reader, she said, so we had a lot in common, she loved books. She liked movies, but only the *French ones*, because *they always make me cry!* Bibi was cool, we clicked right away, and she was real easy to talk to. Of course, I had only one question for her: *Do you like Ingmar Bergman?* I was surprised when she said: *No, I really hate him!* I didn't believe her at first. *I hate Bergman with a passion that I can't describe!* She called him only by his last name, she never said his first name once, which was kind of odd. *He's a joke in my country, his movies are trash,* Bibi said, *he's the Swedish Spielberg!* I had to laugh at her comparison, she was droll, funny, and she said exactly what was on her mind. She couldn't understand the fascination that we Americans had for Bergman. *His films are shit,* she yelled, *they're soap operas, and I hate them!* I didn't agree with her, but I told her that I did, because I didn't want to fight over Bergman. Duke disagreed with us, and he let us know about it: *You are both wrong, they're not soap operas, they're passion plays about life that need to be told.* We are missing Bergman's genius, he said, or, we are too blind to see it. *It's all in his writing, and his words, they allow the shifts in mood to occur while the action stays still, and this is what makes his movies so magical!* I was willing to listen to Duke's defense of Ingmar Bergman, but he was kind of beating around the bush, talking nonsense, and he wasn't making much sense. But Duke was just being his difficult Duke, and he was beginning to get on my nerves. Bibi assured me that most Swedes hated Bergman. *It's our dirty little secret,* she said with a devilish grin, *so we keep our true feelings hidden inside.* The Swedes like to hide everything, even their hate is hidden inside. But Duke kept praising Bergman's films, almost sucking up to him, like he was his agent. Then all of his sentences became questions. *Why don't you like Wild Strawberries? Have you ever seen Autumn Sonata? What is your favorite scene in Persona?* He named off every Bergman film, one by one, like an auctioneer. For some reason, Bibi got really angry with Duke, but he didn't care, he kept on talking about Bergman, he wouldn't stop. But I didn't want to fight about Bergman, so I finally agreed with him. I must say, Bergman's films do have their charms, but most of them have no real fire. They burn low, like warm embers, they smolder and smoke, until they go out. *Wild Strawberries* is a one of his best films, and one of my favorites. *Persona* is a pretty slow go, but the ending is genius. *Autumn Sonata* is an absolute mess, and it made me cry my eyes out. I appreciate his sappy style, he likes to jump right in, and he loves to take chances. but he gets on my nerves. *The Seventh Seal* was my favorite film by Bergman, and Bibi agreed with me. But Duke wasn't so sure, he had another film on his mind, and that wasn't it. Bibi looked Swedish: she was very tall, very blond, and she had very blue eyes. She was real sure of herself, almost cocky, but I liked her vibe, she was fun and weird, in a good way. But the one thing about her that got on my nerves was her fake Midwestern accent, which drove me nuts! I don't know why she talked like this, she could barely finish a thought, without saying *you know* after every sentence. *I love Scenes From A Marriage, you know, it's one of his best films, you know!* Bibi's Chicago accent sounded ridiculous, she was from Stockholm, and she couldn't hide it. Duke had no problem with her fake accent, because he was in love with her, so, to him, she sounded like a nightingale. They were a funny couple, they were total opposites, so they seem to fight a lot. As the night went on, after I got to know Bibi, her guard went down, and she revealed another secret to me. *I'm sorry, it's all a big lie, you know! I really love Bergman, you know! I didn't want to tell you, you know!* She had been lying all this time, because she didn't want me to find out the truth. She couldn't help herself, she said, she loves Bergman, and she wasn't ashamed of it. *Persona is one of my favorite films, I'm obsessed with Liv Ullmann.* Bibi loved her acting and her screen presence, and the way she revealed herself on-screen. Perhaps I was being too hard on Bergman, I thought, his films aren't that bad. But Bibi's accent was making me crazy, so I tried to tune her out, but I couldn't. She sounded like a broken record, as she went on and on about *Persona*. Then I noticed the paint. For some reason, Bibi had green paint on her hands, but she ignored the paint, like it wasn't even there, so I ignored it. I could barely remember anything about *Persona*, I saw it years ago, so I let Bibi talk. The film is a love story about two women: Alma, a nurse, and Elisabet, an actress. It's not a complicated plot, but it takes a little time to understand it. The film can be described in four words: Alma talks, Elisabet listens. Bergman was sly, he made the two women resemble each other, so their two faces blend to make one face. He uses a split screen, which makes Alma and Elisabet look like Siamese twins. That is always Bergman's plan, he wants to pull a fast one on his audience, and he always finds a way to do it. Bibi was fun to talk to, but she was getting too emotional. *It's one of my favorite films*, she weeped, *I've seen it a hundred times!* Bibi wouldn't shut up, she was being obnoxious, so I finally ditched her. What can I say, she was driving me crazy, *you know!* Bibi and Duke left the party around midnight, I didn't see them again, they never said good-bye, which was strange. But Duke's victory party went on without him, and it only got crazier, until nobody wanted to leave. The dancers danced, the talkers talked, and the spillers spilled. Yes, Alabaster spilled his Cognac everywhere. When my wife's favorite song came on, we made a beeline to the dance floor, she'd waited all night long for this song, so she wasn't going to miss it. My wife jumped up and down like a kid, she lost herself in the music, as she spun in circles. All of the movers and shakers of the city were there that night, and most of them were drunk or half-naked. After my wife's favorite song ended, she wanted to leave, so we headed to the door. I wanted to stay, but she wanted to leave, so we left. But it's better to leave a party too *early*, she told me, than to stay too *late*. Alabaster always stays too late, so I get jealous of him. Like most victory parties, Duke's party ended up the same way, with the cops at the front door. As we were going down the stairs, the boys in blue were coming up the stairs. We left at the perfect time, before the shit went down, we got lucky. It got out of hand, people were arrested, and the rest is history. The next morning, Alabaster was livid, he couldn't believe what had happened. *The stupid cops ruined my damn party,* he screamed into the phone. I expected his call, he always calls me the day after a party, to get the gossip. *The cops are idiots, they didn't have to shut down my party! I won't let this one go, some heads are going to roll!* The party was a fire hazard, the cops told him, and there had been too many noise complaints, so they had no other choice. They had direct orders from the top brass, to do *whatever is necessary*, they said, in order to keep the peace. Alabaster knows people in the fire department, who could have helped him with his fire problem, but they didn't answer their phones. All of the lines were busy, or dead, and no one answered. *I feel like a big sucker, I won't be ignored! I have to do something, to teach them a lesson!* He had called city hall, he said, and left a message in the Mayor's office, but nobody was calling him back. I told him to *let it go*, and not to dwell on it, but he wouldn't listen to me, so he kept on ranting about the cops. *I have nothing against the cops, I know they were just following their orders, but they didn't have to be so rude to me! The party still had a few more hours left, and the sun was just coming up!* But the party had to end *sooner or later*, I told him, so why not *then?* The off-duty cops inside the party couldn't convince the on-duty cops to let the party go on, they had orders, so they shut it down. Alabaster wouldn't shut up about the cops, he was rolling, so I let him roll. *My dear boy, last night was such a blast! It was just like the good old days of SoHo, before it turned into a shopping mall! Nowadays, the cops don't let you do anything in this city, it used to be much more fun! The city has gone to shit, they won't even let you throw a victory party!* Alabaster was mad, and hurt, but he would get over it. He had to get over it, I told him, because if he didn't, he would hold a grudge against the cops. *It wasn't their fault, they had to shut down your party,* I said, *and it was a great party, so you should be happy.* Yes, he was happy, but he was also sad, he said, and he had a little secret to tell me. *My dear boy, you're not gonna believe it, but I have to confess this to you, and I need to tell you the truth. I didn't mean to do it, I never intended to do it, I swear, it just happened.* What did he do? *It was a mistake, I should have hung up!* Hung up on who? *I'm the one who called the cops. Yes, I called the cops on myself. I didn't want to do it, but I had to, I had no other choice, I was vandalized!* What was he talking about? Why would he call the cops on himself? But he did, he was proud of himself, he said, and he didn't care if people found out the truth. *I had to do it, because some asshole ruined Duke's paintings!* Someone had spray painted green bananas on the paintings. *What am I going to do with these paintings? I can't sell them, they're worthless!* Alabaster was upset, but he sounded like his normal self, and he was a little too upset, I thought, which seemed a little fishy to me. I could smell him through the phone, he was not telling the truth. *Who would do such a thing? It was one of Duke's crazy friends, I know it, I told him not invite them to the party!*

Of course, the bananas could be removed, it was only spray paint, so it would be a pretty easy thing to do, I told him. He knew that the paint could be taken off, but he didn't want to listen to me, he was being a drama queen. Let me tell you, Alabaster loves drama, it's in his blood, and he searches for it. *The paintings are lost forever, I can't salvage them, they have to be destroyed!* He sounded off his rocker, he knew that they could be cleaned, but he still was acting dumb. I smelled fish, but I didn't know what kind. *Duke got arrested last night! And Bibi did too!* Arrested for what? *They were doing graffiti on the side of a building, so the cops locked them up. I had to bail them out this morning. I knew Bibi was trouble, I should've warned Duke about her, she has him wrapped around her finger!* Of course, Alabaster blamed Bibi for their arrest; Duke did nothing wrong, he was the innocent victim. *The cops picked them up on Wooster Street, they were painting on the side of a bank building. They almost got away, but they didn't run fast enough. Bibi is out of her mind, she's a kook, I don't see what Duke sees in her!* Just like a runny faucet, Alabaster wouldn't stop blaming Bibi for everything. *My dear boy, I must confess, I have another secret to tell you, I know who vandalized Duke's paintings.* He was all over the place, he sounded drunk. *I know who painted the fucking green bananas on the paintings! I know the truth, I saw it with my own two eyes.* Alabaster sounded flabbergasted, he was out of breath. *Bibi did it!* Bibi did what? *She vandalized Duke's paintings!* I didn't believe him, but he was adamant about it. *I know she did it, and I'm sure Duke helped her do it!* But then I remembered the green paint on Bibi's hands, I had forgotten all about it. *Bibi was the leader, Duke was just along for the ride!* I had to laugh at him, this was funny stuff, so I couldn't stop laughing. *I told Duke to stay away from her, but he wouldn't listen to me. She has total control over him, I feel powerless. Last night was supposed to be Duke's night, not Bibi's night!* I don't know why he blamed Bibi, it wasn't fair,

I'm sure Duke had something to do with it. Yes, I did see the green paint on Bibi's hands, that is true, but that didn't make her the mastermind. Bibi and Duke were both there, so it was both of their faults. Duke was no innocent bystander, so some of the blame has to go to him. I didn't know this at the time, but Bibi was a pretty well-known painter in Sweden. She turned out to be a famous street artist, named *OLUST*. She was a household name in her country, so everybody had heard of her. I found all this out later, when Bibi told me her life story. She had come to the United States on a dare, *a double dare*, she said, in order to *make a name* for herself. She wanted to be popular here, just like she was back in Sweden, she said, *but New York is a hard nut to crack, you know!* When she first arrived in the city, she fell in love with the street art, and DAB's green monkeys were her favorite. She was obsessed with these monkeys, she said, *they spoke to me*, so she fell in love with *DAB*. They became her guardian angels, and they protected her in this concrete jungle. I also remember those green monkeys, I mean, they were everywhere; downtown, uptown, anywhere you looked, you saw them. Before *DAB* got famous, Duke roamed the streets without a care in the world. He could plaster half of the city in just one night. His style was one of a kind, it made you laugh and think at the same time. His green monkeys asked simple questions, so they needed simple answers. Back then, his punchlines were never revealed, so the joke was always on you. *DAB* made his name bigger with his green monkeys; after them, people started talking about *him*. It was hilarious, Duke became a mystical street cowboy, and he was here to save us all. In the beginning, *DAB* was anonymous, so he could get away with anything, but after that summer, when his green monkeys invaded the city, he became a moving target. There was a heatwave, but the green monkeys kept us cool, they were everywhere, so the city got flooded. *DAB* had one question for New York City: *Do you want to dance?* I don't know what the green monkeys meant by that, but it made me laugh. But that was then, and this is now, the times have changed. Alabaster was right about Bibi, it was her plan to paint the green bananas on Duke's paintings. She confessed to me later, when she spilled her guts, that she had planned the whole thing out in advance. Bibi went to Duke's victory party with the spray can and stencil already in her purse. *It was my mission to make my mark in this city, and nothing was going to stop me,* she said. Duke knew nothing about her plan, he was blind to it all, he was just there to support her. *I came up with the idea all by myself, without any help from Duke.* I didn't believe her, I never will, but I had to, because I knew Duke, and he was no pushover. After the victory party, when the dust finally settled, these paintings became a hot commodity. There were only twenty of them, so their prices went through the roof. A wild frenzy erupted when these paintings came on the market, every serious collector was blue in the face, and they were all desperate to own one of the paintings. Luckily, for Alabaster, he became the sole proprietor of the so-called *Green Bananas*. He had total control over the paintings, so he showed them off. After their arrest, Duke and Bibi became an *art duo,* and the city fell madly in love with them. And they fell madly in love with the city, so their street art was everywhere. Duke and Bibi were made for each other, but *DAB* and *OLUST* were not. They were like fire and water, so their duo didn't last that long, only a couple of months. After they broke up, Bibi moved back to Sweden, and she became even more famous than before. *OLUST* is now the Swedish Warhol, she has millions of fans that buy her art. Let me tell you, the Swedes are thieves, they steal everything, even their art! They take a little bit of this, a little bit of that, then they come up with their own Swedish version if it. Instead of Warhol's yellow bananas, now, we have Bibi's green bananas. It seems like a joke, I know, but it's not, it's all true! Bibi paints a hundred paintings a week, she can't paint them fast enough. *OLUST* has become a gallery star, so her paintings are now her bread and butter. Unlike Duke, Bibi loves being famous, she can't get enough of it. After the hype died down, Alabaster sold the Green Bananas, all twenty of them, to some lucky collector in New Jersey. I still saw Duke, here and there, at the random cocktail party, but that's about it. He seemed sad, he really missed Bibi, and he wanted her back, he told me, but she didn't want to come back. His new set of paintings are even dedicated to her; they're beautiful double portraits of women. They are painted in his playful style, which I like, and a looseness, that is all Duke's own. When I first saw these paintings, I didn't like them, but with some time, they have grown on me. They are very large, painted thick with oil and acrylic, they look like quicksand paintings. My wife doesn't like Duke's new paintings, *they all look the same*, she says, but she likes his other paintings. She does have a point, they do all have the same color combinations. But my wife is very picky about her art, she tends to hate everything, so I take it like a grain of salt. But she loves Ingmar Bergman, and her favorite film of his is *Persona*. Which is strange, because Bergman is a minimalist, and my wife is a maximalist. My wife is more of an Elisabet, I think, than an Alma, because she hates to talk. But, then again, she loves to listen, so maybe she's an Alma. The one scene in *Persona*, that I don't understand, is the best scene in the movie. While Alma is watching Elisabet sleep, she suddenly hears a man screaming outside, so she goes to see who it is. Alma finds Elisabet's husband in the back yard, but something is off, because he addresses her as if she is Elisabet. Is he confused? Why does he think Alma is his wife? I don't get it, it baffles me, am I missing something? Bergman is a master at this, he hides his intentions, until it's too late. I have watched this scene many times, and I still don't know what it means. *I'm not your wife*, Alma tells him, but he ignores her, as he begins to tell her about the love that he has for Elisabet. I don't know why he doesn't recognize his own wife, but the scene is pure magic. Is Alma another woman, or is she his wife? *We must see each other as two anxious children*, he tells Alma. It's a confusing scene, but Bergman wanted it that way. Is she Elisabet or Alma? It's a question with no answer, which isn't right, but Bergman is a big tease, and he likes to jerk you off while you're in the dark. Don't get me wrong, I like the movie a lot, but that scene is a riddle. When Alma admits to Elisabet's husband that she is in love with him, I almost threw up. Of course, Bergman shoots their love scene like a peeping tom, with tight angles and creepy close-ups. As they make love, Elisabet sits right next to the bed, like a bird on a wire, she watches them silently, while they devour each other. This scene still sticks in my brain, I can't forget it, it's inside my memory bank. Bergman is a bully, he likes to beat me up, but I won't let him. When I woke up, I was refreshed, and I felt wide awake again. I felt like a new man, I had to tell someone, so I told my wife this: *We must see each other as two anxious children*. She barely looked my way, she didn't say a word, she ignored me, like I was invisible. It was supposed to be a joke, but she didn't take it that way, she didn't even smile. Yanko had been driving like a man possessed, with his foot on the metal and his eyes on the prize, so we were making very good time. Yanko and my wife had talked almost nonstop for the entire trip, so I was tired of listening to them. I needed some peace and quiet, but I couldn't find any. Brothers and sisters really know how to talk, I mean, that's all they do is talk. To hear them talking for hours, in a foreign language, while being stuck in this car, was a slow and painful torture. I barely got any sleep, so I was still groggy, I wanted silence, but I got the opposite. I tried to tune them out, so I closed my eyes again and I tried to relax. Then I started counting sheep, but it was useless, because my mind was still thinking about *Persona*. Bergman's words were still floating around in my head: *I'm not like you, I don't feel like you!* Alma tells Elisabet. Bergman is a brute, he likes to make you cry, and one of the best scenes in the film is a tearjerker. It is the split screen shot of Alma's face and Elisabet's face, where the two halves of their two faces become one face. It's a sneaky slight of hand, he pulls a fast one, and you don't even notice it. Yes, *Persona* is one of my wife's favorite movies, so we watch it nonstop. A lot of women love this film, but most men hate it. I mean, you can only watch so much Bergman, before you want to kill yourself. Do the Swedes really hate Bergman? I don't know, I can't really tell, but they seem respect him. The filmmakers in Sweden are well-respected in their country, and they're given the proper amount of time to find their *vision*. They have plenty of time to nurture it, to study it, to master it. No, this doesn't happen in America, our filmmakers have no time to spare, they are starved for time, and they only have dollars on their mind. America only loves one-hit-wonders and blockbusters, so that's all we make. Tell me, who is the American Bergman? It's Woody Allen–they say that he's one of our best, but I don't think so. He has been jerking off America for the last fifty years. I don't dislike his movies, but I don't like them, either. He made a few good films, and two great ones, but so what, now, he makes trashy pulp. Allen is no Bergman, he never was, and he never will be. I couldn't sleep, so I opened my eyes. It was a beautiful morning, the sun was just coming up, and the sky was cherry red. I felt lucky to be here, and I couldn't wait to get to the Black Sea. I'd already waited too long, so I was ready for my vacation to finally begin. Bulgaria reminds me of Texas: it is arid, wide open, and every town looks like a truck stop. Bulgarians are very proud people, they're real hot blooded, just like Texans. They like to talk the talk, and walk the walk, if you know what I mean. Most of them are cocky and full of bullshit, they run too hot, like life is passing them by. And they remember every last word that you say to them, so be careful what you say. They don't forget anything, you have to watch what you say around them, because they will hold you accountable for each word spoken. I was happy to be in Bulgaria, but my wife was happier. *I'm finally back home*, she said, *to the place that I belong.* This trip was making her feel very sentimental, because she had made this same trip many times before. Her family has always gone to the Black Sea, so she had many great memories. In many ways, this return trip was kind of a homecoming for her. When she left Bulgaria, it was under a cloud of regret, and I don't think her family has ever gotten over it. Her decision to come to America is still a sour subject for them, and they still don't talk about it. But she was finally back to the place where she was born, so she was back into her family's grace again. Love is like a shooting star; it burns hot, it glides, it fizzles, then it falls to the earth. Lucky for me, my love was still burning hot, so my wife is a white light, without her, there is only darkness. She had finally come back home, at last, and I didn't want to get in her way. The three of us were hungry, so Yanko stopped at the next town. The truck stop was called EKO, but it looked just like a 7-Eleven. The store was empty, there wasn't a customer in sight, except for the cashier. When we walked in, she looked spooked by us, as if she hadn't seen people for days. There was country music playing in the store, which made me laugh, I could've been in Texas. The products in the store looked like the same stuff that you see in America, but everything was written in a foreign language. When I went over to the magazine rack, I picked up the first rag that I saw, which was a gossip magazine called *Xopa*. It was just like *People*, but it had Slavic people in it. I leafed through the pages, shamelessly wasting my time, as I searched for anything of interest. There was nothing but pictures of Bulgarian movie stars, in weird poses, and they all looked so damn sad. Their perfect white teeth made them look happy, but their frowns betrayed them. I didn't recognize anyone in the magazine, they looked familiar, in a movie star kind of way, but I couldn't come up with any names. Then I saw a real star, I couldn't believe it, there he was, in full color–it was the one and only Woody Allen! I couldn't stop laughing, I was surprised to see a picture of him in Bulgaria, but there he was, in his khakis, oxford shirt, and wool jacket. Why is Woody Allen in this magazine? I didn't want to think about Woody Allen, not on my vacation, so I put it back on the shelf. *Xopa* can do whatever it wants, he was there for a reason, I told myself, and I had to accept it. I was hungry, I wanted peanuts, but I couldn't find any, so I settled for some Cracker Jack. It's not my favorite, but I love the prize that you get at the bottom, so I bought a box. When I got back into the car, I needed some air, so I rolled down my window. As soon as I did, the smell of shit hit me like a brick, it was unbelievable, it stunk really bad. The smell was coming from the dumpster, it smelled just like a dead dog, it smelled like Texas. I couldn't take it, so I rolled my window back up. As soon as my window went up, my wife and Yanko started screaming at each other. I don't know what they were fighting over, I didn't care, but I had to listen to them, I had no other choice. I tried to ignore them, but they never shut up, I was trapped, it was a nightmare. I really didn't want to eat the box of Cracker Jack, I just wanted my prize, so I poured the sticky nuts onto my lap. When I finally got to the bottom of the box, I unwrapped my prize. I was like a kid again, without a care in this world, I felt fancy free. I was happy with my prize: a compass. It was a cheap toy, but I was overjoyed with it, because I was a winner! It was made out of plastic, but it worked just fine, so I knew exactly where we were headed. Yes, we were driving east, we were about to turn south, and we were on our way to the Black Sea. Yanko had bought a few bottles of *Ayran* in the store, which was some sort of yogurt drink, that all Bulgarians claim to love. My wife loved it, too, so she also had a few bottles. I hate it with a passion, it tastes like sour milk and raw eggs, so I never drink the stuff. Yanko had a heart of gold, but he was suspicious of me; I don't blame him, because my wife is his sister. I get it, he only wants what is best for her, but he was getting on my nerves. When I married her, I took her away from Bulgaria, so it has always a little awkward with him. When Yanko was pulling out of the parking lot, he suddenly stopped the car and put it in park. I didn't know what was happening, so I looked out the window to find out. I couldn't believe it, there was a woman standing by the side of the road, under a big oak tree, and she was waving at the passing cars and lifting up her skirt. She had on a pink miniskirt, with black stockings, and she was in red stilettos. She looked like prostitute, but I wasn't sure, so I didn't say anything. But my wife had a whole lot to say, and she said it: *Look at that woman, I can't believe her, what is she doing out here? Why do they let her do this on their property?* Then my wife went into a long rant about prostitution. I tried to ignore the prostitute, but I couldn't, because my wife wouldn't stop talking about her. It was ridiculous, she was critiquing her sense of style, as if she was a model on some runway. We were only a couple of miles away from the Black Sea, I was almost there, so I didn't have to wait that much longer. But Yanko wouldn't move the car, he just sat there in the parking lot. Why was he not driving away? I was ready for my vacation to begin, it was only a few miles away, so I was ready for the car to start moving. While we were sitting there, a red truck pulled up next to our car, and the driver started yelling at Yanko. He kept shouting *Kolko, kolko, kolko?* He wouldn't stop, he was going nuts. *How much, how much, how much?* I was confused at first, I didn't understand what he wanted, but then I got it: he wanted a date with the prostitute. He thought Yanko was her pimp, which was hilarious, but before he could get a word out of his mouth, the guy gave us the middle finger, then he drove off. Yanko looked surprised, he started laughing, then I looked at my wife, and I started laughing. This was like a scene from a Fellini film, it was pure fantasy, I had never seen anything like this before, so I was laughing my ass off. When the guy circled back around again, I got a little nervous, as he drove by us, I could see a big smile on his face, so I wasn't that worried. He did a couple of donuts in the middle of the road, then he slammed on his breaks and he skidded to a stop. Of course, the car ended up right in front of the woman on the side of the road. He waited a couple of seconds, when he got out of his truck, he looked in our direction, then he did a little dance in the sand. The guy walked straight up to the woman, as he grabbed her cheeks, he kissed her on the mouth. She didn't seem to mind the kiss, because she kissed him back. I couldn't believe what I was seeing, it was too good to be true. The prostitute made the next move, a power play, which I didn't see coming. When she picked the guy up, she threw him over her shoulder, then she carried him back to his truck. She took total control of the situation, it was a sight to behold, but I couldn't stop laughing. When they got to the truck, she tossed him into the passenger seat, he squealed like a pig. Then she jumped into the driver's seat and closed the door. It got hot and heavy almost immediately, as they started having sex, the guy screamed out in ecstasy. They were at it for a solid two minutes, then they collapsed into each other's arms. I was speechless, I didn't know what to say, but my wife was saying a lot, so I let her say it. As she went on and on about public nudity, I couldn't stop laughing, but Yanko had seen enough. The show was over, he said, it was time to leave, so we left! Life is like a prostitute, I thought, she only comes when the price is right. But I didn't want to think about prostitutes, I wanted to get to the Black Sea, and Yanko drove as fast as he could, so we got to Primorsko in no time. When we got into town, instead of going to our hotel, we went straight to the beach. Yanko's wife and kids were already there, so it only made sense. I couldn't believe it, I'm finally *here*, I said. I really wanted to jump into the water, I had come all this way, so I ran into the sea with my wife. As the cold waves crashed into me, I felt overwhelmed by their power. I took a deep breath, and, without any fear, I dove into the water. When I got deep under the surface, I finally opened my eyes. It was unbelievable, everything was so crystal clear, but the salt burned my eyes. I wanted to close them, but I didn't, I kept them open. I could see my wife's legs kicking underneath the water, but I saw no other signs of life. The sea was empty, I was surprised by this, because my wife had told me that the Black Sea was full of life. After a few minutes, some small fish finally appeared from out of the blue, but my wife wouldn't stop kicking her feet, so they swam away. She needed to relax, she was stressed out, she needed to unwind. Our vacation was just beginning, so she still had some time left on the clock. She is always thinking about her job, she's a company woman, and the higher-ups have already *noticed* her. It's too late for her, because once your bosses notice you—your life is over! You become their possession, a trophy, and you are now *theirs* to keep. My wife is a highly regarded member of their *team*, and as her reward, she gets to attend *more* meetings, *more* seminars, *more* lunches, and *more* dinners. Well, that's how she explains it to me. She doesn't mind it, she says, because *I love my job.* I envy her commitment, she really does what she loves, so she thrives. *Time is money,* they say, *and money is time,* whatever that means. To tell you the truth, I don't know that much about my wife's job, but I do know time, and my time was running out. Yes, she's on the fast track to the top, *I'm almost there*, she tells me, but I really don't know what the *top* even means, so it goes over my head. My wife has described her job to me, but I still don't know what she does there. I did meet the higher-ups, only once, at the Fony Christmas party. It's a night that I won't soon forget, because it got me into trouble with my wife. Christmas parties are alll the same: they start off with eggnog and yuletide, and they end with vomit and hurt feelings. I had nothing against the Fony bosses, I swear, but on this night, they had something against me. This party is etched into my brain like a bad trip. I did nothing to them, it was all *their* fault, I told my wife, but she didn't believe me. I mean, it was such a random attack, I didn't expect it, so I was caught off guard. I was standing next to the buffet, minding my business, when my wife's bosses started messing around with me. They were drunk as hell, blitzed out of their minds, high as kites. Let me tell you, they're two of the biggest assholes that I have ever met. The one boss, named Fred, was rude as hell and a total jerk. I couldn't believe him, he kept cursing at me, taunting me, saying stupid jokes about me. Then he asked me if I had seen the cocktail sauce; when I told him *no*, it didn't go over so well. He suddenly went crazy, all out nuts, and all hell broke loose. It happened so fast, I had no time to react. As soon as he dumped his plate of shrimp over my head, I knew that I was in trouble. I didn't know what to do, so I just stood there like a statue. Fred gave me a big smile, then he punched me in the stomach. It wasn't that hard of a punch, but I still went down. When I looked up, he was already walking away, so I was lucky that night. Of course, the other Fony employees started laughing at me, it was all a big joke to them, and I was the butt of it. I'll tell you this, these Fony higher-ups don't give a damn about your feelings, they do whatever they want. Now, I smelled like shrimp, which didn't bother me, but I knew that it would bother my wife, so I was nervous. I waited for my wife to come back from the bathroom, but she never came back. I had lost her, she was nowhere to be seen, where was she? The Fony party was very crowded, and very dark. so it was impossible to find her. *Where is my wife?* I said, as I walked around the ballroom. The Fony employees ignored me, like I wasn't even there. *Where is my wife?* I got nothing from them, just stares, they didn't care, they were too drunk to care. They were all drunks, and most of them were out of their minds. They were wild animals, and they wanted to kill something, so I had to be careful. They were completely out of control, they had already torn down the Christmas tree, and the decorations were smashed all over the floor. While I searched for my wife, some old guy named Roy came up to me and he started asking me questions about the New York Stock Exchange. I had no idea what he was talking about, it sounded like gibberish to me, so I had nothing to say to him. I just stood there like a dummy, as I nodded my head like a duck, he rambled on about the state of the market. What can I say, he kept on talking to me, so I kept on listening him, I didn't want to be rude. He wouldn't shut up, he went on and on about the right time to buy and sell stocks. Eventually, I got lucky, he got bored with me, so he quit talking. Then, I got unlucky, when he got really mad at me. My lack of financial knowledge had upset him, that is my guess, and that's when he took a swing at me. I was on guard, so I ducked his punch quite easily, which made him even madder. Then he threw another punch, but he missed me, he was too slow and too drunk. After a few rounds of this, he got bored, and he gave up on me. As he stumbled away like a dodo bird, I gave him a pat on his back for the effort, I had no hard feelings. I really needed to find my wife, so I kept looking for her. While I walked around in a circle, I kept saying my mantra to myself. *Where is my wife?* I need find her. *Where is my wife?* I will find her. *Where is my wife?* I want to find her. Then I got lucky, I finally found her! I couldn't believe it, there she was, I jumped for joy. Of course, I found her on the dance floor, I should have looked there first, but I didn't. I was so happy to see her, but when I told her about Fred and Roy, she didn't believe me, she said I was making the whole thing up. *Fred would never do such a thing*, she said, *and Roy is too professional for that kind of outburst*, which made me laugh my ass off. She believed Fred and Roy over me, I did nothing wrong, but it was *my fault*, and I was to blame. My wife seemed to have a great time at the party, but my night was turning into a nightmare. I couldn't believe her, she got it all wrong, *I'm innocent*, I told her, but my pleas fell on deaf ears. I will never go to another Fony Christmas party, because these folks are out of their minds. While I was under the water, my mind swam around, and I kept hearing Alabaster's voice: *My dear boy, you must cleanse yourself in the Black Sea.* It was agreed upon in advance, I guess, that I would skinny-dip in the sea, and I had to honor my vow. *We are born naked*, he told me, *so we should die naked.* Alabaster loves to be naked, and he wants you to be naked, too! I didn't want to be naked, but I had made a vow to him, so without even a second thought, I took my swimsuit off. The water felt like a second skin, as it caressed my naked body, I was in bliss. The salt content in the Black Sea is very high, so you can float with almost no effort. One is scientifically *lighter* in this body of water, but I felt *heavier*, as if my naked body was somehow holding me back. Kundera called this feeling *unbearable*, but I had to disagree with him, it was quite bearable. As I drifted, my mind felt separated from my body, I was floating, and the hands of the sea were pulling me deeper and deeper underneath the water. I was just a vessel drifting from one place to the next place; the waves told me where to go, I had no control. But then Kundera popped back into my mind. I'm never free of him, he's like seaweed that I can't get rid of, I thought. Since I was floating with the unbearable heaviness of being, I let go of myself and I let the sea take me. Am I touching the water, I asked myself, or is the water touching me? I didn't know, but the question needed to be answered, so I went down deeper. After a couple of minutes of this, I was out of breath and I had to come up to the surface. We all want what we don't have, so I wanted air, and that's when I stuck my head out of the water. I don't know how long I was under the water, but now, I wanted to be on top of the water, so I started floating on my back. I had my reasons to float, I wanted to be free, I went with the tide. I have done many foolish things, but I always live with the consequences, so I was ready for anything. But today was different, I was on my vacation, I didn't want to think about anything serious, I just wanted to relax. I floated for a while, I don't know for how long, but when I finally opened my eyes, I heard my wife screaming at me. I had drifted off, I was naked, and my wife had a problem with this. But before I could say anything, she had something to say: *Why in the hell are you naked? My family is right over there! I told you not to embarrass me in front of my family! Are you crazy?* So what, I'm naked, I thought. *I can't believe you! Where is your swimsuit?* I didn't have a clue where my suit was, it wasn't in my hands anymore, so I guess I lost it under the water. Now, she had a reason to be

95

angry with me. I still didn't think that it was such a big deal, I tried to explain it to her, by telling her that it was Alabaster's fault, *he told me to do it*, but she was not having it. She was livid, pissed, and she was loosing her shit. *I told you not to do this to me, you never listen, are you out of your mind?* I was laughing at her, she was funny, I had to laugh. But I got lucky, because I suddenly saw my swimsuit, it was pretty close to me, maybe ten yards away, stuck on top of some seaweed. *There's my swimsuit, I'm going to swim to it,* I yelled to my wife, in order to reassure her. When I started swimming towards it, my wife began screaming at me: *No, don't go, come back, it's too far away!* The current was very strong, I tried to fight it, but I was losing the battle. My wife was really upset, I could hear her screaming for me to come back. *Come back, come back, the current is too strong, why are you not listening to me?* I wanted to come back, but I was too close, I couldn't stop now, so I kept on swimming. I was only a few feet away from it, but the current was pulling me farther away from the shore. I had to take my chance, I was so close, I was almost there. I butterflied the rest of the distance, and before I knew it, I had snatched up my swimsuit. When I finally had it in my hands, I looked back at my wife and I yelled: *Don't worry about me, I got it!* When I slipped my swimsuit back on, an immediate sense of relief came over me. I'm a pretty good swimmer, so I had nothing to worry about, but the waves were splashing me around like a rag doll. I wasn't afraid of the water, I was more afraid of my wife, so I started swimming back to shore. But before I could save myself, the stupid lifeguards wanted to save me first. Yes, I could now see three lifeguards swimming towards me, and they meant business. I couldn't stop them, they were coming for me, and there wasn't a damn thing that I could do about it. I'd seen the greasy lifeguards on the beach when we got there, and they looked oiled up and ready to go, so I knew what to expect next. They were swimming fast, it was only a matter of time, I thought, before they got to me. On the beach, they were loud and proud, in the water, they were bold and beautiful, and they coming to *save* my ass. *Go back, I can make it, I don't need your help!* I said. But it didn't matter what I said to them, it was too late, they were coming full steam ahead, so I had to get ready to be saved. I was getting tired, but I didn't know what to do, they were swimming as fast as sharks, and they smelled blood in the water, nothing was going to stop them. The closer they got to me, the more fearful I got of them, because these muscled meatheads looked deadly. Most lifeguards are oiled-up idiots, they never listen to you, and they love to scream at you. *I'm fine, I'm not drowning, go away, I don't need you!* I screamed at them. But they were in a frenzy, so they completely ignored what I said, and they just kept on coming. One dude approached me from the front, while the other dude attacked me from the back, and the third dude came up from the bottom. I had no way of stopping these meatheads from ripping me apart, so I had to try and save myself. I didn't need their help, I didn't want it, but they didn't care what I said, they were going to save me, no matter what, with or without my help. I was a dead man, and there wasn't a damn thing that I could do about it. *Stay away from me*, I yelled, *I don't need your damn help, I can make it on my own!* I don't know if they understood English, so I tried it in Bulgarian, but that didn't work either. I was waving my hands in the air, to show them that I was fine, but that didn't do anything. They had a job to do, and that's what they were going to do, they were going to save me. They were suddenly right on top of me, I was trapped and I had nowhere to go. While one lifeguard grabbed my arms, the other one held my legs, and the third one put me in a chokehold. I was thrashed around like a piece of meat, they had trained hard for this, so I was no match for their tight muscles. I was like chum to them, they didn't care, as they pulled my body every which way. When they pulled me under the water, I panicked, and I swallowed a lot of water, too much water. At that moment, a deep fear came over me, I might die today, I thought. Yes, they were saving me, but they had no regard for my life, I mean, they were literally drowning me. As I was fighting them off, a strange calm came over me, and everything went silent. While my body was at their mercy, my mind was somewhere else, so I quit struggling and I let them save me. These oiled-up idiots reminded me of the Three Stooges, they were too much, I couldn't stop laughing at them. I don't know how they did it, but Moe, Larry and Curly got me up on their raft. As soon as I felt the oily rubber on my butt, I knew there was a problem. I couldn't believe it, I don't know how it happened, but I was naked again. During the rescue, my swimsuit had gotten ripped off, so I was laughing my ass off. In the face of death, you have to laugh, I thought, what else can you do? The Three Stooges didn't know what to do with me, I was now their *prize*, but they still had to get me back to the beach. They kept yelling at me in Bulgarian, I had no idea what they were saying to me, so I tried English again, but that only made them angrier. When I tried to get off their raft, they wouldn't let me, I was now their prisoner. Yes, they were on a mission, I could see it in their eyes, and they were going to complete their mission. I had no choice, they were taking me back to the beach, and that was that. I felt pretty stupid sitting there naked on the raft, but I had no escape, so I just sat there. I could see my wife standing on the shore, and there was a large crowd with her, which made me feel uneasy. I couldn't help but remember what she had said on the plane: *Please, whatever you do, don't embarrass me in Bulgaria!* I was in big trouble, no doubt about it, but it wasn't my fault this time. I had no control over these lifeguards, it's their fault, I thought, not mine! But I knew my wife, she would blame me, so I had to do something. The waves were getting real choppy, so the Stooges had trouble holding onto the raft. By this time, Curly was already out of breath, he was bobbing up and down like a pelican. Larry had swallowed a ton of water, so he was fading fast. And Moe, well, he was so oiled up, he was slowly losing his grip on me. I don't think they were real lifeguards; they looked like lifeguards, but they acted like pro wrestlers. I was trapped on the raft, but I wasn't going to let the Three Stooges drown me, I had to take a chance, I had to save myself, so I took it. I took a deep breath, then I stood up on the raft. My naked body sparkled in sun as the light danced off my skin, I was ready, it was time. When I jumped, I screamed at them: *First one on the beach wins a prize!* I did a perfect dive into the water, as I split the wave in half, I dove deep under the surface. I started swimming for my life, but the water was heavy, it was now mixed with suntan oil, so I was at a disadvantage. I looked back to see how the Stooges were doing, and, to my surprise, they were right behind me. I don't know how, but they had recovered their strength, and were now hot on my tail. I was in a race for my life, I was swimming as fast as I could, but they were catching up to me. I had to conserve my energy, I swam at a steady pace, not too fast, because I didn't want to get tired. But the Stooges couldn't keep up with me, they were weak swimmers, so I left them behind in no time. I felt as nimble as a dolphin, I was too fast, and I didn't have a care in the world. But the closer I got to the shore, the closer I got to my wife, so I got real nervous. Yes, I still had my *naked* problem, but I had no choice, I had to get out of the water. As I was swimming, I kept hearing my wife's voice in my ear: *Please, whatever you do, don't embarrass me in Bulgaria.* I didn't want to embarrass her, but what else could I do, I couldn't stay in the water, because if I did, the Stooges would kill me. I was in real danger, and I knew it, so I couldn't stop swimming. If I stopped, the Stooges would drown me, I had to *save* myself, I said, it was my only chance of survival. I was swimming and laughing at the same time, which is a hard thing to do, but I did it anyways. I started getting water in my mouth, that was bad, then the water went up my nose, which was even worse. I started choking, but I couldn't stop laughing, I was choke laughing to death. The Three Stooges have always made me laugh, so I wasn't surprised that they were making me laugh now. They were pure slapstick, I was choking, the whole thing was a wet farce, I was laughing. When I went under the water, I knew that I was in trouble, I was drowning, but I couldn't stop myself. I didn't want to die in the Black Sea, I wanted to live, but if I had to die, well, then I would die here, I told myself. As I took my last breath, I felt my body go numb, then a deep presence came over me. Underneath the water, I was in a wet dream, I was in a green paradise, I was in a blue bliss. No, I didn't see God, it wasn't some deity, no, it was nature, and the Black Sea was now alive. When I opened my eyes, a school of fish had surrounded me, and they were nibbling on my body. As they tickled me with their salty embrace, a million lips kissed me all at once. I could hear my heart beating, it was ticking like a clock, I was struggling, fighting for my life. Then the tiny fish started lifting me up to the surface, I didn't want to go, but they kept pushing me, so I had no choice. As soon as my head came out of the water, I didn't feel them anymore, and the fish let go of me. I'm not sure how long I was down *there* under the water, time didn't exist, it was outside of time, time meant nothing, only my next breath meant something. But in the back of my mind, I still heard my wife's voice: *Please, whatever you do, don't embarrass me in Bulgaria.* When they finally dragged me out of the water, Moe had both of my arms, Larry had one leg, and Curly had the other leg. I felt manhandled like a dead fish; I was naked, but they didn't care, because I was alive. I was *saved*, but I didn't need any CPR, I was fine, I just needed some air. I was still kind of out of it, I didn't remember being in the water, let alone, the *drowning*. This farce went on for a couple more minutes, until the Stooges finally let me go. I was butt naked, but I had no place to hide, so I just stood there like a fool. Most of the people on the beach looked bored by the rescue, but my wife was ecstatic. To my surprise, she had a big smile on her face, and she was laughing hysterically, which made me a little nervous. When she handed me a towel, she hugged and kissed me. I couldn't believe it, she was calm, she wasn't mad, and she was laughing, too! This didn't seem like my wife, she appeared to be a *new* wife. Then she started taking pictures of me, I felt like a prized piece of meat, she even made me pose with the lifeguards. But something seemed fishy to me, it just didn't smell right, why was my wife not embarrassed? What is going on here, I thought, am I in a dream? No, it was no dream, she had changed right before my eyes, and she was now my new wife. I couldn't figure *her* out, it must be Bulgaria, I thought, she feels more free here, more loved, so she was acting like a different person. My wife made me take a ton of pictures with the lifeguards. I mean, it was ridiculous, but what could I say, I was just happy that she wasn't upset, so I just stood there and took the pictures. My story even made the local paper the next day, the headline read: *Naked American Tourist Saved!* Yes, I was *saved* from the clutches of death, the story said, by three local *heroes*, who almost *died* while doing their duty. I couldn't believe it, and I didn't want to believe it, but I had to believe it, because the newspaper said that it had happened. Our hotel was right on the beach, so our room had a perfect view of the Black Sea. The place was shabby chic, postmodern, and a little run down. Yanko was a longtime guest there, so we got two of the best rooms in the hotel, on the top floor. As soon as we got to our room, my wife brought up my swimsuit mishap. Now, she was *embarrassed* by my naked stunt, and very mad, but I wasn't buying her charade, because I had the photos to prove it. She looked happy in every picture, and she is smiling in every one, so I didn't believe a word that she said. I really wanted to forget about this unfortunate incident, I was over *it*, but my wife wouldn't stop, she kept talking about it. She must have talked for an hour, I listened to her, but I didn't believe her, she was just being difficult. After she was finished talking, we took a nice nap, we were both tired, we needed some sleep. When we woke up, we took showers, got dressed, then we went out for dinner. Yanko chose the restaurant, it was filled with locals and tourists, so it was packed. They served traditional Bulgarian food, Yanko said, the fish was fresh, the meat was local, and the cheese was the best in town. We started off with tomato and cucumber salad with feta cheese, fried sardines with feta cheese, sauteed spinach with feta cheese, and red peppers stuffed with feta cheese. Let me tell you, the Bulgarians *love* their feta cheese, and they put it on almost everything, Every dish had feta cheese on it, it was unbelievable, it was feta heaven! Then Yanko did a toast to my wife and I, he said some kind words about us, I was very touched. He spoke about family, love, marriage, and he recited a Bulgarian poem. If you don't already know by now, Bulgarians love poems, and they can recite one at the drop of a hat. Yanko is passionate and gregarious, unlike his wife, Iskra is quiet and aloof. She had barely said a word to me, and she had this sideways look on her face, like she was sizing me up. She was calm, cool, and collected, so it was hard to read her. Yanko and Iskra seemed very close, they had known each other since first grade, and they had an unspoken bond. They had two kids: a son, Petar, and a daughter, Mascha. They were young teenagers, but they acted like sixty-year-olds. When I first met them, they creeped me out, but then I got to know them, and I got used to them. They were very intelligent, real clever, and they asked brainy questions with an existential bent. But they were born hustlers, and they already knew a thing or two about life. Petar was a pest, he was too big for his britches, he was a know-it-all. Mascha seemed more mature, and she had an old soul, if *old* is the right word for it. She was wise beyond her years, and she already had deep a knowledge of herself, which made her easy to talk to. Primorsko is an ancient town, and it has been here for thousands of years, so the local roots run deep. It has been a host to many different Ages: the Neolithic Age, the Copper Age, the Iron Age, the Industrial Age. And it has been invaded by some of the great invaders; conquered by most of the great conquerers; looted by all of the great looters. You have to salute Primorsko, because after all this bloodshed and war–somehow, the town is still here! The second day of my vacation is always better than the first day. I become more open, more relaxed, and more willing to explore. So, on the second day, I woke up with a purpose, I wanted to get to know the locals. Primorsko reminded me of Key West, it was made for the tourists, but built by the locals. It was a very kitsch town, almost tacky, but in a good way, if you know what I mean. The locals run the show during the day, so it moves at a snail's pace, but when the night comes, the tourists take over the place. The locals and tourists exist together, day and night, without much conflict. They have learned to share the town, so they live in harmony. In the morning, they sit together in cafes, with frappes and cheese pastries, while the town goes about its business. During the day, the tourists wander around the markets and buy handmade trinkets, and the locals work hard to please them. At night, the locals disappear, and the tourists party everywhere. But, on this morning, my second morning, after breakfast, I went to buy a new swimsuit. Yes, my old one was lost at sea, and it wasn't coming back, so I needed a new one. Some things just disappear, they never come back, and my swimsuit was one of them. It was under the abyss, gone forever, and it would never return again. I had to accept it, it was *my* fate, so I bought a new swimsuit. I was ready for the beach, and my wife was too, but there are four beaches in Primorsko, and we didn't know which one to go to. Of course, my wife wanted to go to all of them. Yesterday, we were on North Beach, so today, we decided to visit Central Beach. It's the most popular beach, the so-called *family* beach, my wife said, so it's always very lively. Yanko loved this beach, it was his favorite, because the vibe was so family oriented. When we got there, we tried to find a nice open spot on the sand, but the beach was very crowded, so we settled for less, it was a tiny square spot by the water. All of the sunburnt families looked like sun-dried tomatoes. As they played in the water, the wind blew their umbrellas down the beach, while the seagulls stole their food. Central Beach was too crowded for my taste, but what could I do, this was Yanko's favorite beach, so I had to stay here. *Today is chess day*, I told my wife, and she agreed with me. Yes, it was time to play a game of chess, we were finally ready to have some fun. My wife and I are chess addicts, so we can play anywhere, and this beach was the perfect place, I thought. But chess is a deadly game, it can ruin your life, and it can even kill you. *I don't fuck with chess, chess fucks with me,* the saying goes. But I'm still in the honeymoon phase of the game, I'm a novice, a student of the game, so I don't expect to win every match. I play for fun, I play to get better, I play to learn. But a lot of players play to *win*, so I lose a lot of the matches. And today, I wanted to start off slow, I wanted to try out some new moves, and I didn't want to stress out about it. My first opponent was Petar, then I played Mascha. I wanted to relax, I wanted to think, so a game of chess was the perfect thing to do on this beach. *I'm only a beginner,* Petar said with a grin, *so you better take it easy on me.* But after a couple of matches with him, I knew that he was playing me for a fool. I loss every match, he was a pro, it was a lie, this kid wasn't a beginner. He knew exactly what he was doing, and after he won each match, he would dance around like a spoiled brat and yell: *I win, I win, I win!* I was his sucker, he played with no mercy, so he destroyed me. Of course, I got stressed out, but I couldn't stop playing. When I got tired of Petar, I switched to Mascha. But she was ready for me, so she beat my ass, and she was even better than Petar. She was played like maniac, she was on fire, so I was toast. After my first loss to her, a checkmate, I was ready to quit, but I didn't. We were playing for ice cream, so I already owed Petar two cones and Mascha one. I was down on my luck, I was in a sticky hole, I needed to win one. I didn't want to lose another match, but I was unsure of my strategy. I didn't want to look weak, so I pressed on, I couldn't help myself, I was addicted to it. Let me tell you, when I start playing chess, I can't stop, I keep playing. The game is a matter of life and death, it's kill or be killed. You play in order to play another day, but losing is no fun, so I was getting tired of losing. But I only had myself to blame, I walked right into their trap, I didn't see it coming. These kids were greedy, they didn't know when to stop, they craved more sugar, so they kept playing with me. But I had to beat them, at least once, I told myself, I really needed it. I don't like chess, I love it, I need it like a drug, and Mascha knew this, so she played like a dealer. I started off with a good offense, but chess is a game of defense, so I got into a deep hole. I was running out of squares, I had no place to go, I had no chance of winning. Ingmar Bergman loved to play chess, it was one of his favorite games. *The Seventh Seal* begins with a game of chess. It's such a great way to start a film, with only a couple of moves on the chessboard, he sets his story into motion. A Swedish knight, back from the cold Crusades, returns to his homeland, only to find his country has been taken over by the Black Death. How did Bergman come up with such a great idea? *Death*, a monk-like figure, has come to the beach to take the knight's life away. But in the hope of starving off his demise, the knight challenges death to a game of chess. Of course, death accepts his challenge, and, thus begins one of the best chess matches in cinema history. The first three words spoken in the film are by the knight: *Who are you?* It's such a great question to ask. And death replies: *I am Death.* I was feeling the same thing at this moment, I was dying a slow death, and Mascha was torturing me. I was using a queen and knight combination, a solid strategy, which usually worked for me. But Mascha was too good, she countered me with a bishop and rook combo, so she was killing me. I'd misjudged her power, my plan was all wrong; and her pawns were very strong, unlike mine, I was down to just one. Without my other pawns, I had no real strength, I was left with no protection at all. I had nowhere left to go, I could only run for my life. I should have quit playing, but I didn't, I had to play until the end. Mascha had no sympathy, none, she wanted to punish me, and that's what she did. I felt like a chump, a loser, a fool. *Why me?* I mumbled. Mascha heard me, so she told me: *Why not you?* She was right, the chess gods will do whatever they like to me, and they did! First, she took my queen, then, with a smile, she snatched my last pawn. I was helpless, I was suffering, I was almost dead. When my king was finally taken, I was relieved, I had had enough. *I win, I win, I win, I want my ice cream!* Mascha screamed. You have to accept your destiny, so I had to accept mine: I had a lot of ice cream to buy. I assured them that their ice cream was on the way, but they kept screaming for it, which was making me mad. *Don'y worry, when the ice cream truck comes by,* I told them, *I'll buy your damn ice cream!* But they didn't want to hear what I had to say, they just wanted their ice cream. I couldn't believe it, it was impossible, how did I lose every match? I'm better than this, I thought, *I know I am.* I didn't play that well, it just wasn't my day, so I lost. I had played too much chess, I was beat, I felt completely drained, and I was ready for a nap. *It's only a game,* I told them, *you win some, you lose some.* They were laughing at me, I was a big joke, they were rubbing it in my face and being obnoxious. I couldn't take it, they kept screaming for their ice cream, they sounded like little babies. When the ice cream truck finally appeared, I gave them some money and they bought their ice cream. *Leave them alone, they're just kids,* my wife said, *why are you bothering them?* I'm bothering them? That is a joke, I thought. I didn't care if they were kids, they were *little hustlers,* I told her, but she didn't believe me. Of course, it was *my* fault, she said, I was to blame, and I got what I deserved. I tried to tell her my side of the story, but I wasn't getting anywhere, so I gave up. I was done with chess, done with kids, done with ice cream, and done with this beach, so we finally left. When we got back to our hotel, we took hot showers, changed our clothes, then we went out to dinner. This time, Iskra chose the restaurant, and we ordered what she told us to order. If she said, *eat this,* we ate it, if she said *drink this,* we drank it. This was my kind of restaurant, it had no pomp and ceremony, it was all business. I couldn't believe it, we were in and out of the place in an hour, and we were completely stuffed. After dinner, we went straight back to our rooms, then off to bed. I was out like a light, I slept like a baby, and I didn't have any bad dreams. We got up very early the next morning, at the break of day, it was another beach day, so we were excited to see the next beach. We were going to South Beach, the best beach in town, a local told me, so I couldn't wait to hit the sand. After we got breakfast, we took a bus to the beach. It was pretty nice, I liked it, it reminded me of Brighton Beach. Vodka and volleyball ruled the place, so the beach was very loud. Most of the locals came here, which was a good sign, my wife said, that it was the best beach in Primorsko. It had a cool vibe, and it has a swim-at-your-own-risk rule, with no lifeguards, which made me very happy. It was filled with some crazy people, and they were having tons of fun, so we spent the next few days there. We had the same routine every morning: wake up at eight o'clock, get coffee and breakfast from the bakery, then walk to South Beach. I loved every minute of it, so did my wife, it was late summer, which made the days linger in the wind longer. This kind of beach made you feel lazy and hazy, so I had plenty of time to read. This was the perfect beach for *TULOB*, but I didn't want to get sucked into Kundera's abyss again, so I put my book down. I had been using *it* for a pillow, but it was getting too hard for my head. Why should I be so afraid of a book? I shouldn't be, it was just ink on paper, I thought. So I picked *TULOB* up again and I opened the first page. Then I read each word out loud, as they tumbled off my tongue like dice, I screamed with laughter. Kundera has some big balls, so he mentions Nietzsche on the very first page. He knew that it would ruffle some feathers, but he didn't care, he did it anyways. I swear, after you read the first page, you can't unread it. Kundera is a piece shit, so he stinks like shit. He knows how to hook you, with only a couple of words, you take the bait. *I hate Kundera, he stinks shit!* I yelled out loud. But nobody on the beach even looked at me, they didn't care what I said, this was

South Beach. When I turn the page, and I see the name Parmenides, I bust out laughing. Let me tell you, Kundera knows exactly what he's doing, he's a real pro. Most people will shit their pants if you mention a Greek philosopher; so, of course, he mentions one on the second page. The Greeks rule me with their words, I spoon myself when I read them, they open my mind wider and I go deeper into it. Their words flow through me, but I still question them, so they fill me with doubt. The Greeks can send you to an early grave if you let them, but I don't let them. But if you study them long enough, you start to understand them. Kundera loves the Greeks, and their cosmological theories, because the proof is in the pudding, he says. I have to agree with him, he's right, the Greeks are a bunch of freaks. They're a bunch of drama queens, with something to prove. *Did he want her to come or did he not?* As soon as I read that line, I was hooked, and Kundera knew it. South Beach is made for a book like this, so I took full advantage of it, and I started reading *TULOB* again. I wanted to read it, but I couldn't, because this guy started screaming at me. *Ebi se, ebi se, ebi se, ebi se!* I tried to ignore him, but it didn't work, he kept on screaming. *Fuck you, fuck you, fuck you, fuck you!* I couldn't believe it, this jerk was cursing at me. He was getting on my nerves, but I didn't want to get into it with him, so I played nice. But he was out of his mind, he was drunk as hell, and he could barely stand up. When I took a closer look at him, I couldn't believe it, this guy was a policeman. What in the hell was he doing? As he sat under his yellow umbrella, he cursed at me, while he chugged beer after beer. When he stood up, I got nervous, but he was standing about ten yards away from me, so if he tried to do anything, I still had time to react. He was dressed in his full uniform, and he was losing his shit. I wasn't that worried about him, but I had to be on my guard, in case he did something stupid. Kundera has written so many crazy things, but this sentence is absurd: *Our internal reality is an endless argument against the void, and our external reality is a constant fight against the absurd.* He can't help himself, I swear, he writes like a bird on a wire. *Was it better to be with Tereza or to remain alone?* This was a silly question, and I didn't have the answer, so I put my book down. *TULOB* would have to wait, I had other things on my mind. When I looked at my wife, she gave me a big smile, which melted my heart. Love is so simple, I thought, it's a smile from your wife, on a Black Sea beach. I just wanted to chill, but the stupid policeman wouldn't let me. He was now chugging a bottle of vodka, he could barely stand up, as he swung his arms around, he started spinning in a circle. When he came to a stop, he started cursing at me again, and telling me to get off *his* beach. It was just my luck, to have a drunk cop yelling at me, on such a beautiful beach. No, today was not my lucky day, it was my unlucky day, so I had to deal with this drunk idiot. This policeman was out of his mind, he had some major problems, and *I* was one of them. I couldn't stop laughing at him, he was acting like a crazy fool. I was in the middle of an absurd comedy and I didn't even know it. Life is a sketch, Kundera says, of a much bigger picture. I disagree with him, to me, life is an Indian miniature, painted by a blind person. Yes, life can be real messy, and it's filled with many regrets and missed opportunities, but the beauty of reality is always worth the pain. My wife was also reading a book, it was *Anna Karenina*, which she had been reading for the last year and a half. She can't finish the novel, she says, because it's too sad of a story. Yes, Tolstoy can be a hard read, he is complicated, he can overdo it, but a year and a half was plenty enough time to read a novel. My wife is a tough cookie, she likes what she likes, and nobody else was going to tell her who or what to read. I mean, you have to have some guts to read Tolstoy on your vacation. When I read Tolstoy, back in the day, I always felt like a criminal. His novels are crimes, when I read them, I'm always guilty of something. Tolstoy is a guilty pleasure, and just like a drug, you have to him at your own discretion. My wife is very brave, she always has been, and nothing scares her. I don't know how she did it, but she ignored the drunk policeman, and she kept reading her book. I couldn't ignore him, so I couldn't read my book, because he wouldn't stop yelling at me. I was getting tired of his shit, I couldn't take him anymore, I had had enough of him, and I was about to lose my cool. When the policeman pulled his beach umbrella out of the sand, I got alarmed, when he started swinging it around like a sword, I got ready for a fight. He must have screamed *fuck you* at me a hundred times, then he got tired, and he stopped. As soon as the policeman stopped screaming, my wife stopped reading, which seemed kind of odd. *Quit teasing him, you're only going to make him mad*, my wife told me, *why are you bothering him?* I couldn't believe it, I was guilty in her eyes, *I'm innocent*, I said, *I didn't do anything to him!* She didn't believe me, she was taking his side. *I was just reading my book, minding my own business*, I explained, *then he started cursing at me.* My wife wanted the whole truth and nothing but the truth, but she didn't want to listen to my truth. Then things took a turn for the worse, when the policeman started to charge me. I had two options, I could run or fight, so I chose to fight. I was ready to fight him, but he wasn't ready to fight me. He was too drunk, every time he took a step forward, his leather boots would sink into the sand. He looked like a wounded penguin, as he wobbled around in a circle, he started balling his eyes out. He was drunk, and he wouldn't stop crying, which only made things worse. I felt bad him, so I tried to calm him down, but he was hysterical. *What do you want from me?* I said. He slurred something back to me, but I couldn't understand a word of it, he was too drunk to talk, but he wasn't too drunk to make me laugh. As he swayed back and forth like a palm tree, his breathing got real heavier, and his boots sunk deeper into the sand. I was tired of listening to him, I didn't want to listen to him anymore, I wanted him to shut up. But this time, I got lucky, when natural selection intervened for me. Darwin did it! Well, he didn't do it, a dog did it! Yes, believe it or not, a tiny Chihuahua saved the day. It came out of nowhere, it was like a speeding bullet, and it was on top of the policeman in a matter of seconds. He had no time, or no chance, to react to the dog; he was no match, he was dead meat. The Chihuahua's teeth were as sharp as nails, and his jaw was like a vice grip, as it latched onto the policeman's's leg. He tried his best to shake the dog loose, but it wouldn't let go of him, so it became a battle for survival. I couldn't stop laughing at the policeman, it was like a comic strip had come alive. He put up a good fight, but he was no match for this dog, so he went down in less than a minute. The Chihuahua had no mercy on him, it was hard to watch, as his upper body got mauled, he screamed out in agony. But the tables turned in a flash, it was too late, when the dog's destiny intervened. I don't know how it happened, but it happened right before my eyes. Somehow, in the frenzy, the policeman got a hold of the Chihuahua's neck When he stood up, he had the dog in his hands, he looked real cocky, then he did the unthinkable, he broke the dog's neck. The Chihuahua didn't have a chance, it was over in a matter of seconds, when the policeman killed it with his bare hands. All I heard was a high-pitched yelp, then there was complete silence. The dog was dead, but the policeman didn't care, when he picked up the dog's carcass, he held it above his head, then he screamed: *Fuck you, I killed you!* It was a surreal sight, he was in shock, as he taunted the dead dog, he danced around like a drunken fool. But the Chihuahua's revenge came in spades, it was written in the cards, that it would have the last laugh. Yes, I saw it with my own eyes, I couldn't believe it, when the dog's owner came running across the sand. He brought some swift justice to the policeman, he really let him have it, when he beat the shit out of him. He punched him into a bloody pulp, he looked pretty bad, but I don't think he felt a thing, because he was too drunk to feel anything. It took the policeman a little while to get up, but he eventually got up to his feet. He was stunned, he didn't know what to do, so he gave me a bloody smile, then he said; *Fuck you too!* He didn't say anything else, he seemed out of words, and out of beer, so he gathered his stuff, then he stumbled away. I was grateful to the Chihuahua, it had saved me from the policeman's wrath. Who knows what that policeman would have done to me? The dog's owner was in tears, he looked crushed, as he cradled the tiny corpse, he stroked it like a genie's lamp. This sounds like a bad movie, but it isn't a movie, this is the real deal, I mean, this is Bulgaria for you. The policeman got what he deserved, I guess, it was written in his cards, but the dog didn't deserve this kind of death, he deserved better. In Greek terms, it can be explained as: *what is* and *what is not*. Parmenides would say, that the dog is positive and the policeman is negative. In Tolstoy's mind, the policeman is the hammer and the dog is the sickle. Of course, for Kundera, the policeman is heavy and the dog is light. Was the policeman real or was he just a figment of my imagination? I couldn't tell, the sun was hot, and I was feeling dizzy. Did a dog really die right there in front of me? I think it did. Was I seeing things with my *new* eyes? I didn't have a clue what I was doing. But that was South Beach, it was the best beach, so anything could happen there. When we went back to our hotel, we had a few beers, then we went out for dinner. Yanko suggested a popular Bulgarian beer garden, so that's where we decided to go. But it was more of a dance hall, with a kitchen, than a traditional beer garden. It had a huge dining area, with long tables, wooden benches, and there was a small stage in the middle of the hall, where the folk dancers performed. When we got there, the restaurant was filled to the rafters, and they were packed in like pigs in a pen. After waiting for almost an hour for a table, we were finally seated in the main dining area, right in the front of the stage. As soon as I sat down, Petar and Mascha started laughing at me. They were acting silly tonight, they were on a sugar high, so they were playing games with me. I didn't trust them, I knew something was up, and I was ready for anything. And that's when Petar told me to *get ready* for my surprise. What surprise? I was confused. But then I looked down, and when I looked up again, I was attacked by a swarm of flies. They were everywhere, I couldn't get them away from me, it was ridiculous. They went in and out of my ears, nose, and mouth; I couldn't stop them. Petar and Mascha howled like wolves, they wouldn't stop laughing at me, it was all a big joke to them. I don't know why the flies only attacked me and nobody else, for some unknown reason, they were attracted to me. I couldn't swat them away fast enough, they were playing with me, and having fun at my expense. When the flies first appeared, I couldn't ignore them, so they really bothered me. But once I got used to them, I ignored them, then they didn't bother me anymore. It was just a matter of time, I thought, before they got bored with me. So, after a few minutes, they got bored and they left me alone. *What you ignore, will ignore you,* Alabaster says, so that's what I did. It was hard to concentrate, because the music was so loud, and everybody in the place was shouting at each other, so you had to shout in order to be heard. This wasn't a fun time, it was a shouting match. The restaurant had communal picnic tables, so everybody sat together and ate family style. It reminded me of a TGI Fridays, but a more kitsch version of it. It had a festive atmosphere, it was one big party; but looks are deceiving, so it had some major problems. After sitting there for about an hour, with only warm beers and flat soft drinks on our table, the food was nowhere to be seen. We were hungry, but the kitchen was a little *backed up*, the waitress told us, because of a *minor* grill problem. The rest of the staff didn't seem to care, they walked around like zombies with nothing to do. I was starving, but what could I do, the grill was down, so I had to wait for my food. *The grill is being fixed as I speak*, the cheeky waitress told us, *your food is on the way.* She sounded like a robot, it was a lie, I could tell, she had to say it, it was her job. Then the folk music started, and the rock music was turned off. When the performance began, a couple of teenagers came out and they started dancing their routine. They were dressed in traditional Bulgarian folk garb, but they didn't seem to have a clue what they were doing out there. As they danced around like bumbling idiots, they made strange animal noises, which made the audience go crazy. They looked really absurd, they were out of their minds, but I couldn't take my eyes off them. They were making fools of themselves, but they seemed to be having a lot of fun, so I didn't mind watching them. Then they started making obscene gestures with their hands, which was weird, but the audience didn't care, they still yelled for more. What can I say, they were funny, so I couldn't stop watching them, And, best of all, they made me forget about my food. Yes, they did their best to entertain us, but after a few numbers, it just wasn't enough, we needed our food. I was starving to death, and there was still no food in sight, I didn't know what to do. Our waitress seemed unconcerned by the delay, and unwilling to tell us the truth. She did finally tell me a little secret, but she told me to keep it to myself. *I'm sorry, this happens every night,* she confessed, *we need a new grill, but the owners don't want to buy one.* I was impressed by her candor, it was refreshing, because people never tell you the truth. *I'm just the messenger, I have nothing to do with the kitchen,* she said. It was completely out of her hands, it was not *her* fault, and she wasn't gonna take the blame, so it was the kitchen's fault. Even Yanko was upset, which made me laugh, because he had been the cool one for the entire trip. All this waiting was getting to him, he was famished, and he looked mad as hell. He was about to lose it, he was ready to explode, so I tried to calm him down. *No one should have to wait this long for a damn meal,* he said, *this is not how you run a restaurant!* They're having a grill problem, I told him, but he didn't want to hear about the grill, he just wanted his food. It was all a big mess, and everybody was in a horrible mood, so I tried to think positive thoughts. The kids were crying out for the food, and the men were cursing for the food, but the women didn't seem to care about the food, they were dancing in the aisles. The folk music was making only the women dance, and nobody else. Women have more patience than men, they know how to wait, unlike men, they can't wait for anything. They were dancing on the stage, on the tables, almost everywhere! I was so hungry, I would have done anything for a piece of food. But I didn't have to do anything, because the music stopped, then the waitress yelled: *Dinner is served, are you ready to eat?* She looked a little too proud, I thought, when she announced the good news, I mean, she had nothing to do with the arrival of our food, but she was taking full credit for it. Everybody ran back to their tables, and the food was finally served. But when our dinner arrived, there was a big problem, it was burnt to a crisp. Everything was charred; the chicken, fish, lamb chops, steaks, even the vegetables. Was this some kind of joke? After all this time, I thought, and the joke is on me. No, it wasn't a joke, the food was real, and it was all well done. But nobody at the table seemed to care, they were devouring it like it was their last meal on earth. Yanko and Iskra were too hungry to care, and Petar and Mascha didn't care, and my wife surely didn't care. I didn't care either, it was too late to care, so I swallowed my meal whole. Not a word was spoken between us, we were too hungry to talk, we ate like pit bulls. I finished every last morsel on my plate, this mammal became animal. The waitress stood by our table with a cocky smile on her face, she was completely amazed at herself, as if she had done her good deed for the day. She looked forward to this moment every night, I thought, when she could stare across the restaurant and see all of *her* happy customers. She loved this feeling, I could tell, it was on her face, it was her moment of zen. After everyone was done with their food, the dinner plates were cleared, then dessert was served. I was having the Bulgarian chocolate cake, which our waitress had recommended; it was the *house* specialty, so I ordered it. But before my cake could be served, there was a special treat, she said, there was a fire walker, and he was going to walk on fire. I couldn't believe it, this place was ridiculous, but I wanted my cake, so I had to watch him. A small fire circle had been set up right in front of the stage; it didn't look very hot, the coals were barely glowing. It was more a circle of ash, than a circle of fire. When the fire walker appeared, he was dressed in a white tuxedo and a black top hat. He looked more like a magician, than a fire walker, which made me laugh. When he took his shoes off, he left his socks on, which seemed kind of strange, but I was willing to give him a chance. *In the name of the holy ghost,* he declared, *I will walk on the fire!* I didn't know what to do, laugh or scream, so I laughed. He seemed a bit too zealous, and his bravery was way overboard. Because his fire was not a fire, it was a smoking sandpit, the danger level was very low. He stood there like a fat king, he took his hat off, then he put it on the edge of the stage. It didn't seem to matter to the audience that the fire wasn't hot, they still cheered him on, which made his confidence grow. He stood there in his filthy socks, smiling at us, like we were his loyal subjects. When he started reciting a poem, I almost lost my shit, and I burst out laughing. It was by some Bulgarian poet from the 16th century, my wife told me, and it was a poem that all Bulgarians knew by heart. As he read it, the audience recited the words along with him. I could barely understand him, he spoke too fast, and he slurred his words. Yes, the words got murdered, but the audience didn't care, they were with him all the way. *What in the hell is he saying?* I asked my wife. She told me to be quiet, and to *let him finish*, so I stayed quiet and I let him finish the poem. I wanted my cake, but the poem was very long, so I had plenty of time to think about it. As he went on, I began to imagine the cake, it was a little too sentimental for my taste, but it seemed made from the heart. *Where is my cake?* I said. My wife told me to shut up, she didn't want to hear about my cake, she wanted to hear the fire walker's poem. I needed my cake, but it was nowhere to be found, so I had to wait for it. But then the wind picked up, and the ashes began to smoke like a chimney. Of course, I inhaled some smoke, I didn't mean to, and now I felt nauseous. It was getting too smoky for me, but the guy standing next to me wanted more smoke, and he was full of hot air, so he began to heckle the fire walker. He was screaming all sorts of rude things at him, but the fire walker ignored the heckles, and he kept reciting the poem in a very loud voice. Poetry is nice, it can be hot stuff, but fire is better, because it burns hotter. The smoke was unbearable, I couldn't see in front of me, so I could barely see my wife. When the fire walker finally finished his poem, he took a couple of steps into the ashes, then he said: *With mind over body, I will now walk on the fire!* He was still wearing his socks, which made him look ridiculous, so he had a difficult time walking. As he dragged his feet through the ash and sand, he walked around the circle a couple of times, then he stopped. It only took him a few seconds, so he had plenty of time to bask in his own glory. It was his time to shine, he couldn't help himself, he had to show off a little. But then he ran into a slight problem, he couldn't move, and it stopped him in his tracks. His feet had sunk into the sand, he had found a soft spot, it was like quicksand. Now, he was stuck, but he didn't care, it was his show, and the best was yet to come. While he wiggled in the sand, he jumped out of his socks, when he took one step forward, he fell like a tower. It was a quick trip, as his body belly-flopped, he landed face first into the ashes. When he hit the sand, a big plume of dust exploded around his body; he rolled a few times in the warm ashes, then he stood up. I couldn't stop laughing at him, he was hilarious, he was a comic genius! His white tuxedo was now a black tuxedo, which made him look like a penguin. The fire walker had a huge smile on his ashy face, so his teeth looked whiter than white. It was all part of the show, I guess, because he had us in the palm of his hand. Let me tell you, he knew how to milk an audience, he had absolute trust in himself, and a blind confidence in the outcome. He milked the moment for what it was worth, he took a few bows to the audience, then he said a few words in broken English: *Thank you people, the show no more, I'm happy, now you tip me!* I couldn't believe him, he was out of his mind, there wasn't even a fire to walk on, I thought. When he passed his hat around, he smiled at me like a beggar, he looked pretty sad. I just smiled back at him, I didn't give him any money, what else was I supposed to do? Most fire walkers do it for the thrill of it, but this one only did it for the tips. But I couldn't be mad at him, he had to make a living, and this was his job, so I had to respect him. When the music started up again, the folk dancers came back out again, they looked really hyped up this time. The audience cheered for more, they didn't want the show to end, so for their finale, they brought a horse onto the stage. It wasn't a real horse, it was two kids dressed up in a horse costume. I couldn't stop laughing at them, they were too silly, they looked like a joke. The kid up front, with the horse's head on, was wearing rubber fishing boots, which were painted to look like the horse's front legs. The other kid in the back, he had on the back half of the horse, and his boots were also painted like legs, but they were ripped apart, so I could see the kid's skinny knees sticking out. They were both attached in the middle with black duct tape and long belts to a leather saddle. There was a third kid, he was wearing a cheap cowboy outfit, he looked like a cheap Lone Ranger. When he was jumped up onto the horse, I lost my shit, I couldn't stop laughing. And everybody in the audience was laughing at them too–even my wife was laughing. For some reason, Petar and Mascha weren't laughing, they looked mad and sad. They didn't think the show was funny; *the horse looks fake, and the cowboy is stupid!* Petar said. I didn't care what he said, the horse was funny as hell and the cowboy was a hoot, I thought. *The horse and cowboy are dumb, they don't look real!* Mascha said. She was already a realist at such a young age, I felt bad for her. The two of them were acting like little brats, and I was getting tired of their shit. What is real, what is fake? I thought. They were beginning to sound like a broken record, so I tuned them out and I tried to enjoy the cowboy and horse show. Then the fire walker came back into the picture, when he jumped on the stage, he did a crazy dance in a circle. This time, he had a fire torch in his hand, which put me on edge, because I didn't trust him with fire. As he twirled the torch like a baton, the flames flashed through the air in unison. Bulgarians love to make a scene, and this fire walker was mugging up this one. They really like to show off their muscles, to be the star of the show, so they're born performers. It's in their Thracian blood, they can't help it, they're very theatrical people. They were born to fight. And they like to fight to the death, and they hate to lose. This fire walker was really hamming it up, he was showing his fire, if you know what I mean. Up and down, and all around, he spun his torch into the air, and he caught it every time. He was pretty impressive, but I had seen his act before, so I knew that it couldn't last. Each time, he tossed the flaming torch into the air, he caught it with no problem. He did it again and again, it was amazing, he almost made it look easy. Then he did a trick, he caught the torch behind his back with only one hand. The audience went nuts, we couldn't believe our eyes, he was a real pro. He still looked filthy, he was covered in black soot from head to toe, but this fire walker had some skill. I couldn't believe that this was the same fire walker from before, because this one had some skill. Let me tell you, he was a much better fire *thrower* than a fire *walker*, and he really knew how to play with fire. I was wrong, I misjudged him, I guess, I had to admit it. But, then again, deep down, I knew better, I had seen his act before, so I knew this couldn't last forever. It didn't take too long, it happened so fast, in a flash! On his next toss, the fire torch went too high, and his luck changed in an instant. I could tell by the look on his face that he was in trouble, because he looked scared straight. When the torch went up and peaked, it came down like a kamikaze, as it crash landed onto the stage. But there was a slight problem on deck, when the torch finally came to a stop, it settled was right under the horse's behind. Of course, the bushy tail caught on fire almost immediately, and it was engulfed by the flames. Yes, the fire walker had done it again, once more, I was in awe of his incompetence. This was his best show yet, I thought, he had outdone himself. If you wait *long* enough, Kundera says, the inevitable will eventually *happen* to you. He is right, but I couldn't wait any longer, and I was too eager to see the fire walker's next move. So I just sat back and I watched the fun unfold before my eyes. I must say, his will to entertain was impressive, he was born to do this, and he was showing the world his proof. Some people don't care if they put on a great show, but this fire walker was a born entertainer, so he was doing his best to entertain us. Let me tell tell, Kundera would have a hissy fit if he had to come up with a horse tale. And he surely wouldn't know what to do with a horse tail that is on fire, it's much too hot and unpredictable for him. Kundera says silly things, but this one takes the cake: *What should happen will always happen.* I mean, you can't make this stuff up, when the kid in the back realized that his tail was on fire, he panicked, and he tried to put it out, but to no avail. The kid in the horse's head tried to run away from the tail, but he couldn't, because they were still strapped together. They were stuck in a no win situation, so they started running in circles like idiots. The kid in the saddle was in the most danger, as they went around and around, he hung on for his dear life. Then something happened that I didn't expect: our waitress saved the day. Yes, she wasted no time, as she grabbed hold of the horse, she ripped the belts off the saddle. I didn't expect this from her, she surprised me, she had no fear in her eyes. When she cut the duct tape, they were finally freed from each other. The horse's head went one way and the horses's behind went the opposite way, so the cowboy in the saddle had only one way to go and that was straight down. He hit the floor like a brick, and he didn't get up. The horse's tail was still on fire, and he saw only one way out of this mess, which was to exit stage left. Before he jumped right off the stage, he took a running leap, as he flew like an asteroid through the air. A flaming tail is an amazing sight, so I couldn't pull my eyes away from it. He glided like an arrow until his arc started to curve down, then his final descent began. He was brave and dumb to do this, but he had no choice, he was on fire. He came down pretty fast, it didn't take him that long to hit the ground. Or, should I say, to hit my funnybone: because he landed right on Petar and Mascha's table. I couldn't stop laughing, I was in tears, it was a perfect landing. Our waitress saved the day again, when she yanked the flaming tail off the horse's behind, then she stomped the fire out. The kid was lucky that she was there, she saved him from some serious injury. He looked a little embarrassed, so I kept on laughing at him. What can I say, he looked ridiculous, but he was alive, so he was happy. The kid looked at me like I was crazy, but if something is funny, I can't help but to laugh at it. But Petar and Mascha didn't think anything was funny, and they didn't laugh. They both have old souls, but they're still young at heart, so they weren't laughing. They looked really upset, which was expected, but they were lucky, because they didn't get hurt. The horse's head was long gone, but the horse's behind was now crying on the floor. I wanted him to stop crying, but I couldn't stop laughing, which made my stomach hurt. When the show was over, it was time for dessert, I was ready for my cake. Then the fire walker started collecting his tips, but the audience wanted more, and they kept cheering for him, so he ran back on the stage. First, he did a couple of cartwheels, then he did a back flip. But the folk dancers had seen enough, and they weren't having it; they grabbed the fire walker by the seat of his pants and they proceeded to toss him off the stage. Lucky for me, he landed right on top of my table, so I saw the whole thing up close. When he got up, he didn't look hurt, he looked happy. He took a bow to the audience, then he went around with his hat and he collected his tips. He was being greedy now, I swear, some people will do anything for a tip, they have no shame. *One has pay to play*, Alabaster says, *or play to pay.* And the next day, I paid in full, because I woke up like a sick dog. I had food poisoning, I was a horrible mess, but no one else got sick, just me, which seemed almost impossible. When I got up, I felt dizzy and nauseous, I wanted to sleep it off, but my wife wanted to go to the beach, so I had to go with her. The last beach on our list was Perla Beach, which turned out to be my favorite beach. It's a very secluded beach, with a hidden cove, a stone pier, and, best of all, no greasy lifeguards. It's off the beaten path, so it takes a little effort to get there, but it's well worth the trip. There is a derelict mansion on the property, that sits on the overlooking cliff, which used to be the summer home of the former communist leader of Bulgaria, Todor Zhivkov. The property is in bad shape, but the house is still standing, because it was made with steel and stone. When you first arrive there, a private cove awaits you, which is hidden by a wall of trees. This beach is something special, there is a secret hidden in the sand, and it is your job find it. Once you are *here*, then the secret is revealed. The mansion is now just a distant reminder of a lost past, a communist past, that most Bulgarians want to forget about, my wife told me. After Zhivkov was ousted, everything inside the house was looted and ransacked. In a matter of hours, all of his riches were gone, but the actual house stayed intact. Steel is strong and stone will last forever, so this house would be here for a very long time. It was built in a modern style, with granite, marble, steel, and wood. It looks like an alien spaceship on the cliff, it is a strange sight to behold. The wood was removed years ago, so only the earth stones and steel remained. Zhivkov lived like a king, and Perla Beach was his private paradise. But now, it is open to the public and anyone can come here. You can sun yourself on Zhivkov's beach, and you can swim in the same Black Sea that he swam in. When you're on this beautiful beach, time slows down, it lingers longer, so it makes you more calm. On Perla Beach, I was at peace, and all my troubles seemed to drift away with the wind. Today, I was in a good mood, and it was time to swim, so I jumped into the water. The beach was almost deserted, it was fantastic, there was no one else around except my wife and I. When I jumped into the swell, I was caressed by the blue waves, as they took me under, I was now floating away. The lure of the Black Sea had brought me here, so I was overwhelmed with emotion, it was everything that I had hoped that it would be and more. I was swimming in it, and it was finally swimming in me, if you know what I mean. *I'm the Black Sea and the Black Sea is me!* I screamed out loud. After diving in and out of the sea, I felt baptized, so I got out of the water and I went back to our blanket. I was a *new* man, I was *now* wide awake, I was *nobody* but me. My wife had picked the perfect spot on the beach, it was away from everyone else, and we had our privacy. I was ready to read, I had the time, and I had my *TULOB*, I was literally in literary paradise. Yanko and Iskra had gone for a walk with Petar and Mascha, so there was no one to bother me. *You must go back to nature, and cleanse your sins in her water,* Alabaster told me, and that's what I did, I thought, I came here to Perla Beach. I was *here* at last, I wanted to take it all in, and I wanted to remember it. I had *TULOB* in my hands, but I didn't want to read, I wanted to see, so I put it down, and I just stared at the sea. But temptation is a bitch, and I was tempted to pick my book up again, and that's what I did. But, this time, it felt light in my hand, not heavy, like before, so I opened it to a randon page and I read this sentence: *It's not too late, it's never too late*. Kundera really knows how to get under my skin, when I read those words, I wanted to punch him in the mouth. *It's not too late*, that stung me like a bee, *it's never too late*, that is too sweet for me. But I was on Perla Beach, so Kundera had no control over me, and I was free to do whatever I wanted. *TULOB* is a big tease, he likes to tease you with his sweet words, and I didn't want to be teased by him, so I didn't let him. But Kundera is a master beekeeper, so it only took him one sentence to sting me: *Sabina knew of nothing more magnificent than going off into the unknown*. I wasn't ready for these words, I was caught off guard, and they shook me to my core. Kundera is a sugary writer, but that sentence is just too damn sweet, I thought. Kundera is a big softy, he likes to shape you, until you are putty in his hands. What can I say, he taunts me, he plays me, he whips me. He knows me very well, inside and out, so I was in big trouble. Like a hungry hawk, he swoops down on me, and I am carried away by his words. Hawks will go after anything that moves, and they usually get their prey, so I was dead meat. Kundera is the hawk, and I'm the rabbit, I thought, and I'm running as fast as I can. I didn't have enough time to read *TULOB*, so I put it back into my pocket. When I looked at the sea, I saw my past floating away, as the waves crashed on the shore, I heard my future yelling at me. I was in a trance, I was in a tsunami, I was in a tornado, and I was completely present. I felt new and old at the same time, I was alive but dead, I was somewhere in between the two. Kundera can bite you like a cobra, but squeeze you like a python. He is deadly, one he gets a hold of you, once his venom is in your bloodstream, you are dead! Within seconds, his toxins are injected into you, as the polypeptides spread through your body, you are slowly paralyzed by his words. I was done with Kundera, and I was done with *TULOB*, so I had nothing to worry about, I told myself. I just wanted to chill out, I was feeling mellow, I was as free as a bird. But before I could relax, Mascha and Petar came back, so my peace was sadly interrupted. Of course, they wanted to play chess again, which didn't surprise me, but I wasn't in the mood. *No more chess for me,* I said, *I don't want to play anymore.* But they didn't believe me, they kept nagging me to play, so I ignored them. Life is like a game of chess, it takes some skill, but most of the time, it's just pure luck. And I knew all about luck, because I was lucky to be here on Perla Beach, I had won the lottery. *How did I get here?* I didn't have a good answer, and it was a miracle that I had made it this far. Perla Beach is a bucket list beach, and I knew it, so I was grateful to be here. *I love you Perla Beach!* I screamed out. It's such a simple phrase, but it's so hard to say out loud. I was in heaven, and my wife could tell, so she reached over and she gave me a kiss. It was the perfect kiss, because it was exactly what I needed at this moment. I've been to many beaches where I don't belong, they are no fun, but this wasn't one of them, I belonged on Perla Beach. This is the perfect beach, I thought, where I can lose myself and find myself in the same day. I could read any book here, it was so peaceful, and the people don't bother you. I could even read the so-called *classics* here, they would be easy to read here on this beach. I've read most of them, but I can't pick my favorite one: Camus' *The Stranger*; Gombrowicz's *Ferdydurke*. Miller's *Tropic of Cancer* and *Tropic of Capricorn*; Nietzsche's *Zarathustra*. The list is too long, so I won't name them all, but any of them would be perfect for this beach. Of course, Kundera's *TULOB* was on the list, and in my pocket. I had no choice, he had power over me, so I had to read it again. When I opened the book to the next page, I read this: *But was it love? The feeling of wanting to die beside her was clearly exaggerated: he had seen her only once before in his life!* Is my wife a *Tereza* or a *Sabina*? I asked myself. I still didn't have an answer yet, so I kept on reading the words. I got lost in the poetry and sucked into the drama of it all. Yes, *TULOB* is a dark and funny labyrinth, and, just like New York, it's filled with a few unsavory characters. I try to stay away from them, but the sickos always find me. I let Alabaster deal with the crazy ones, so I don't have to worry about them that much. Let me tell you, this world is full of them, they're everywhere, and they don't take *no* for an answer. I can smell them coming from a mile away, they smell just like shit. I try to avoid most of them, but it's hard, because they stink up everything. *New York is a big bowl of shit*, Alabaster likes to say, *with a sour cherry on top!* He's right, and we all have to eat it everyday, without any complaint, because this is how it works. Well, Alabaster knows how to *make* it work, and he works *it* all the way to the bank. *I get up every morning,* he says, *I have my coffee, I feed my cat, I put on my boots, then I step in shit for a living.* I swear, Alabaster can make anything sound romantic. I know his job is hard, it never ends, but he loves it with a passion. It's the perfect job for him; he loves to chit and chat, to wheel and deal, to wine and dine. The dinner parties and fundraisers get to him, but that's all part of the business, he says, so he does it with a smile on his face. I could never do his job, I mean, I've seen it up close and personal, and it's not for me. Alabaster is an absolute saint, he deals with the collectors for me so I don't have to do it. It's not an easy thing, because these deranged people will disturb you at any hour of the night, and they have no boundaries. They don't care, you're *their* dealer, so you have to listen to them no matter what. I still remember one collector trip in particular that I took with Alabaster; we went to see this rich doctor in New Jersey. I didn't want to go with him, but he made me go, so I had no other choice. He was going on one of his *personal* visits, where he saw a collector's collection in person. He wanted to show me *the wheel of the deal,* he said, and *the nuts and the bolts* of the business. *This collector*, a gentleman named Mr. Shadi, *was a serious collector with a deep wallet.* His summer house was on the Jersey Shore, on Long Beach Island, and he was only there for three months of the year, so this was the perfect time to visit him. Alabaster really wanted me to meet Mr Shadi, I needed a collector like *him*, he told me, because he would be very *beneficial* to me at this point in my career. I was all for it, I had nothing else to do, and nothing to lose, so we headed down to the shore. Mr. Shadi was the real deal, *he loves to buy art*, Alabaster said, so I was dying to meet him. Mr. Shadi was all class, he had hired a limo for us, which made the trip quite comfortable. When we arrived at his house, Mr. Shadi greeted us at the front gate. Alabaster told me to call the doctor by his proper last name, *Shadi*, which meant happiness in Persian. If that's what Alabaster wanted me to call Doctor Happiness, then that's what I was going to call him. This was supposed to be a serious visit, so I was on my best behavior, but when I saw Mr. Shadi's house, I lost my shit. His house was a modern monstrosity of glass and steel, it looked like a shipwrecked cruise ship. It was beyond gaudy, or kitsch, it was a spectacle of wealth. The house was by some famous Argentinian architect, but it didn't matter who designed the house, it was a pile of junk. The first thing that Mr. Shadi showed me was his speedboat; I couldn't believe the size of this thing, it was gigantic, more like a rocket ship on water. Then he showed me his Olympic-size heated swimming pool, that had a diving board and a slide. His car garage was the size of an airplane hanger, and it was filled with old classics from the past: a Ferrari, a Jaguar, a Porsche, a Rolls Royce. Mr. Shadi was very proud of his car collection, it was his favorite hobby, he said, and the most fun. His car collection was impressive, and with all the original parts, they were in mint condition. But Alabaster didn't seem impressed by the cars, they were *too old* to drive, he said, and *not driven* fast enough. He has met the richest of the rich, so cars are just cars. *Money makes the world go fast*, Alabaster likes to say, *but sooner or later you will run out of gas*. He's been in this business for a long time, words mean a lot to him, he likes to talk, so I let him talk. He will do anything to buy and sell his art, and money is only a means to his end. He makes a good living, but the art is what matters to him, so the money is irrelevant. For Alabaster, being rich is having a pastrami sandwich on rye and a beer in Central Park. Money is like a tree, *it rots from the roots*, he says, so he goes where the money takes him, and this time, it took him, and me, to New Jersey. When Mr. Shadi opened his front door, the first thing that I saw was a Botero painting. I love Botero, so the sight of one of his large ladies made me giggle, I was beside myself, I couldn't believe he had one. She was in the living room, hanging over a massive fireplace, and I couldn't take my eyes off her. I gazed at her rounded curves like a jealous boyfriend, she filled me with joy, and her tiny hands and feet made me feel happy inside. Then Mr. Shadi showed me his Barnett Newman, which was a huge canvas, it dwarfed me when I stood by it. Yes, it was one of his famous red paintings, with blue and black, and it was very rare, so I don't know how he got a hold of one. There was also a Warhol painting of cantaloupes in the den, which was much too pretty to take seriously. Mr. Shadi's house was stocked full of masterpieces, and he loved to show them off. The Yves Klein sponge relief in the foyer made me feel blue, because it seemed so lonely there on the wall. And the Henry Moore stone sculpture in the kitchen made me feel angry, the whole thing was covered in black grease, it needed a good cleaning. Mr. Shadi's collection was all over the place; he had Danish furniture next to Japanese china, Tiffany lamps mixed with 18th Century bronze sculptures. It was a total mishmash of centuries and styles, I couldn't wrap my head around his taste, it was quite unusual. The back of his house had floor-to-ceiling windows, so there was an amazing view of the Atlantic Ocean. There was a spiral staircase in the middle of the sitting area, which circled up to the second floor game room. The Italian tile floors were layered with Persian carpets and the walls were covered in Gothic tapestries. Mr. Shadi's house was making me feel dizzy, his taste was beyond kitsch, it was post-kitsch, so I couldn't see straight. It had a decadent charm and it oozed warmth, but it reminded of a hookah lounge. Mr. Shadi was a very talkative guy, most doctors love to talk, so I let him talk. He had been living here for the last forty years, when he came here in 1980, after the Iranian Revolution. His father had died in a Tehran jail cell. First, they beat and tortured him, he said, then they killed him *like a dog!* His father was arrested on some fake charge that had nothing to do with him, it was all *a big lie*, but they didn't care, *they killed him!* Mr. Shadi had been married only once, and was now happily divorced and having *the time of my life*, he bragged. He was a short man, but he was very stocky, with broad shoulders, so he looked like a water buffalo. He was debonair, and he had a lascivious gait, he was always on his tip toes, which made him walk like a prissy peacock. He was wearing a red Speedo, with white boat shoes, and he was covered in suntan lotion, so his skin glistened like a hotdog. This was the ideal bachelor pad for the ideal bachelor, and Mr. Shadi was letting it all hang out, if you know what I mean. He was part Romeo, part Tarzan, and part Zorro, all rolled into one, and he was living *his* American dream. Like most doctors, he didn't have a care in the world, he had a nonchalant attitude about life and death, so his jokes were dark and dirty. He had a daily vitamin routine that kept him *nice and clean*, he told me, *on the inside and outside.* He took twenty pills in the morning and twenty at night, but was still trying to find the right dose, *to keep the edge off.* Then he wanted to show me his cherished wine collection, so we went down to his underground wine cellar. It was filled with all the *great* years: *1961, 1978, 1982, 1994.* Mr. Shadi was very proud of his cellar, he had spent a lot of money on it, so he really wanted to show it off. I didn't care what great *years* he had hidden down there, they were just random numbers, so they meant nothing to me. He had *a real passion for wine*, he said, and *an obsession to acquire* only the greatest years. Rich doctors have the money to burn, so he bought up most of the best vintages that were available on the market. While Mr. Shadi and Alabaster were discussing the greatest wine years, I took a tour around the cellar. It was a real mess, and it was stuffed with all sorts of miscellaneous junk: gold coins, silver tableware, fine jewelry, fur coats, porcelain vases, bronze sculptures. This was supposed to be a wine cellar, but there was barely any room for the wine. I took a left turn, a right turn, then I came upon a metal door. I tried to open it, but it wouldn't open, it appeared to be locked. I tried again, but nothing happened, it was really stuck. I felt a little nervous, like an Egyptologist in a dusty tomb with no way out. I didn't know what else to do, so I kicked the door, but it didn't budge. When I tried the knob again, the door suddenly unlocked itself. When I swung the door open, I couldn't see what was inside, it was too dark. I looked for a light switch but I couldn't find one, so I walked into the darkness. It smelled musty, and I could smell the scent of oil paint in the air. As I looked for the light switch, I ran my hand up and down the left wall, but I couldn't find it. Then I did the same thing to the right wall, and, lo and behold, I found the switch. When I flipped it up, a bright light flickered on. For a moment, I was blinded by the light, but then my eyes adjusted to it. As soon as my eyes came back into focus, I saw the paintings. I was flabbergasted, I couldn't believe my eyes, there they were: *The Green Bananas!* Yes, I recognized them right away, they were Duke's paintings. Why are they down here in this dusty cellar? I wanted to know. Did Mr. Shadi really buy all twenty of them? It didn't make any sense. I'm sure he had his reasons why they were here, but I didn't want to hear them. The paintings were covered with a large tarp, so I couldn't get a good look at them, which made me want to see them even more. First, I undid the top clamp, then the bottom clamp, but as soon I did that, the tarp fell to the floor. The mystery was finally solved, after all this time, I had found the so-called *Green Bananas*. Well, they really found me, I mean, I was just here for the ride, so blame it on fate. But I had to make sure that they were real, so I took a look at the signature on the bottom of a painting. Yes, I knew it, I was right, it was signed Duke A. Barn-stable. Then I saw Bibi's green banana, and that verified the painting for me, so I was satisfied. Why are Duke's paintings down here in the cellar and not up there in his house? I was stumped, I couldn't think of a reason. Duke would be appalled if he saw his paintings down here, I thought, he would be mad as hell. No living painter deserved to be hoarded like this, it was a crime, and a crying shame. Mr. Shadi had too many paintings for his own good, it was ridiculous, how many paintings did one man need? If you ask me, no more than five or six, so the doctor was way beyond the limit. He was out of his mind, he was greedy, and he didn't when enough was enough. I wanted to take a closer look at the paintings, so I pulled a couple of them out and I leaned them on the wall. I picked one painting out from the bunch and I gave it a good look. I contemplated the painting in my mind's eye while I looked at it, then I ran my fingers over the surface of the canvas, I wanted to feel the texture of the paint, it felt just like shark skin. Up close, the painting felt alive, it was breathing, it was talking to me. Duke's brush strokes were now more visible, the colors reminded me of flesh: they were blue, pink, purple, red. Even Bibi's green banana was more vivid up close; the closer I got to it, the greener it got. Yes, Mr. Shadi was living the American dream, but it was a spoiled rotten dream. Why was he hoarding these paintings? It didn't seem fair, it was unfair, I thought, that one man should own so many paintings. Mr. Shadi had bought the paintings fair and square, I get that, but he was being a greedy bastard. I was starting to get mad, but it was silly, because I had no control over Doctor Happiness. It was his life to live, not mine, and that was that. I took one last look at the painting, then I put it back into the pile. I had seen enough, seen too much, and I didn't want to see anymore. I fixed the tarp, closed the door, and I found my way back to the front of the cellar. Mr. Shadi and Alabaster were now discussing America, I had nothing to say about it, so I stayed quiet. Mr. Shadi *loved* Iran with a passion, he said, but America was his *real* home. He went on and on about our land of plenty, and about how *lucky* he was to be here in this country. He was really laying it on thick, it was too much, I couldn't take it any longer, so I excused myself and I got the hell out of that cellar. It was time for lunch, and Mr. Shadi was cooking hamburgers and corn on the cob, which were two of his favorite American dishes, he said. The doctor was a likeable guy, but he acted like a car salesman, he liked to fudge the truth, he made things up on the spot, in order to make himself look good. *When I first came to America, I ate corn on the cob and hamburgers for a year,* he told me, *and nothing else.* I didn't believe him, I wasn't buying his corny story, it sounded a little too meaty to me, if you know what I mean. A few of Mr. Shadi's *friends* were stopping by for lunch, so he had pulled out enough corn and hamburgers to feed a small family for a week. When he rolled out the grill, he sprayed the coals with some unknown fluid, then he lit it. I don't know what was in that bottle, but the fire was five feet tall in a flash. Of course, his so-called friends were all very beautiful women, and they were all very young. It was like a slumber party from around the world; there was a Brazilian, one from France, another one from Japan, and two Polish twins. They were all in their early twenties, so the age difference between them and Mr. Shadi was at least forty years. He was living the good life in spades, five times over, and he had *his* friends to prove it. He had the big house, the huge yacht, the art, the fancy cars, the wine cellar, the hamburgers and corn on the cob, but, most of all, he had the girlfriends. I have to say, they were all really nice and very sweet, but it got confusing after a while. The sun was shining, I was hot, so I jumped into the pool. His girlfriends didn't want to swim, they were too busy jockeying for position, they just swooned around Mr. Shadi like dogs in heat. I tried to talk to them, but they didn't want to talk to me, only the Japanese girl (*Yumi*) gave me the time of day. I liked her the best, she gave off a good vibe, she was very confident, whip-smart, and she had a good head on her shoulders. She was here on a work visa, and she had a long list of things that she wanted to do in America. *I'm looking for a sincere man*, she told me, *with a good heart,* and finding a husband was on the top of her list. The young lady from France (*Margot*) was cocky as hell, and a rude prude. She wouldn't shut up, and she kept telling Mr. Shadi about some *creep* that disrespected her. He listened patiently to her creepy story, he even held her hand while she talked. He was a good listener, he never interrupted her, so she never stopped talking. The Brazilian (*Benedita*) was sexy in a Brazilian kind of way, she was all boobs, butt, and thighs. I couldn't take my eyes off her, for some reason, she was mesmerizing. She had beautiful skin, she was ripe like peach, and a fireball of fun. She had a huge unicorn tattoo on her lower back, and a rainbow on her shoulder, but the hummingbird on her left breast was the best. She was a typical Brazilian, wild and crazy, so I had to keep my eyes on her. The two Polish sisters (*Pola* and *Olga*) looked like twins, but they were only *cousins*, they said. I didn't believe them, because they looked exactly like each other. And they talked at the same time, I didn't trust them, so I tried to ignore them. One was playing good cop, the other one bad cop, and they wouldn't stop talking to me. *We party the Polish way,* they said in unison, *so we like to party hard!* I didn't know what they meant by that, but they had really high voices, so they sounded like dolphins. Was this a threat to party or an invitation to party? I didn't have a clue, but I was all ears. But the twins were very entertaining and fun to watch. They were playing hard to get, but Mr. Shadi didn't seem to care about their motives, he was open to interpretation, so he let them talk. He was being nice and mellow with them, which put them at ease, so they slowly began to drop their charade. But they were all here for Mr. Shadi, it was a free-for-all, and, sooner or later, one of them would be the declared winner. Who would win Mr. Shadi's heart? I didn't really care, but it was funny to think about. Yes, love is a mystery–a crime, it can never be solved. Mr. Shadi was still up for grabs, he was just waiting for the right woman, and they all knew this, so they were doing their best to be his wife. They all had a chance, but my money was on Yumi, she had the best shot at his heart, I thought. The Polish twins had come to party, they had a bottle of Polish vodka, and they were doing their very best to finish it. When they handed me a glass, I was happy, then they poured me a shot, I was thrilled. I was real thirsty, so I chugged it. Then I slammed a second shot, which went straight to my head. I was feeling good, but when they pulled out two joints, I felt much better. They lit them at the same time, I didn't know which joint to smoke, so I smoked them both. I was in heaven, I swear, the Polish twins were angels. But before I could enjoy my high, I was ambushed by Margot. When she yanked the joint from my fingers, she took the biggest toke ever, then she blew the smoke into my face. I couldn't believe her, she was a stingy bogart, and a human carburetor. Every time she exhaled, her smoke would go into my face, she was French, she was rude as hell. But I felt bad for Margot, because she had zero chance with Mr. Shadi, she was too greedy. She was just like him, they would never get along, they're too alike, I thought, they would kill each other. And Margot is too proud to beg, I can tell, so she was in no man's land. Then Yumi came over and whispered something into Mr. Shadi's ear. She was a real pro, she knew exactly what *he* wanted to *hear*, so that's what *she* told him. She was very sure of her abilities, and she knew how to conserve her energy, so she was the horse to beat in my book. To be noticed, they say, is to be possessed, and Mr. Shadi was all hers. He was already spoken for, and she wanted the rest of his girlfriends to know this, so she never let up, she just kept on coming. But Benedita was not about to be left out of the race, she moving fast, and she doing her best to get noticed. She was all oiled up and ready to go, she was now topless, and she was jumping up and down on the diving board like it was a trampoline. I couldn't take my eyes off her, and Mr. Shadi couldn't either, so we both watched her do backflips into the pool. When she leaped up and down, she would squeal, then jump into the water. I was drenched from her splash, I was soaked like a wet noodle; but I was thinking about bananas, not noodles. Yes, the *Green Bananas* were still on my mind, I couldn't get them out of my head. Mr. Shadi is one greedy son of a bitch, I thought, and he lives in a dream world. I couldn't understand him, there was no logic to his madness, if anything, he was illogical. The art business is a dubious business, the collectors are shady by default, so anything goes. *There is always time for caviar and cocktails,* Alabaster says, *when the time is right.* Collectors love to eat and drink whenever they can, they always indulge, so the art world is full of intoxicated gourmands. Mr. Shadi is one of them, he can't get enough, and he buys anything that his fat heart desires. He will swallow anything that you give him, he can't stop himself, and you can't stop him, so he gets fatter and fatter. Alabaster loves this business, and he knows how to deal with the really fat cats, unlike me, I just linger around like a rat. But all painters need their cheese, I need mine, and I have to pet these fat cats every once in a while. I have tried to climb the ladder as fast as I can, but a painter can climb only so high, then he must descend and come back down. I'm on my descent, I think, on the other side of the mountain—and I'm hanging on for dear life. Before I know it, in no time, I'll be safe and sound on the ground, I thought. Alabaster has been my Sherpa on this journey, but the cheese has been all mine. We're a team, and, as a team, we have touched the top, and now we're falling back to earth. You can't stay at the top forever, sooner or later, you must tumble down to the bottom. If Sisyphus can do it, then I can do it, I thought, if not today, then tomorrow. The world is a mountain, I climb it everyday, but, one fine day, I won't want to do it anymore. When I'm a rolling stone, then I'll be free, yes, as free as a bird in the sky. But you can't stop a collector's appetite for art, *when they get hungry,* Alabaster says, *no painting is safe!* Yes, they want what they want, and they have the money to spend, so they have no limits. I feel bad for the collectors, I really do, because they have all the time in the world, but they don't know what to do with it. They have no mountain to climb, and no mountain to descend, but they have a plane, so they can fly over any mountain. Besides that, they own the whole goddamn mountain! Yes, every painter and every dealer is the world have one thing in common: we're both at the mercy of the collectors. They're a bunch of hungry cannibals, if you ask me, and they're always looking for something to eat. Let me tell you, these colletors can really make meal out of you, if you let them. Mr. Shadi was now the center of attention, as he talked to each girlfriend, they would laugh like robots every time he said something. I couldn't believe it, he had all five of them in a trance, they were in the palm of his hand, and all their eyes were on him. I tried to talk to the Polish twins, but they ignored me, so I let them off the hook, I ignored them. I have to say, Benedita was doing her best to impress Mr. Shadi; she was now doing yoga in the nude. I love Brazilians, I really do, because they only do what they feel, and it usually involves nudity. nothing less. They don't care what other people think about them, they only care about themselves, so they live life to their fullest. As soon as Alabaster went inside the house, Margot came over and sat down next to me. For some reason, she started talking about Victor Hugo, who was *her favorite writer*, she said, because he was the *easiest to read*. Easy to read? What the hell was she talking about, she was out of her French mind, she was nuts! Hugo is not an easy read, and, he wrote poetry, too, which makes him even harder to understand. He was madly in love with himself, he couldn't get enough of his voice, so it all came out in his verse. I didn't want to talk about Hugo, but that didn't stop Margot from talking about him, she was a human wrecking ball and she wouldn't shut up. I just zoned out and I let her talk to herself, which is the best thing to do with someone like Margot. Luckily, after ten minutes of Hugo talk, Alabaster came back out, so I didn't have to listen to her anymore. But Duke's paintings were still on my mind, I couldn't get them out of my head. Why was Mr. Shadi hiding the Green Bananas? It made no sense, it seemed senseless, and it was selfish of him to hoard them all. Yes, he was a *serious* collector, but that didn't give him the right to be so greedy. Duke had painted the paintings in good faith, and this was his reward: a dusty wine cellar in New Jersey. It just didn't seem right to me, so I had to do something. I should steal the paintings, and bring them back to Duke, I told myself. But Mr. Shadi wouldn't even notice that the paintings were gone, so it didn't matter, it was a complete joke. What else can this man possibly want? He had everything his heart desired. Serious collectors never worry about the price of a painting, it's never an issue, they don't fuss over the zeroes, it's their obsession, so they buy whatever they want. But no painting is theirs forever, and the smart collectors know this, but the dumb collectors don't. The smart ones buy their art like they buy their wine, they buy only the best years. And the dumb ones buy their art like they buy their cars, they buy only the fast cars. One can be smart or dumb about it, but it doesn't really matter to Mr. Shadi, because he doesn't care what something costs. He was one rich son of a bitch, and the rich always get what they want, and now, Mr. Shadi wanted to go to Atlantic City. *It's time to gamble,* he said, *it's time to some play poker!* I didn't want to go, but he wouldn't take no for an answer, so I had no choice, I had to go to Atlantic City. Alabaster just smiled at me, like he'd seen this go down a million times before. Mr. Shadi's boat was as big as a battleship, and he had come up with a great name for it, it was called: *It's About Love.* When I saw that on the back of the boat, I laughed my ass off. The boat should have been named: *It's About Money.* I had never seen anything like this, his fully-stocked yacht had every non-essential luxury that one could ever want. Mr. Shadi was a free spirit, with a big heart, and a fat wallet, so he really knew how to have a good time. I had nothing against him, he just wanted to be happy, like the rest of us. He was living his happiness, and this boat was proof of that, which made him look even more silly. And it was a super fast speedboat, so we got there in no time. When we docked at the hotel casino, you could tell that Mr. Shadi was a prized guest, because the staff was waiting there for him. They acted liked sheep as they greeted him one after another. They showed him a lot of respect, it was unbelievable to listen to them talk. *Welcome back Mr. Shadi, we missed you! Mr. Shadi, it's so nice to see you, where have you been?* It was a little too much, I thought, but Mr. Shadi seeemed to like being fawned over like some puppy dog. He was hungry, so we went to his favorite Japanese restaurant: *Fuji Fuji.* It was one of these *teppanyaki* restaurants, where the chef cooks your meal right there in front of you. I had been to one before, so I was prepared for the comedy to come. As the chef prepares your meal, he slices and dices all the ingredients, then he tells you stupid jokes. *I really love this place*, Mr. Shadi said, *it's even better than Benihana!* He told me that the whole staff was from Japan, but I didn't believe him, because half of them were American. Some people love to tell stories, and Mr. Shadi is one of them, so he started telling us about his first visit to Japan. On this particular trip, he met his first love there. *Hitomi fell from the sky, it was love at first sight,* he said, *I met her in Tokyo, on summer vacation, at the Tsukiji fish market!* I didn't believe a word of it, he was talking out of his ass, the whole Tokyo love story sounded fishy to me. *She was standing between the tuna and salmon, so she caught my eyes right away!* He talked about Hitomi like she was from another planet, she didn't seem real to me. I wasn't buying his story, it was filled with too many holes, and his timeline didn't add up. And Yoshi, our so-called Japanese chef, sounded

Spanish to me, so Mr. Shadi's story was falling apart by the minute. Yoshi's wisecracking jokes started almost immediately; he didn't hold no punches, he even went after Mr. Shadi. Like bullets from a gun, he fired off three zingers in a row. I couldn't stop laughing at him, he was funny as hell, and his Spanish accent was killing me. But I didn't care where Yoshi was from, because his jokes were funny in any language. Then he started asking Mr. Shadi questions about Tokyo, but he couldn't answer any of them. But Mr. Shadi didn't care, he just babbled on about Hitomi, which seemed to make Yumi mad. *I kissed her at the Imperial Palace, and her lips were like honey, when the cherry blossoms were in full bloom!* I didn't believe him, because his summer love story sounded like an early spring story, so he was off by a few months. Yes, it could have happened, it is plausible, but Yoshi wasn't believing any of his bullshit. He was on a roll, so his jokes were coming faster and faster, and they were hitting his target every time. Was Mr. Shadi ever in Tokyo? I don't know, but Yoshi didn't think so, so he was ripping him apart. But it didn't matter if Mr. Shadi had ever been there, because he knew how to time travel, I could see it in his eyes, and it was written all over his face. *Hitomi was my cherry blossom, she was a sweet treat, I will always remember her!* Mr. Shadi's story was nice, but it was a little too kitsch for me, so I was getting tired of hearing it. *Kitsch*, there's that damn word again, I hate how it sounds, but I can't do nothing about it. But then when he started talking about some other people, which kind of through me off; I wasn't prepared for three new characters in his story. There was *Hachiro*, his best friend; *Makoto*, his lawyer; *Asami*; his driver. He met them in Tokyo, *on the same trip*, he said, which only made things worse. He went on and on about them, he wouldn't shut up, so I had to listen to him. What happened to Hitomi, what happened to the pupil of his eye? Somehow, I don't know why, she had gotten lost in his story, and he quit talking about her. This can happen, from time to time, when you talk too much, so I had to give him a break. But Mr. Shadi didn't care what I thought, he was too busy talking shit, so he forgot all about Hitomi. The best storytellers know how to lie right through their teeth, they do it with a smile on their face, so Mr. Shadi was smiling his ass off. But his smile didn't bother me, his stupid story did, and I was tired of listening to it. He wouldn't shut up, while he got drunk on sake, I nodded along, as his story got more outrageous. He was talking like a giddy tourist, he had no idea where he was headed, so there was no end in sight. The joke was on me, I was trapped in a nightmare, and I didn't know how to get out of it. Finally, Mr. Shadi came to his senses and he stopped talking, which was a relief to us all. Yoshi is a master at his craft, so it was time for the real fun to begin, he began splashing Mr. Shadi with his water bottle. Then he started telling fat jokes, and bald jokes, but they didn't seem to bother Mr. Shadi, he took it like a man. When I glanced at Alabaster, he had a big grin on his face, like he had heard these jokes before. He is used to stupid jokes, they are his bread and butter, but they never make him laugh. He was now discussing Proust, his favorite writer, with Margot, and she was having a hissy fit. Why do women love Proust so much? I don't know what it is about this man, but they love him to death. Don't get me wrong, I like Proust, but I don't *love* him like they do. I live in the present, not the past, so the future is all I think about. I was having a good time, and Yoshi's food was very tasty, but the Polish twins were having a great time. They were already on their third Manhattan, so they were getting pretty loose. The twins were starving for attention, they were really showing off, but I was beginning to like them. They were fun to be around, they knew how to *party* hard, and they didn't take anything too serious. Benedita was in top form, she already had her two coconuts lying right on top of the table. I tried to ignore them, but I couldn't, they were looking at me, I didn't want to be rude. She was trying her best to get Yoshi's attention; as she flirted with him, she did a wild samba in her seat. Let me tell you, Brazilians are the best *teasers* in the world, they know how to tease the life out of anything. Yoshi was smitten with her, it was written on his face, so now he wanted to show off. I didn't blame him, this was his time to shine, to show his nuts and bolts, it was now or never, I thought. When he took his spatula out, he flipped a huge prawn into the air, and he said some dumb joke about flying shrimp. As it twirled in the air, it reached its peak, then it fell back to earth. The prawn came down like a laser, and it landed right between Benedita's two coconuts. It was an amazing trick, I was laughing my ass off, Yoshi had done it again. While she fondled her breasts with her hands, she screamed: *Obrigada!* When she grabbed the prawn from between her coconuts, she smiled like a barracuda, then she bit the head off and she sucked out the insides. She did it with one big gulp, as she swallowed the salty juice, she moaned to herself, then she ate the rest of the prawn. After she was done, she licked her fingers like a cat, as she let out a *meow*, she scratched her nose with her paw. Luckily, for Mr. Shadi, Benedita had taken Yoshi's attention away from him, so now his eyes were only on her. I liked Benedita, she knew how to have a good time, and she had a real lust for life, which made people notice her. And Yoshi had finally noticed her, so he had forgotten all about the rest of us. It's funny how fast you can forget someone when you don't think about them. I was getting tired of Yoshi, he was turning into a big ham, so I was ready to leave. But he still had one last thing to do, he had to collect his tips, so he passed a wooden bowl around the table. *I did my tricks*, he said, *now it's time for my tips!* I had to give him his props, his food was really good, and his jokes were even better. He had entertained me, so I tossed a twenty dollar bill into his bowl. *Domo arigato*, Yoshi said. Then he said it again, *Domo arigato!* He wouldn't stop saying it. *Domo arigato!* He kept bowing to me, thanking me, smiling like a bank teller during a robbery. Of course, Mr. Shadi handed him a hundred, he had no hard feelings, it was all in good fun. He didn't hold any grudge against Yoshi, he was too rich for grudges, so it was all forgiven after dinner. *I'm feeling real lucky tonight, I can feel it in my bones,* Mr. Shadi said, *it's time to gamble!* After the bill was paid, we made our way to the main poker room. As soon as we sat down at the table, Mr. Shadi became a different person; he was no longer nice and mellow, now, he was mean and rude. Atlantic City is just like every other casino city in the world, so it was filled with a bunch of losers. They were stumbling around the place, in a daze, with sad faces, and some of them were even crying. I saw a few winners loitering in the corner, but the losers ruled this place. How can you tell a loser from a winner? Well, they stink! I can smell a loser coming from a mile away. I have a great nose for them, they all smell the same: they smell like booze and bitter regret. And this casino smelled like a slaughterhouse, I wanted to leave, but Mr. Shadi insisted that we I play poker with him. He was a serious poker player, he meant business, I was trapped. His girlfriends wanted to play the slot machines, but he wouldn't let them, he made them play poker. He was an above-average poker player, he told me, and he had won in all of the major poker cities: Las Vegas, Macau, Monte Carlo. *The more I play, the better I get,* he bragged. But he had a right to be cocky, he had just won a big tournament in Singapore. *It took me ten hours to win the damn thing, and gallons of coffee, but I did it!* But now, his main game was backgammon, *I play in all the major tournaments,* he boasted, *and I'm ranked in the top fifty.* I didn't believe him, but Alabaster vouched for him, so I to believe him. Also sitting at the our poker table were two older gentlemen; one was dressed up like a cowboy, and the other one looked like a cop. The cowboy had on jeans and boots, and the cop was in all black leather. When the dealer dealt us our first hand, he mumbled something, but I couldn't hear what he said. Then he said it again, but this time I heard him, he said: *Are you ready to lose your money?* When I heard him say that, I burst out laughing, because I always lose at poker, I never win. He knew me better than I thought, so, yes, I was willing and able to lose my money. But this time, I wanted to beat Mr. Shadi, so I needed to play the odds better. I'm ready, *bring it on,* I told the dealer, give me my cards, it's now or never! The dealer gave me one of those devious smiles, you know the kind, like he knew what cards were coming next. He looked bored as hell, so I made him wait a long time until I placed my bet. I was in no rush to lose, and I still had plenty of chips, I wasn't going anywhere. But he was a fortune teller, he already knew my future: I was going to lose all my chips. It didn't matter what cards he dealt me, I was never going to win, so I just had fun. But I was playing the odds this time, I forgot, I needed to focus on Mr. Shadi. I wanted my next card, so I placed my bet. *Make me a winner,* I whispered to the dealer. He laughed in my face, then he said: *I can't perform miracles.* Once a loser, always a loser, I guess, so he had the upper hand. I was going to lose, I could see it in his eyes, and when the card came, I lost the hand. I hate poker, it's a stupid game, why do people play it? Poker should be fun, but it's not, it's a long and winding grind. I just wanted to have some fun tonight, so that's what I was going to do. But Mr. Shadi was having no fun at all, he was taking it too seriously, like it was a game of life and death. *I'm here to win, and nothing is going to stop me,* he told me. Mr. Shadi was very competitive, whenever he won a hand, he would yell at the dealer: *I win, I win, I win!* But when he lost a hand, he would scream: *Fuck you, fuck you, fuck you!* The dealer had to warn him a few times for cursing, but Mr. Shadi didn't seem to care, because he kept cursing at him. The cowboy and the cop told him to calm down, but he didn't want to listen to them. The two gentlemen were old friends, the cop told me, and they were only here for a few days of fun. The cowboy was from Buenos Aries, and the cop lived in Los Angeles. Let me tell you, the most important thing in poker is not luck, or skill, no, it's who sits next to you. When to bet, when not to bet, when to bluff, when not to bluff, means nothing compared to your poker table neighbor. If the guy or gal sitting next to you is a lunatic, well, then your night is a total bust. Atlantic City is full of lunatics, but we got lucky, because the cop and cowboy had perfect table manners. I have to say, they were a real delight to sit next to, and they told great stories. But Mr. Shadi was being a real asshole, so the dealer was going to teach him a lesson. When he dealt him three bad hands in a row, Mr. Shadi lost it, he turned into a powder keg. Everybody at the table was having a fun, except for Mr. Shadi, he looked miserable. He wanted to win so bad, you could see it in his eyes, he needed to win, or else, he was going to die. He didn't care what he had to do to win, no, matter what, he was going to win. *I'm going to win my damn money back, even if I have to stay here all night!* I tried to calm him down, but he was acting crazy, so it was useless. As he cursed the dealer, he blamed him for his bad cards, then he stood up, and he started waving his hands in the air. He looked real silly, but he had to win, he said, *I will win, sooner or later, I will win!* For Mr. Shadi, winning was the only way, and it didn't matter how much money he had to spend to win, he just wanted to win. He was getting out of control, he was losing his shit. I, on the other hand, didn't have a care in the world, because I knew that I would never win, I always lost, so it didn't matter to me. I expected to lose, I didn't want to win, but if I did, then I won. But Mr. Shadi was here to win, he had to win, but he was acting like a loser. He would play, until he started *winning*, he said, even if it took him the whole night. You win some and you lose some, but Mr. Shadi was losing them all. He had no luck at all, he lost every hand, and he lost a lot of money. But he didn't care about the money, money meant nothing to him, *winning is everything,* he said. I couldn't stop laughing at him, he was hilarious, he was acting like a fool. The cop was pretty quiet, but the cowboy was a talker. He owned a book store back in Agentina, and he was a walking encyclopedia of literary facts. Once he got rolling on a subject, you couldn't shut him up, all he did was talk. Of course, he loved the South American writers: Borges, Cortazar, Allende, Marquez, Neruda. But his favorite writer that he was really obsessed with, the one that he read the most, *the writer that I most adore,* he said, *is Danielle Steel!* He has read all of her books, but he had three favorites: *Family Ties, Five Days in Paris, Matters of the Heart.* He knew everything about her, I couldn't believe it, and he knew every last detail about her personal life, too. He knew where she was born, how many children she had, he even knew her house address. He loved her so much, because she was a genius, he said, and he couldn't live without her. *She has sold over 500 million books worldwide, and she is the most popular writer of all time.* I didn't believe him, but he wouldn't shut up, so the lies kept coming. Then he started telling me the story lines from her novels, which made no sense to me, I couldn't follow them. *A fine man named Peter Haskell had everything that he desired.* What was he talking about? *Maxine Williams met a new woman in Paris.* I was confused. *I can't believe*

148

who was with Annabelle Worthington. I was really lost, I couldn't follow his stories, I was tired of listening to him. I tried to concentrate on my cards, but the cowboy wouldn't stop talking about Danielle Steel. *Once you read one of her books,* he told me, *you have to read them all.* I didn't believe him, that sounded like a lie to me. I wanted to play poker, but the cowboy wouldn't let me, he kept talking to me. I didn't want to read any of her books, I told him, but he wouldn't shut up about. *Danielle Steel is a writer's writer, she lives to write,* he yelled into my ear, *and writes to live!* I live to read, and I have never read any of her books, so what does that say about me? Well, it says, *I'm a reader's reader,* I told him. He looked confused, like he didn't know what to say to me, I had stumped him, I guess. Danielle Steel is just like Kundera, I thought, she's knee-deep in kitsch, and she can't get out of it. They're cut from the same cloth, they use the same words to seduce you. The cowboy had read every one of her books, so he was an expert on her life. Her readers love her, *because she knows what we want, and what we don't want,* he said with a smile. Did she really sell 500 million books? That is an insane number of readers, how did she sell so many books? It sounded almost impossible, but the cowboy swore that it was true. *She's the greatest writer of all time, and the most popular, I will love her forever!* The greatest writer of all time? Well, that was kind of pushing it, it was all *a matter of taste,* I told him, but I knew nothing about Danielle Steel, so I let him talk. Then Alabaster and Margot started fighting over Flaubert, which seemed like the French thing to do at a poker table. It was going to be a long fight, because Flaubert is a dark and dirty swamp, so they were going to be in it for a while. Yumi had won the last two hands, so she was now discussing her winning strategy with Mr Shadi. The Polish twins had somehow escaped to the slot machines, so their seats were cold and empty. By this time,

Benedita was already sitting on the cop's lap, and fondling him like a stripper. She was a fireball of fun, the world revolved around her, so everybody got burnt by her. The dealer was getting tired of us, but this was his job, he had no choice, he had to deal us cards. He had utter contempt for Mr. Shadi, when he dealt him his card, he said: *I really hate you.* Mr. Shadi didn't seem to care anymore, he was blinded with winning, so he didn't say anything back. He had lost thousands of dollars, but that wouldn't stop him from playing through the night. After too many losses to count, Mr. Shadi's bad luck started to change into good luck, so he won a few hands. Then he won a few more hands in a row, and a few more, and lo and behold, he doubled his money. His luck had surely changed, it was unbelievable to watch, as the poker gods shined on him. *I win, I win, I win, I win!* Mr. Shadi screamed. He was acting crazy, he kept flipping the dealer off, cursing at him, and the dealer had no choice but to call for security. Mr. Shadi was acting like a madman, he was kind of embarrassing to watch, but it was also funny as shit, so I was laughing my ass off. When the casino guards came out, the dealer looked happy as hell, but after a few minutes, he turned really sad. As soon as he realized that Mr. Shadi knew the guards, his demeanor changed, and his big smile turned into a big frown. *Hello Mr. Shadi, it's so nice to see you, it's been such a long time, how have you been? We missed you, welcome back, what seems to be the problem?* The poor dealer looked devastated, he was livid. When Mr. Shadi pulled the two guards to the side for a private talk, the dealer almost lost his mind. After a few minutes, the guards came back and they had a nice talk with the dealer. I only heard a snippet of it, but I heard enough, they informed him that he would be moving to a *new* table. The dealer didn't know what to say, he looked flabbergasted, so he didn't say anything. Mr. Shadi was really lucky, he was playing with fire, I thought, he better watch out, because the next time might be very different. Then the dealer gathered his stuff and he was led away by the guards. Mr. Shadi deserved to be kicked out of the casino, but he was a so-called high roller, so his dealer problem was immediately fixed. He now considered himself a proven *winner*, he was *back* in the black, so he was ready to leave. A casino is like a dungeon, it's hard to find your way out of it. I wanted to get out, find an exit, I needed some fresh air. But before we could leave, we had to find the Polish twins, they were missing in action. Somewhere along the way in this story, they got lost, and it was time to find them. We didn't know where they were, after a few circles around the casino, we finally found them in the hotel lounge. They were dancing looked like drunk hyenas, you couldn't miss them, as they squealed with laughter. The sign above the bar said that it was *Trash Disco Night,* whatever that meant. The place was packed with losers, they were drinking to forget. Pola and Olga were doing some sort of Polish chicken dance, and the bar patrons were going nuts for it, as they cheered them on. They really knew how to dance like chickens; to groove to the seedy beat, they jerked up and down, then they did the splits. I couldn't stop laughing at them, they were double the trouble, and double the fun. Then they did something that they shouldn't have done: they jumped on top of the bar. Of course, they started dirty dancing with each other, and the crowd couldn't get enough of it. The cop surprised me, when he jumped up on the bar and he started dirty dancing with the twins, I didn't expect this from him. The cop looked ridiculous up there, but the crowd loved him, as they cheered for more. When I stepped up to the bar to get a drink, Alabaster and Margot were bitching about Balzac, which made me giggle to myself, because he had some big balls, and they didn't like it. Alabaster hated him, and Margot loved him. Balzac can be a real bore, I mean, if you let him get into your brain. When I looked around the lounge, I saw an absurd human comedy, it was humanity in action, but, in reality, it was a human nightmare. The chicken dance was hot, but then the twins started doing a Polish striptease on the bar, and it got even hotter. They fondled the cop like a pogo stick, he was beyond funny, he was a lark! Then he started taking his clothes off, which made the crowd go wild. Before you knew it, he was down to only his leather thong. I was a little worried about him, because he was really drunk, and he could barely stand up. Where's the cowboy when you need him? I said. He was nowhere to be found, he was missing in action, and he needed to get his friend off this bar. The music was really loud; the bass was too high, and the treble was too low, so it sounded like shit. But the cop didn't care, he loved the sound of the music, he was *feeling it*, as he danced like a horny monkey. The twins were sandwiching him like a Polish hot dog, and he was loving every minute of it. But he took it too far, when he started kissing the twins without their permission. Then he did the unthinkable, he did a free dive off the bar. He flew head first through the air, the strobe lights flashed, as he crashed to the floor like a meteorite. I didn't see him land, but I heard the scream. He landed on some poor guy with the full weight of his body, it was pretty ugly, all I heard was: *Help me, help me, help me!* As soon as I heard his voice, I almost didn't believe it, but then I saw the voice, and I bust out laughing. It was Mr. Shadi! He was lying flat on his back, he was spread out on the floor like a tunafish sandwich, and he looked like a mess. He was dazed, he didn't seem to know where he was, he was out of it. When he got up to his feet, he slowly came to his senses. He didn't appear to be that hurt, he was more drunk than hurt. Balzac would have a field day with this lounge scene, I thought, it's right up his alley. He wrote like a happy pig, he oozed warmth, so this was the perfect place, because it was hotter than hell. Then the cop lost his damn mind, he started attacking Mr. Shadi, he was punching and kicking him, while laughing at the same time. The cop was wasted, he could barely stand up, but he was connecting with a lot of the shots. Mr. Shadi tried to defend himself, but the cop was too strong for him, so he got the best of him. After they rolled around on the floor for a few minutes, the bouncers came out and separated them. Mr. Shadi got the worst of it, his nose was bleeding and his lip was cut. The cop looked untouched, except for a few scratches on his neck. The bouncers wanted to throw the cop out, but Mr. Shadi knew the bouncers, so he told them to let him stay. After the dust cleared, the cop apologized to Mr. Shadi, and then everything was kosher. I must say, Mr. Shadi was really cool about it, he showed a lot of compassion, he wasn't upset, and he even helped the cop put his clothes back on. But the cop was still sloshed, he could barely stand up, so we needed to find the cowboy. *It's no big deal, everybody gets drunk,* Mr. Shadi told him, *it happens to the best of us.* I was surprised by Mr. Shadi's patience, because he hadn't shown it before. The cop looked like a sad puppy without the cowboy by his side, but I wasn't that worried about him, because the cowboy would be back, I thought, sooner or later. As soon as I ordered my drink, the cowboy came back. He had been in the restroom all this time, he said, but I didn't believe him, because he smelled like vodka and cigarettes. I could already imagine the story that Alabaster was cooking up about this night, it was written all over his face. Of course, Mr. Shadi would be the *loser*, and the cop would be the *winner*. Alabaster has a way with words, so I couldn't wait to hear his tall tale about the cop and the cowboy. After we found our way out of the casino, we went back to the boat. The ride back was nice, because nobody said a word. But then Mr. Shadi started yapping about his fight with the cop, and he wouldn't shut up about it. He was being real cocky about it, and he wanted us to know that he had won the fight. *I taught that cop a good lesson, he needed an attitude adjustment, so I gave him one!* I wanted to say something, but I was too tired, I let him talk. *I didn't want to beat him up, but I had no choice, he was being a real asshole.* When we finally got back to Mr. Shadi's house, the sun was just coming up, and he wanted to make us a *real* Iranian breakfast. I didn't know what that was, but I was hunger, so I was willing to wait for it. Let me tell you, this breakfast was ridiculous; it took him one hour to prepare it, and one hour to cook it. There was too much food, so the kitchen table was covered with piles of food. It was quite a spread, it was a lapse of luxury, and Mr. Shadi was very proud of it. I couldn't believe the size of this breakfast: there was Maine lobster, Canadian salmon, Italian truffles, Kumamoto oysters, and Russian caviar. It was an Iranian feast, fit for an Iranian king and his girlfriends, and there was just too much food, I thought. The food was good, but the Iranian coffee was great! It was a special Iranian *blend*, he said, from his favorite coffee shop in Tehran. I loved every cup, it had the most intense flavor, it tasted like cumin and cardamon mixed with hash. I couldn't get enough of the stuff, I was already on my third cup, so I was now wide awake. As I buzzed around the kitchen, I couldn't help but notice the Polish twin's identical plates of food, which only had caviar and truffles on them. When they swallowed the fish eggs and fungi, they would moan to themselves, they sounded like two vacuum cleaners sucking in air. The twins were in ecstasy, and they wanted me to know it. Margot wasn't that hungry, she said, but she was poaching down salmon like it was going out of style. Benedita was starving, so she was eating oysters like a machine, and she had two whole lobsters in front of her, too. She was oiled up and ready to eat, she was just getting started on her breakfast ritual; everytime she picked up an oyster, the juice would drip on her breasts. After she swallowed each oyster, she would giggle to herself. then shout: *Que disse?* She was teasing me, but I didn't have anything to say, so I just watched her eat. Yumi didn't want to eat, she wanted to leave, she was tired, she wanted her bed, she said, so she was going home to sleep. I was sad to see her go, I was just getting to know her. Mr. Shadi was lucky to have her, she was a keeper, but she was *sleepy*, so she left. If life is an eternal rotation of souls, then I was spinning out of control, I thought. It's either in the cards or it's not, plan and simple, there are no buts about it. Mr. Shadi was rich enough, so he had some cards up his sleeve. He was a lucky son of a bitch, he could buy anything that he wanted. I could only laugh at him with envy, because I wasn't so lucky, I was unlucky. If the cards hold all the answers, then his next card was an ace, and mine was a deuce, I thought. Mr. Shadi needed to win, I didn't, so he needed everything, I just needed to stay alive. Why is he hiding the Green Bananas from the world? It made no sense, and that made me mad. Why is he so greedy? He wanted more, he was sick. But he didn't see it the same way, these were his paintings, so he was going to do what he wanted with them. He could have bought just one painting, but that wasn't good enough for him, he had to buy all of them. None of this made any sense to me, but, then again, nothing that Mr. Shadi did made much sense. Most collectors are out of their minds, they're completely insane, so Mr. Shadi needed a straight jacket. I don't understand collectors, they really baffle me; they like to *talk* about art, but they don't like to *look* at art. And Mr Shadi was a talker, and a big pain in the ass, so I was tired of listening to him. They never look at art, they love art, but they hate to look at it. They can have a deep conversation about it, but they can't look at it. They love to talk nonsense, and when they want to impress you, they will always bring up Picasso. The collectors have all the time in the world, they never sleep, so they can talk forever. There are three types of collectors: the good, the bad, the ugly. Well, there is a fourth kind, and Mr. Shadi was it, he was the *best* kind of collector, Alabaster said, because he only buys what he loves. Yes, I could see what he loved, it was everywhere, I mean, he loved everything! Why did he buy the Green Bananas? Because he loved them so much? I don't think so. If he loved them so much, then why were they down in his wine cellar? It didn't make any sense, but most things in life don't, so you have to let them go. Why did I bring *TULOB* with me? I still didn't know why, but I didn't care, because I didn't have the time to read it. *TULOB* is like a drug, I *need* it, I *want* it, so I *read* it. If you read it once, I swear, you'll want to read it twice. And, if you read it a third time, like me, then you will go insane. It's the kind of book that makes you go crazy; it's a simple love story, but it's so much more than that. It's a comedy of kitsch errors, and a song and dance number all rolled into one. Some love stories begin in a bed, some start on a beach, while others take to the road in an car. But, if you're unlucky, like me, the love story appears in a book. I love *TULOB* with a passion, so it loves me back. Let me tell you, after you read the first page, you will be dead on arrival. I swear, I fell in love with the book. What can I say, Kundera's prose touches my funny bone, so he always makes me laugh. I've read all of his novels, but *TULOB* is by far the funniest one. Speaking of funny, watching Benedita eat her oysters was hilarious, I was laughing my ass off. Every time she sucked an oyster out of its shell, there would be a loud slurp, followed by a deep moan, when she swallowed it. There is an art to eating oysters, and Benedita was an artist, so she devoured two dozen in less than five minutes. She was mesmerizing to behold, I could have watched her eat oysters all day long, but then *Betty* showed up. Yes, she was another one of Mr. Shadi's girlfriends, and she was here for her Iranian breakfast, she said. Betty was one of these an all-American girls, you know the kind, with blonde hair, blue eyes, and boobs. She had some big bazookas, I couldn't tell the size, but they were humongous. Were they D's, G's, E's, or F's? I don't know how big they were, but she was showing them off. She had on a white t-shirt, with no bra, so her babies were crying for attention. Betty was attractive, if you liked beauty queens, she was all fake: her boobs, hair, makeup, tan. She was all dolled up in eyeliner, when she posed, she did it like a real pro. She was starving, she said, so she went straight for the food. She was of Hungarian descent, Mr. Shadi said, which explained her goulash breakfast plate. She had a pile of everything, she barely said a word, she was too busy eating. But Mr. Shadi wasn't too busy, he went straight in for a kiss. It was hard to ignore her boobs, they were in the room, so you had to look at them. I could tell that they were fake, but I didn't care, but Alabaster did, so when he saw me looking at them, as he winked at me, he said: *God bless America!* I couldn't stop laughing, it was the perfect line, I thought, at the perfect time. I wanted to get to know Betty better, but I didn't have the chance to, because Alabaster was ready to leave. I was kind of relieved when he told me that the car was on its way. I was tired of listening to Mr. Shadi, but now he was talking about cooking a traditional Iranian dinner, so I was tempted to stay. He didn't want me to leave, but I had no choice, the car was on its way. Betty inhaled her food like a lion, she was all teeth, as her boobs bounced up and down like balloons. While she was eating, time seemed to slow down, only her mouth moved. But when you eat that much food that fast, time becomes irrelevant, as the hunger is filled up. After Betty finished her food, she started up a conversation with me, and she told me a little bit about herself. She was a Southern belle, she said, *I'm real bossy and I always get what I want!* She had a snarky attitude, but she was kind of funny, and she had a good sense of humor. She was a registered nurse, and she loved her job, she said, *because I get to help people.* She used those exact words, so I couldn't stop laughing. She was a healer, and a yoga instructor, *I love to heal people with my hands,* she told me. While I listened to her talk, I could only stare at her boobs, because they were staring at me. She had spilled some food on her t-shirt, there was a stain right by her nipple, and now I was distracted. The stain had a round shape to it, it was curved, so it kind of looked like a heart. *I do yoga in the morning and I do yoga in the evening,* Betty said, *and I run on the treadmill during the day. I have tried to get Mr. Shadi to do yoga or run with me, but he won't!* She wouldn't shut up, she was a ticking time bomb, and she was ready to explode. I could have stared at that stain on her t-shirt for the rest of the afternoon, but it was time to go, Alabaster said, the car was here. When I said goodbye to Betty, she gave me a big hug and a wet kiss on my mouth, then she pressed her breasts into my face, and she said: *Kiss these babies goodbye!* I didn't know what to do, or say, so I didn't do anything, I just stood there like a scared little boy. Betty was definitely in the lead now for Mr. Shadi's heart, I thought, and the rest of his girlfriends knew it. While Betty nibbled on my ear, I just smiled like an red-bellied woodpecker, while Mr. Shadi watched. Betty was here to *help* him, I could tell, she was here to *heal* him, too, so she was teasing him on purpose. Mr. Shadi needed to learn a lesson today, and Betty was teaching him one. And with Yumi out of the picture, she was here to claim her trophy. I know this story is pretty kitsch, and I sound just like Kundera, but I can't myself, I'm a sucker for his style, so I have to say it: *Miss Betty wanted to possess Mr.*

Shadi's Iranian heart. No, wait, now I sound just Danielle Steel! It isn't fair, he has no chance in hell, I thought, if she wants his heart, it's all hers. But it was time to leave, so Mr. Shadi walked us to the front gate. As we were making our way out through his yard, Mr. Shadi suddenly stopped for a moment and he stood silent. There was a small fig tree right by him, and it was covered with a bright yellow bird net that seemed too big for the tree. Then he told us to be quiet, as he leaned into the tree, he bent his head down, in order to get closer to the net. He stood there in silence, like he was listening for something, but I didn't hear anything. Then I heard it, there was a peeping sound, it was a bird. When I bent down, I could hear faint chirping, but I couldn't tell where it was coming from. But then Mr. Shadi saw it, there was a tiny bird trapped under the net, and it was trying to get out. I could see it, but it was very small, so I wanted to get closer to it. I couldn't tell what kind of bird was in front of me, but it was desperate to get out. When the bird finally saw me, it started chirping louder, it looked terrified. But it was trapped, it needed some help, so I had to try and free it. I couldn't just leave it here to die, no, I couldn't do that, I had to do something else. Let me tell you, there is nothing sadder than seeing a bird trapped in a net. Birds were made to fly, and this one couldn't, so I had to leap into action. *It's now or never,* I mumbled, *it's live or let die!* I had to free this bird, it was my duty, and nothing was going to stop me. When I grabbed the net, I could see the bird's tiny eyes staring right at me, they were asking me for help. First, I grabbed the net with my right hand, then I untangled it with my left hand. It was a good plan, but the bird went limp on me, so now there was a sense of urgency. The net was messed up, I tried to untangle it, but time was running out, I had no choice, I had to tear the net apart with my bare hands. It didn't take me too long, the bird was now only a couple of inches away from me, and I could feel the feathers in my hand. But my luck ran out, I was ambushed by Mr. Shadi, when he snatched the bird from my hand. It happened so fast, I didn't have enough time to react, I had no warning, so I didn't have a chance. He looked like a crazed ornithologist, he just smiled at me, then he gave me a big wink. I didn't know what to do, smile or wink, so I did both. Then Mr. Shadi did the unthinkable, he broke the bird's neck. I couldn't believe it, I was in shock, how could he do such a thing? The poor bird didn't have to die, this was uncalled for, it didn't need to end this way. Alabaster just stood there with no emotion on his face, like he had seen him kill birds before. *I had to teach this one a lesson, it was acting too big for its britches,* Mr. Shadi said. Then he nonchalantly stuffed the dead bird into his back pocket. Danielle Steel would have a field day with this story, I thought, this is *her* kind of story. Why did Mr. Shadi have to kill the bird? He didn't have to do it, he could have just let it go, but he didn't, he killed it. I should have stopped him, but he was too fast, I didn't have enough time. It wasn't my fault, but I felt guilty for some reason. Time is brutal, it can run right over you, just like it ran over that poor bird. But at this moment, on Perla Beach, it was all about the living, the *now*, so I had nothing to worry about, I was in harmony with the world. I didn't want to move from my spot on the beach, this was the perfect spot, I thought, the perfect place to relax. But *TULOB* was still in my head, Kundera would never let me relax, not for one second. He's always there, deep inside me, always laughing, as he teases me with his prose. He knows too much about me, the good and the bad, I can't hide from him. I don't want to think about *TULOB*, but I can't help it, it follows me everywhere. Kundera knows what I like, most writers *know* their readers, so I'm always putty in his hands. Of course, at the very end of the *TULOB*, Tereza and Tomas's dog gets cancer, and it has to be put down. For some reason, their female dog has a male name, she is named after Anna's husband, from *Anna Karenina*. When I first saw the dog's name, Karenin, it didn't make any sense. Why did Kundera choose that name? Well, so his readers would have to wonder about it. It's such a silly thing to do, but he couldn't help himself, he had to do something kitsch. Why didn't he name the dog Anna? I mean, that would have been the natural thing to do, but his ego wouldn't allow him. Kundera always goes for the heart, never the soul, so the dog had to die. Kundera is a pro, he knows exactly what he is doing, and nothing is gonna stop him from doing his craft. And there is also a pig in *TULOB*, named Mefisto. No, really, that is his name, I'm not lying to you. Kundera wrote a damn pig into his novel, isn't that a bitch, he did it again, just to mess with me. But I didn't want to think about a pig, or a dog, not today, not here on Perla Beach. At this moment, I wanted my mind completely empty, so all of my thoughts could evaporate into the air. When I looked at my wife, I had no words to describe my love for her, I only had *TULOB*. If I couldn't say it with my own words, then I would have to let Kundera say it for me. I thumbed through the book, in search of any passage that could describe the feeling that I had at this moment, but I couldn't find one. The devil must have been in the ink, because my hands were on fire, as the words seared me. Then I found the passage that I was looking for: *But this time he fell asleep by her side. When he woke up the next morning, he found Tereza, who was still asleep, holding his hand. Could they have been hand and hand all night? It was had to believe.* He can express it much better than I can, I thought, his words say what I want to say. I love to read a novel more than once, because the second time, I like it much better. I know what to expect, I can wander around more, I can explore the loose ends, and see where they lead me. When I'm lost in a story, I start to notice small details about the plot, that I didn't see the first time. I used to be sane man, until I read *TULOB*, after that, I became insane. You have to be an idiot to read the same book twice, what can I say, I'm an insane idiot! When I read *TULOB*, I swear, I die a little bit every time. I'm sure, when it's all said and done, *TULOB* will kill me in the end. Any book can kill you, but this book was killing me page by page. Before Kundera, there was Kafka, before that, there was Kerouac. Yes, I've read the three K's, three times over, and they draw blood every time. Kundera is a killer, he's no joke, he can kill you with just one passage. After Kafka, I was put on trial, and I was found guilty. I can never escape K's clutches, he's like a noose around my neck, he will always be there. Kerouac killed me a long time ago, when I got sucked into his road trip lifestyle. It took me years to recover from it, my body got battered and bruised. But today was different, I didn't want Kerouac's words, or Kafka's, I wanted Kundera's words, so I kept searching through *TULOB*. I read page after page, I got lost in them, I was helpless, I couldn't stop myself from falling in love. Then, I found the words that I was looking for, they were right there in front of my eyes, I couldn't believe it: *He had gone back to Prague because of her. So fateful a decision, resting on so fortuitous a love, a love that would not even have existed had it not been for the chief surgeon's sciatica seven years earlier.* I don't know why these words spoke to me, but they did, especially these three words: *because of her.* Yes, because of her, my wife, I thought, I was here on this beach. It was that simple, without her, I wouldn't be here. Kundera had a plan for Tereza; she was planned in advance, so he knew what she would be like. I had no plan, I was on my vacation, and my wife was here with me, and that was enough for me. This was Kundera's story, not mine, I had no control over it, I could only read what was on the page. It was there in black and white, *because of her*, I couldn't deny it. No sciatica, I thought, no Tomas. *No wife*, I said, *no Perla Beach!* My wife smiled at me, but she didn't say anything, she just kept reading book. Kundera is a born liar, he loves to tell tall lies, he can't help himself. He's one of the best liars in the world, so I believe everything I read. He can write with his eyes closed, and he knows how to make you cry tears of joy. Kundera is a monkey with a pen, when he gets hungry, he'll do anything for a banana. He was once a jungle ape, then he evolved into a mountain ape, but now, he is considered a civilized ape. I swing from page to page, without a care in the world, as I do his dirty work for him. *TULOB* is a rotten apple, but I don't care, I still want eat it. I always feel like a worm, as I burrow through it, I get fatter and fatter. Yes, I'm nothing but an worm, down under the loam, *on the road to being*, I thought. I'm boneless and slimy, up and down, I move through the earth without a destination in my mind. I eat everything, and I shit everywhere. Yes, I am what I am, in my DNA, I was made this way, and I can't be anyone else. Earthworms are creatures of habit, and they love to spread their seed in the same spot. They have an uncanny ability to regenerate, so they nourish the soil with their minerals and nutrients. And, what do I do? Well, I read *TULOB* on a beach, then I bitch and moan about it. I couldn't stop laughing at myself, I was acting stupid. *Knock knock.* I said. *Who's there? Time. Time who? Time means nothing to me!* But the joke was on me, I was wasting my time, it was too late, I thought, I was already a goner. I have hope for earthworms, they'll live on, but I have no hope for humans, we'll be extinct in no time. Yes, my time was coming, it was written in the stars, but I didn't want think about death, I wanted to think about life. Today, I wanted to think about love, yes, I wanted think about my wife, who was lying right next to me. She wanted a divorce, but I wasn't surprised, because she always wanted a divorce. She wants to *leave the city*, she told me, *and move to the country*. I always laugh when I hear her say this, because my wife hates the country, and she loves the city. Why lie about it? I don't know why she lies, but she does. Why move to the country, if you love the city? She didn't make any sense, but she didn't want to talk about it. *If you don't move to the country with me, then I want a divorce*, she told me on the plane. I should do what my wife tells me to do, I should move to the country, but I wasn't going to. Alabaster is all for it, it's exactly *what I need*, he tells me, at this moment in my life. If your wife needs the country life, then you should give her the country life. I still remember the day that we got married, it was a quick and easy ceremony. We did it on a whim, as a lark, as a way to show the world that we meant business. Of course, Alabaster showed up an hour late, and he was way overdressed. He was dressed up for a funeral, not a wedding, he was in all black. He had bought my wife two dozen red roses, but he forgot them on the subway, so he turned up with a box of melted cupcakes. Alabaster looked like a magician on a blind date, he had sticky fingers and a top hat. It was easy, the whole thing was over in a couple of minutes, we were now husband and wife. The city clerk should have said: *I now declare you master and slave*, but she didn't. If you ask me, it's too easy to get married, it should be much harder to do it. Before we said our vows, we were two, after the vows, we were now one. Yes, we were now stuck together for all of eternity, there was no escape. *A marriage is a cage*, Alabaster says, *with two birds trapped inside, who are always trying to get out*. And that's why he has never been married, because of the cage, he told me, it doesn't suit him. Yes, my wife and I are constantly trying to get out of our cage, but when we escape it, we always come back. A marriage is an accident waiting to happen, it can save your life, or it can kill you.

This was our second divorce this month, and the third one was on its way, so I knew what to expect next. Yes, we were two birds trapped in a cage, she was a cockatoo and I was a canary, and neither one of us knew how to get out of it. Cockatoos are very affectionate birds, they have an intense curiosity, and they make great pets. But they're sensitive and moody, too, which make them very hard to live with. Canaries are singers, we love to sing all day and all night, so I will sing my song. *I don't want another divorce,* I told my wife, *can't we work this thing out?* My wife didn't want to talk about it, she was reading her book, she said, so she gave me the silent treatment. She couldn't be bothered, she was too busy with *Anna Karenina.* But this was good news, because this gave me more time to read *TULOB,* so I dove right in. *Love is the longing for the half of ourselves we have lost.* When I read that sentence, I burst out laughing. Kundera is a fool, but he's a honest fool, and makes all the difference. Then I read it again. *Love is the longing for the half of ourselves we have lost.* Tears came to my eyes, then I started crying, and I couldn't stop. That sentence made me cry, but I didn't know why, so I cried. But the Black Sea was calling me again, the water wanted me, it was time to swim, so I put my book down. When I ran into the water, the waves hit me like bricks, and that's when I said my mantra: *I am the sea and the sea is me!* As I breathed in the salty air, I said it again, *I am the sea and the sea is me!* I was full of joy, the beach was so beautiful, it was beyond my wildest dreams, I was in heaven. *I'm really here,* I said, *I'm finally in the Black Sea!* Then my peace suddenly turned into dread, when I heard someone yell: *Fire! Fire! Fire!* There was black smoke coming from the back of Zhivkov's house, which gave me a little concern. I was in no mood for smoke, and now there was a lot of smoke, so I couldn't ignore it. The smoke trails looked like black snakes in the sky, they zigzagged their way through the air, as they got higher and higher in the sky. I didn't care about the smoke, but then the plumes got bigger and bigger, so I started to worry. The house was made out of stone and steel, so that wasn't my concern, but it was surrounded by a forest of trees, which was a major concern of mine. The smoke was getting thicker by the minute, so I was getting more worried by the second. If those trees catch on fire, I thought, we will be in some deep trouble, because a dry forest was nothing to mess with. If it did catch on fire, who would put the fire out? We were in the middle of nowhere, so the firefighters would take forever to get here. And, once this fire starts, they will never be able to put it out, I said. Even Kundera doesn't play with forest fires, he knows better, they can burn you alive. But Danielle Steel doesn't care, she's a pyromaniac, and she fights fire with fire. She burns you with temptation, and she sizzles you with soap opera, as her words flow out of her like an inferno. Her books are life savers, and they have saved millions of lives, the cowboy told me, so I had no reason to doubt him. This fire was looking dangerous, but my wife didn't seem to care, she ignored the smoke. She had her Tolstoy, and that's all she needed at this moment, she said, she didn't need a fire. It's just like her, I thought, to choose fiction over fact. By this time, some people on the beach started to get nervous, and they started leaving. I didn't care about the chaos around me, I was at peace, so I blocked everything else out. It worked like a charm, until some crazy lady started yelling at me. *Dovijdane! Dovijdane! Dovijdane!* She kept saying goodbye to me, she wouldn't stop, she sounded like a laughing hyena. I don't know why she was saying goodbye, so I stayed quiet, and I didn't say anything to her. Finally, I saw a fire truck on the horizon, and it was coming down the dirt road. But it wasn't in a hurry to get here, because it was moving at a snail's pace. I was relieved to see it, because the winds had picked up, and the smoke had gotten worse. The beach had become almost deserted, most of the people had run over to the house. I was still at a safe distance, so I stayed on the beach. Slowly, like a tortoise, the fire truck was making its way to us. It was like watching paint dry, it took forever to get here. As soon as I saw the fire truck pull up to the house, I burst out laughing. It wasn't even a real fire truck, it was an ice cream truck, painted to look like a fire truck. There was a small water tank clamped to its roof, with a green garden hose, and a wooden ladder was hanging from the bumper. The three so-called firefighters were dressed in shorts and sneakers, which was kind of ridiculous, because they had no protection for the fire. They looked more like surfers than firefighters, which made me nervous. The one dude had a fire extinguisher in his hand, and the two other dudes were carrying axes; but they didn't seem to be in any rush, because they took a cigarette break. I couldn't believe it, they were unbelievable, I couldn't stop laughing. After their smoke break, they grabbed their gear and headed for the fire. From where I was standing, I could only see the smoke, not the fire, so I couldn't see what was going on behind the house. The firefighters were behind the house for only a couple of minutes, then they suddenly reappeared again, and they returned to their truck. After a brief conversation by the road, they pulled out their cigarettes and they took another smoke break. I was confused, why didn't they care about the fire? The smoke was still billowing into the air, so I didn't understand their strategy, it seemed very reckless. This wasn't the proper way to fight a fire, this was dangerous, I thought. But what did I know, I had never fought a fire in my life, so I had to trust them. The smoke was still coming from behind the house, but they didn't seem that worried about it. Then the surfers got back into their ice cream truck, as they started driving away, I started laughing again. Something wasn't right, but I didn't know what, so I had to find out. I was dumbfounded, as they drove away, the truck backfired, and a big cloud of black smoke floated up into the sky. Why are the firefighters leaving? It didn't make any sense, so I started walking over to the house. I was cautious, because I didn't know what to expect. As I got closer to the house, I could hear people screaming, but I couldn't see anything. The smoke was pretty thick, I had to cover my nose and mouth with my hands. I couldn't see anything, I felt like a blind person, as I creeped along, I hugged the wall for dear life. The closer I got, the louder the screams got, so I had no clue what to do next, so I froze. Yes, I was frozen in place, I couldn't move, as I inhaled more smoke, I got scared. I was lost inside of the smoke, and I needed to get out. I couldn't move, I couldn't see, so I just stood there like a fool. After a few minutes of this, I came to my senses, and I decided to turn back. But before I could move, I was saved. Yes, a hand grabbed me, I don't know whose hand it was, but it pulled me out of the smoke. I couldn't believe my luck, I was being led out of the darkness and back into the light. It was a miracle, before I knew it, I was safe. When I looked up to see my savior, there was no one there, the hand was gone. I was grateful for the help, and happy to be out of the smoke. As I stood there, I pondered my next move, it was now all up to me. But then the wind came, and it changed everything. It was just in time, it was a strong wind, so the smoke started thinning out. It didn't that long, the wind blew most of the smoke away in no time. I was surprised, because the smoke was just there a few minutes ago, where did it go? My mind was playing tricks on me, *I can see now*, I told myself, as I looked around the corner of the house. When I saw the fire walker, I lost my shit! I couldn't believe it, it was the same fire walker from the night before. I was really surprised to see him again, but there *he* was, standing proud and tall. And he had the same stupid smile on his face like before, but this time he looked a little scared. Because this fire pit looked dangerous, unlike the last one, and this one was deep and wide. *Is this a joke?* I said. I couldn't stop laughing at him. And this fire was very hot, it had red hot coals, and it meant business. I didn't trust the fire walker, I had seen his act before, so I was scared for him. This fire pit was not playing around, it was dead serious, it was looking for trouble. Why was the fire walker here? It didn't make any sense to me, but it was the same one, I swear, so I had to watch him. First, he did his fire dance around the pit, as the crowd cheered him on with each new step. He kept going around the fire circle but he never entered it. I could only laugh at him, he seemed very serious, and much more focused than the last time. And, this time, he didn't have his socks on, he was barefoot, which made me even more nervous. He was real brave, but real stupid, too, I thought, because this fire was no joke. I was impressed by his bravery, when he circled the fire pit, he looked like a show horse showing off, as he closed his eyes, he spun around in a circle. The fire dance was great, but he still hadn't stepped into the fire. He seemed like a different fire walker, but it was the same one, so it was only a matter of time before he did something stupid. I didn't have to wait too long, it happened pretty fast, when he announced to the crowd that he would jump into the fire pit. But before he could step into the fire pit, he did one more lap around the fire circle. Then he did it again, he looked like a possessed man as he ran around the fire. Then he did it a few more times, with no problem whatsoever, he was unbelievable. Of course, his luck ran out, he got too cocky, too sloppy, it was bound to happen. He did one foolish thing and it almost cost him his life. *Ladies and gentlemen, I will now walk through the fire on my stilts*, he said. I thought he was joking, but he wasn't joking, he was really serious. When he pulled his wooden stilts out, I laughed, but then he put them on, I cried. His stilts appeared to be made out of thin plywood, they didn't look safe, but what could I do, this was his death wish, not mine. Yes, this would be suicide by fire, no doubt, so it was about to get real ugly. When he stood up on his stilts, he did a pose for the crowd, and he took a bow. Then he took his first step into the fire, he was fine, and he took his second step with no problem at all. I couldn't believe that this was the same fire walker as before, it didn't seem possible, because this one knew what he was doing. He was fearless, unlike the other one, this one was actually walking on the fire. The crowd went wild, as they screamed for more, he ran through the fire again. But I knew this wouldn't last, it couldn't last, because his stilts were made out of wood. Then trouble appeared, when his stilts suddenly got stuck in the sand; he couldn't move an inch, he was now trapped in the middle of the fire pit. The look on his face was priceless, I should have known better than to trust him, but I let my emotions get the best of me. Things got very serious real fast, but I couldn't stop laughing. He had no way out, any wrong move could be deadly. This stupid stunt might be his last stunt, I thought, but it was his fault, I blame him. He didn't seem aware of the danger that he was in, he was kind of enjoying himself, but that wouldn't last long. A few people tried to reach him, but the fire pit was too wide, and there was no way across it. Then his wooden stilts started to catch on fire, he didn't know what to do, his time was running out. *Jump for it,* I screamed, *you have to jump!* But he didn't listen to me, he just stood there, as the flames got higher and higher. He was frozen in place, he looked like a zombie, he couldn't move. *What are you waiting for?* I yelled at him. He ignored me, like I wasn't even there, he was in his own world. He needed to find a way out, because his stilts were being slowly engulfed by the fire. After a few tense moments, he finally came to his senses, and he untied the stilts from his legs. It's now or never, I thought, it's time for action, he has to jump. As he swayed back and forth, he made a fatal mistake, when his feet slipped off the stilts. He had no place to go but down, so he fell like a rock. As he was falling, I made eye contact with him, but it was too late, and he knew it. He came down pretty quick, as he crash-landed into the fire, he screamed: *Pomogni mi!* The crowd let out a communal moan, but we were helpless, we couldn't help him, he was on his own. He wasn't in the fire for that long, fortunately for him, the fire-fighters came back, and they were ready this time, so they drove their truck right through the fire, and they sprayed him down with a fire extinguisher. The fire walker had some burns on his feet, but overall, he appeared to be very lucky. He jumped right up, I couldn't believe it, his clothes were burnt to a crisp, but his body was safe. Somehow, he was still alive, it was a miracle, and I was laughing my ass off. He acted like his fire fall was all part of the show, but the crowd knew that it wasn't, but they still clapped for him. He bowed like a prizefighter after a win, even though he really lost. The fire walker was a born performer, he really knew how to work the audience, so he soaked up their applause for as long as he could. I have to say, he won me over with his showmanship, I couldn't look away, he was a ball of thrills. But this was the same fire walker, so, now, he wanted his tips. The more things change, the more they stay the same, I thought, so I tossed a few bills into his hat. He smiled at me like an alligator, with all his teeth, then he said: *Blagodarya!* No, thank you! He had done his job, he had entertained us, and he was safe, so I was happy for him. But the show wasn't over yet, there was a special surprise, something unexpected was about to happen to the fire walker. While he was counting his tips, he was attacked by some crazy tourist. This nut came out of nowhere, the fire walker didn't have a chance, he was blindsided by this maniac. As soon as the fire walker hit the ground, the guy snatched his tip hat from the ground. I couldn't believe it, he did it so fast, it was like magic. Then, without saying a word, he threw the fire walker's hat into the fire. When the hat touched the fire, it burst into flames. Just like that, the tips were gone. The fire walker was confused, he didn't know what to do, so he just stood there and stared at the fire. I couldn't stop laughing at the tourist, he looked like a lost puppy who had just found his mother. I felt sorry for the fire walker, but it was too late, the cash was gone for good. Then, without missing a beat, the tourist said: *I get my money for nothing and my chicks for free!* Yes, Bulgaria is a wonderful country, I thought, just when you think you are in dire straits, a tourist will do something funny like this. I must say, this guy had perfect timing, he really hit his mark, if you know what I mean. Eventually, the fire walker and the tourist got into a staring match, but the tourist got tired, so he stumbled away. The fire walker didn't say anything to him, he just let the tourist walk away. There was nothing to say, the money was gone, and it wasn't coming back. Some things in life are destined to happen, and this one seemed to be one of them. Yes, this was a big loss, but the fire walker accepted his destiny, so he didn't want to fight. It was in the cards, it lady luck, it blind chance, it was bound to happen. You can call it *fate*, but just don't call it faith, because shit happens, and the future is not known, until it happens. *I love only what a person has written with his own blood*, Nietzsche said. What more can I say? Well, I was sick and tired of Kundera, and sick of *TULOB*, too, so I had to listen to Nietzsche. I didn't want to listen to him, but I didn't care anymore, so I grabbed my book from my back pocket. I was hot from the fire, my blood was boiling, and like a patient

before an operation: *I was ready, willing, and able!* I didn't owe
Kundera anything, I only owed myself, and it was time to end
this charade. It was so simple, so easy, it was just what the
doctor ordered. When I walked over to the fire pit, I paused for
a moment, but I knew what I needed to do next, it was written
in the stars. Yes, I had to throw *TULOB* into the fire. I had no
choice, I had to do it, it was my destiny. As soon as I did it, I felt
a shock go through my body, then there was a flash of regret.
While the book burned, the purple and blue flames made love to
each other, like a two-headed snake, one ate the other, as I said
goodbye to Kundera. *I'm free, I'm free, I'm finally free!* I screamed
to myself. I felt just like that crazy tourist, I had blind faith in
my decision, so I felt nothing but unbridled joy. I was done with
Kundera, and done with his kitsch words and silly sentences, I
was over him! But I was still full of hot air, so I finally exhaled;
when I did, I felt much better, I felt like a new man. *TULOB* was
gone, it was dust, it was nothing but ash, and I was in heaven. I
had no choice, I had to do it, Kundera was getting on my nerves,
and his words were driving me crazy, so I threw him into the
fire. Now, I could really enjoy my vacation, without any distrac-
tion. I didn't come all the way to Bulgaria just to read a book, I
thought, I came here to be with my wife. Yes, it was all *because of
her*, I didn't feel heavy anymore, now, I felt light, yes, I felt as
light as a feather. When I drifted back to the beach, my wife was
still reading her book; I wanted to tell her everything, I had so
much to say, but I didn't want to bother her. I wanted to tell her
about the fire walker on wooden stilts, but she wouldn't believe
me, so I didn't say anything. My wife didn't want to talk to me,
she wanted to listen to Tolstoy. She was still chained to her
Anna Karenina, just like I was once chained to my *TULOB*. But
now I was free, and my wife was enslaved, I could tell, it was
written all over her face. All this divorce talk is silly, I told her,

but she didn't want to listen to me, she just wanted to read her book. *If you want another divorce*, I said, *you can have it!* She didn't say a word to me, Tolstoy had her full attention. I had no chance at all, I thought, she wouldn't listen to me, so I stayed quiet. Then I bent down and I kissed her on the cheek, when she kissed me back, she chirped like a bird. But my kiss wasn't enough to stop her from reading, Tolstoy already had her in his arms. My words were no match for his words, so I gave up and I quit talking. Some books are like fire, they sizzle you, and they burn you for eternity. Once you read them, you are never the same, you are forever burnt by them. *TULOB* had burned me, and *Anna Karenina* was burning my wife, I had no other choice, I thought, I had to get rid her book. Yes, I needed to throw her Tolstoy into the fire, but I didn't have the balls to do it, so I let her read. *TULOB* was gone, but not forgotten, and Kundera would always be there for me, whenever I needed him. He won't let go of me, so I won't let go of him, it was only fair. When I need him, I will read him, but today I didn't need him, so I was happy. But, then again, on Perla Beach, I didn't anything. I was speechless, the beauty of the place was singing to me, so I didn't say another word. The sky was red and yellow, until the sun disappeared behind the hills, then the sky became pink and turquoise. These colors are etched into my memory: they are a prism from my past and my future. If you fall in love with Bulgaria, it will fall in love with you. At this moment, I needed nothing else, only my wife and this beach. After it got dark, we went back to our hotel, and we had cocktails on the balcony. Our hotel was not the best, but the location was perfect, so it didn't matter what it looked like. Our room was shabby chic, post-Soviet, and it was an eyesore, but it was on the top floor, which gave us an unobstructed view of the Black Sea, so we loved it. The view took my breath away, I could see all around me, it was an incredible view from heaven. But, let me shut up, I won't talk about *my* view, I don't want to bore you. I hate it when other people tell me about how great *their* view was, so I won't tell you about mine. They drive me nuts, I get tired of listening to them, they won't shut up about their view, and I usually have to shut them up. Great views are great, but I get tired of hearing about them. So now, if someone asks me about my view, I will always say: *My view was horrible!* I love to say it, when I say it, it freaks people out. I can't get enough of it, it works every time. I promise you, if you had a horrible view, they will leave you alone. I always request a room without a view, but you can't always get what you want, so sometimes you end up in a room with a great view, and this room was one of them. As I stared at the stars twinkling in the sky, they put me into a trance, so I let my thoughts wander. But I had only one thing on my mind: *Insomnia!* Yes, tonight was club night, so we were going out on the town to *Club Insomnia*, my wife said, *so I can dance my blues away!* We had seen these signs all around town, it was supposed to be the best club in town, so we were excited to check it out. And, lucky for us, tonight, there was a guest DJ, a German fellow named *Sir Freud*. At first, I thought his name was a joke, but it wasn't a joke, that was his real name. I had never heard of him, but my wife had, so she couldn't wait to get there. I couldn't wait to hear his music with my own ears, because if he wasn't good, then the club wasn't going to be good. Most of the clubs were located in the center of town, but Insomnia wasn't, it was about a mile away. It wasn't too far out of town, but was in a pretty isolated spot, so the loud music wasn't going to be a problem. It was right on the beach, which made it the perfect spot for a club, and there was nothing else around it. To get there, we had to walk on a beach trail, which was easy to find, the locals said, *if you know where it's at.* Of course, it turned out to be a pain in the ass to find, so our night became a real adventure. Yanko and Iskra decided to join us, which was unexpected, because they never went to dance clubs, they said, because the music was always too loud. While we were getting ready, I had some time to kill, so I played another game of chess. I was bored, and Mascha wanted to play me, so I couldn't say no. Plus, I wanted to win at least one match, it was only fair, I thought. As soon as she made her first move, I was already in trouble. After her second move, I immediately regretted playing her. I was no match for her, I was dead, she killed me. I couldn't believe it, she used the old *Scholar's Mate* on me, which was one of the oldest tricks in the book. I never saw it coming, I had too many cocktails, *I'm drunk*, I told her, but she didn't believe me. I didn't expect a four-move checkmate, I was caught off guard, when Mascha moved her queen into check-mate, she screamed: *I want my ice cream!* Then Petar chimed in: *I want my ice cream!* They wouldn't stop laughing at me, I was funny to them, but I wasn't trying to be funny. *We want our ice cream, we want our ice cream!* I tried to ignore them, but they wouldn't stop. Yes, she beat me fair and square, *but the match is over*, I told her, so *you need to shut up.* She taunted me, as she danced around the room, she wouldn't stop screaming for her ice cream. I was getting mad, they were acting like spoiled brats, and I wanted them to know it. I tried to tell them that it was just a game, but they didn't want to listen to me. No, it wasn't a game to them, this was a war, an ice cream war, and they were winning it! They kept screaming for their ice cream, I couldn't take it, so I gave them their money, and they finally shut up. I should have known better than to play Mascha again, but I'm an addict, so I had to get my fix. I never learn my lesson, I can't say no to a game of chess, and that always gets me into trouble. I'm a sucker for mind games like chess, so I always play them. We finally left our hotel at around midnight, we were ready to party, and ready to dance. But the so-called *trail* from the hotel to the beach was impossible to find, so we got lost. We couldn't find it, it was too dark, we looked everywhere. Yanko had taken the reins, he was now leading the way, so we followed him. But after a while, we began to doubt him, because we were going in circles. I knew it, he knew it, my wife knew it, Iskra knew it, but no one wanted to say anything. After a few more circles around the dunes, things changed quickly, when Iskra freaked out. All of a sudden, she was a different person, just like that, she became a waving lunatic. I couldn't believe my eyes, when she started screaming at Yanko, I was shocked, because I hadn't seen this side of her before. She was cursing at him, calling him an idiot, she was pissed, and she wanted him to know it. I hadn't seen this Iskra, she was crying like a baby, jumping up and down; and she had been the so-called quiet one for most of the trip. She was mad as hell, and totally out of control, as she cursed Yanko out. While she barked orders at him, she ran around in a circle, I tried to calm her down, but she was ready to explode. *We'll get there, when we get there*, I told her, but she didn't want to listen to me, she just wanted to scream at Yanko. He just stood there and took it like a man, he didn't say a word, he couldn't, because Iskra wouldn't let him. Where did this new Iskra come from? I really wanted to know, because this monster came out of nowhere. She rose out of the ashes like a phoenix, she was a raging fire, and nothing could stop her. Iskra was here for her vengeance and nothing was going to stop her from getting it. *She is born again*, I mumbled, *and she is free!* Then my wife told me the reason why Iskra was so upset. I couldn't believe it, it was over a single word, which made her tantrum seem rather absurd. The word was *maybe*, that's right, Yanko said *maybe* to her, and all hell broke loose. How could one word make Iskra so upset? It seemed kind of silly to me, she was over-reacting, she was making a big deal over nothing. But she wouldn't stop cursing at Yanko, so I had to listen to her scream, which only made me laugh even harder. After she was done with this nonsense, she screamed herself out, then she finally stopped screaming. Yanko didn't seem bothered by her outburst, he looked indifferent, and aloof, as he tried to console her. But this *new* Iskra had already been awakened, and her wrath was about to explode, so the fire was coming. Yanko tried to talk to her, but she was in no mood to talk, she wanted her vengeance, and she was going to bring it. When she picked up a wooden log from the sand, I got nervous, then she began swinging it around like a sword, and I got scared. Iskra looked like a goddess warrior, that was about to unleash her power, so I wanted to get as far away from her as I could. But I couldn't get anywhere, because my wife wouldn't let me. Yanko stood very still, with no emotion on his face, as Iskra slashed her sword within an inch of his face. It was unbelievable how close she got to him, but he never moved a muscle. Her attack went on for a couple of minutes, then she got tired, and she threw her sword down. But the show wasn't over yet, she still had a little left in her tank, so she surprised us, when she started running down the beach. She was out of her mind, she was losing her shit. *What drug is she on?* I said as a joke. But my wife didn't get the joke, she just gave me that look, you know the look, the one that meant: *Keep your damn mouth shut!* I didn't say another word, it was time to shut up, and that's what I did. I wanted to dance, but I would have to wait, because Iskra was losing her mind. To read Freud is hard enough, I thought, but to dance to his music, well, that would be easy for me. I didn't have any reason to doubt Sir Freud's skills, but I would have to hear his music in person, then I could make up my mind. Sigmund Freud liked to dance around the issues, he really danced, so it was only natural for me to want to dance my ass off, I thought. When I try to read Freud, he always steps on my feet, and he goes way beyond my pleasure principle. Sigmund was a dancing fool, but he did his thing on the couch, so he never got tired. But tonight was party night, it was Sir Freud's party, and I was ready to dance. I had only one question for him: *Can you make me dance?* That was the eternal question of the night, I thought, because he controlled the music, so my night was in his hands. I couldn't wait to get to Insomnia, but Iskra was still acting ridiculous, and she was now refusing to walk. *I'm tired of your shit*, she screamed at Yanko, *you think you know everything!* I was thinking the same thing, but I was thinking about Kundera, because he was still *maybe* on my mind. If you know him, like I do, then you know what I mean. But I was on my way to hear Sir Freud, so I didn't want to listen Kundera anymore. He was still talking shit to me, but I ignored him, and I only thought about Sir Freud. I just wanted to dance, so I was happy to think about his music. Now, if I had to think about Sigmund Freud, well, that was music that I didn't want to listen to. If you know Freud, like I do, then you know the smell that I'm talking about. Yes, I can smell him coming from a mile away, he smells like a load of shit. Freud's logic is a pigpen of waste, it is a smelly science, so his books smell just like shit. He wrote so many stupid things, but this one really takes the cake: *Talk to me, and tell me everything!* Yes, his talking cure offered some relief to a few people, but it also made millions of people sick. Freud was a dreamer, he liked to make things up, so that's what he did. If you ask me, his *id*, *ego*, and *super-ego* is pure spectacle, it's total nonsense. He was a born entertainer, he loved to perform, so he sold his snake oil to the masses. His theories are confidence games, they make no sense, and most of them are pure rubbish. Freud ripped off Sophocles;

and his Oedipus complex is a sham, it's a comedy of errors disguised as a serious drama. Now, *Oedipus the King* is a real masterpiece, and Sophocles really knows how to tear your heart out with this tragedy. His play is a knife in the heart, about a pain that has no name, and it is all about love. But Freud was a shady plagiarist, and a horny hypochondriac, he was full of himself, so he loved to hear himself talk. When he brought his talking cure over to America, he told Carl Jung a joke: *They greet us with open arms, but they don't realize that we're bringing them the plague.* That sentence would be funny if it wasn't true, but it's true, so it's sad. If we only knew then, I thought, what we know now, we would have sunk their boat! But we didn't know about his silly science, how could we, so now we're stuck with it. But I didn't want to think about this Freud, not tonight, I didn't have the time, I wanted to dance, so Sir Freud was on my mind. Lucky for me, Iskra had calmed down and come to her senses, and she was now standing right in front of me. She seemed to be in a better mood, her meltdown was over, but she looked exhausted. Then, we all got lucky, when Yanko found the secret trail. It had been right there in front of us all this time, behind some bushes, and we didn't even see it. When we finally reached the beach, I was ecstatic, I wanted to feel the sand between my toes, so I took off my shoes. When my feet touched the sand, my worries were all gone, I felt born again. The quartz sand was as smooth as glass, I felt like I was walking on thin ice. The moon and stars were out, so the light sparkled on the waves as they crashed to shore. A beach at night, with no sun, is much different than a beach during the day, it becomes more romantic. In the light of day, the sea is a blue angel, but at night, the sea becomes a black labyrinth. I could smell the scent of rose in the wind, and the sound of the water gave me goosebumps. As I walked in the waves, I splashed my feet just like a little kid, which got my wife's attention, so she grabbed my hand and she told me to stop. When I stopped, I looked into her eyes, and she looked into mine, then she gave me a kiss. It was a sloppy kiss, a teenage kiss, but it was the sweetest kind of kiss, because it was a real kiss. I really needed a kiss at this moment, it was exactly what the doctor had ordered, so I took our medicine gladly. *Love is a kiss from your wife, on a Bulgarian beach, in the middle of the night,* I whispered to my wife. She didn't say a word, there nothing to say, she just gave me a another kiss. A kiss is a kiss is a kiss, they say, but this kiss was from heaven, so I was in the clouds. Words can't say what a kiss can say, so I didn't say anything, I shut my mouth. As we made our way down the beach, I could see Club Insomnia twinkling in the distance, it looked so close, but it was pretty far away. I was almost there, and it was only a matter of time before I was dancing on the dance floor. Yanko and Iskra were walking in front of us, but they were fighting again, so I was ready for anything. My wife and I were walking as slow as we could, because we didn't want to be in the middle of their fight. They were an odd couple, they were fire and water, so they were hilarious to be around. Then the *old* Iskra came back, the crazy one, and she brought trouble with her. As soon as she stopped walking, she started crying, which meant only one thing, that the shit was about to go down! She wanted to say something, I think, but she couldn't get the words out, so she just stood there with her bloodshot eyes. Then she made an unexpected move, when she ran into the water. She still had her clothes on, but she didn't care, she dove right into the sea. *Come back, come back*, I screamed, *where are you going?* But she didn't listen to me, she was in her own world, and it was a very wet world. As she dove in and out of the water, my heart sank every time, because Insomnia seemed farther and farther away from me. She looked like a slippery seal, she was doing flips and tricks, and she was having a good old time. She seemed to be in a trance, she was lost out there, and we didn't know what to do about it. A dream is like a rebus, Freud said, it is a puzzle with pictures. I have to agree with him on this one; I use pictures to represent words for a living, so it makes perfect sense to me. I had some pictures in my mind, but I didn't have the time, so I didn't want to conjure any of them up. No, I wanted to dance, but first we had to get Iskra out of the goddamn water. *Non verbis sed rebus*, I said to my wife. She looked annoyed when she heard the Latin words, but I couldn't help myself, I had to say them. My wife hates Latin, it's a useless language, she says, because nobody speaks it. I didn't know much about Iskra, only that she was Russian by birth, so that told me everything that I needed to know. She was raised in Bulgaria, my wife told me, but she wanted to go back to Russia, *when her time is right*, whatever that meant. She was mad as hell, and she wasn't going to take any shit, and she wanted us to know this. As she jumped up and down in the water, she kept screaming: *Voda, voda, voda!* She wouldn't stop screaming for water, and I couldn't stop laughing at her, so we were both being ridiculous. Yanko just stood there like a log, he didn't know what to do, I felt sorry for him. After Iskra finished her water dance, she came to her senses, and she finally got out of the water. She was a wet noodle, she was completely drenched, and she had seaweed hanging off her back, which made her look like a mermaid. Her dress was all white, so it was now completely see through, and you could see everything. Iskra didn't seem to care, she was showing it all off, and it was making Yanko mad. She had been baptized in the Black Sea, she was now a phoenix, and she was ready for anything. I don't know what going on with Iskra, but it didn't matter, because she was walking again, so I was happy. I could see a bright light in the distance, it was Insomnia, and it looked like a beautiful mirage. When my wife kissed me again, she whispered this into my ear: *I love you, I don't want a divorce!* My wife's voice was music to my ears. I knew she didn't want another divorce, but it was still nice to hear her say the words. *A single metaphor can give birth to love*, Kundera says. What can I say, we think the same way, but we just use different words. *TULOB* is a love story, so his *unknown consequences* and *the soul of man* are two birds of the same feather, I thought. But I didn't want to think about Kundera, or his novel, I wanted to dance, so I needed to get to Insomnia. My wife wanted to dance, too, so we were on the same page. *Two halves will always want to be one*, Plato said. Well, he is dead right on this one, my wife and I have always wanted to be one, but we've always been happy being two halves. Why force unity, I say, when distance is preferred. It was a clear night, the stars seemed to be signaling us in the right direction, so we kept walking towards the white lights of Insomnia. When I was a boy, I used to have the same recurring wet dream: I am walking down a dirt road, I come upon a rusty can in the grass, I pick it up, when I look inside, a big eye stares right back at me; as it begins to cry, the can starts to fill up with water, so I hold it above my head, as the tears fall on my face, I begin to drown in them. Yes, that was my wet dream that I had every night; but I would always wake up at the same exact moment, just when I was about to get drenched with the tears. When I woke up, I would be covered in sweat, and scared to death that the eye was still staring at me. My mother would always come into my room and sit with me, and say: *Close your eyes, go back to sleep, you were only having a bad dream.* But tonight wasn't a dream, it was real, and I couldn't wait to get to Insomnia. Of course, the club was much farther down the beach than we were told, but I didn't care, I would have walked a hundred miles to dance tonight. I was ready to dance my ass off, I could feel it in my bones, and my wife was ready too, so we picked up our pace and we started walking faster. But Yanko and Iskra didn't seem ready to dance, they were ready to fight, so I had to keep my eye on them. I can't explain my dream, I mean, it's way beyond me, and it's impossible to know the full meaning of it. It was a metaphor for love, I think, but what did I know, I was only a boy. I mean, it's like trying to explain the meaning of love; I can try to explain it to you, but there are no words for it, there is only love. Who can explain love? I can't! Nobody can. Freud tried to do it, he worked his balls off and he still couldn't do it. For him, love was an applied science, but no one listened to him, so his love theory never stuck. He never found a way to explain the beginning of love, *why we fall*, so he could never find the ending of love. What is the origin of love? Is it Eros? Is it desire? Is it death? No, love is an eye that stares right back at you, I thought. Yes, I see my wife, so she sees me, and the rest is written in a book. Maybe I've was too hard on Freud, he never killed anybody. Well, he did kill a couple of people, indirectly, but not on purpose. I'm sure, after reading Freud, some lost souls must have jumped off of a bridge ot two. His method is pure madness, and his theories are mumbo jumbo. His books are beyond science, they are *post*-science, and they sound all of the alarms. Let me tell you, if you really want to upset somebody, just mention Freud in a conversation, and see what happens. Say *Freud*, I dare you, if you do, you won't be able to fight them off fast enough. But I didn't want to think about Freud, not tonight, no, tonight I wanted to dance, and that's what I was going to do. In Freudian terms, my need to dance was a form of wish-fulfillment, so I was *willing* it to happen. Yes, I had just one wish, I wanted to dance, and that was the only thing on my mind. When I dance, I let it all hang out, I dance myself clean, if you know what I mean. If you ask me, we don't dance enough, we need to dance more; and people talk too much, they need to talk less, but they don't. Freud was still floating around in my head, so I had a bunch of absurd thoughts in there, that really wanted to get out. My mind was full of them: a wife, a divorce, a fire walker, a cop, a cowboy, dogs, lifeguards, firefighters, folk dancers. Freud was nothing but a bullshit artist, and he believed his own bullshit, so he couldn't stop talking about bullshit. He had some big balls, though, and he loved to show them off. He was a horny voyeur, he liked to watch people sleep, it gave him a big hard-on. Freud had a real kink for privacy, but he loved to kiss and tell, so he let his books do the talking for him. Was Freud's *A Metapsychological Supplement to the Theory of Dreams* meant to be a joke? I mean, after I read it, I couldn't stop laughing. What does that title even mean? Freud was a speed freak, he got his rocks off every day of the week, and he put *it* all into his books. But I wanted to dance, not think, so I put some more speed into my walk, and I started walking faster. If I squinted my eyes, I could see the lights of Insomnia glittering like an oasis in the darkness. The wait was killing me, I had waited long enough, I told myself, and I wasn't going to wait any longer. As we approached Insomnia, I could hear the tribal drumming and deep bass, but I still couldn't tell where the music was coming from. The closer we got to the club, the louder the music got, which made me happy, because loud music is hard to come by, and this was loud music. It was deep and dark, just the way I like it, so my feet were already moving. When we got to the front entrance, it was mobbed with people, so we had to wait in a long line. There was an orange fence set up around the club, that went all the way down the the water, which was kind of silly, because people were just walking around it and getting in for free. I wanted to get in for free, but my wife didn't want to, so we had to wait in the line. There was a red neon sign above the front door, it was blinking the word *OMNI* over and over again, and it was blinding me with the light, I had to shield my eyes with my hands. The sign should have said *INSOMNIA*, but the *I*, *N*, *S*, and *A* were missing, so the joke was on me. *Omnia vincit amor*, I said to my wife. She gave me a smile, then she said: *Carpe noctem!* Yes, love conquers all, I thought, so we needed to seize the night as fast as we could. My wife knew Latin better than I did, but she never spoke it, which was a crying shame. The neon sign was surreal to a fault; with only a few missing letters, Club Insomnia had become Club Omni. But you can't change a club's name in the middle of a story, so I won't, but even if I wanted to, I didn't have the time. On the side of the club was a huge mural of wild animals; it was painted in rainbow colors, so it really popped off of the wall. In big colorful letters, it said: *Welcome to the Jungle!* They had white lights strung up from the trees, which hung like curtains all the way down to the ground. The wooden tiki torches by the front door were burning a little too hot for my liking, so I became fully aware of my surroundings. As the flames wiggled back and forth in the wind, I watched them like a hawk, and I got prepared for any emergency. I had seen my fair share of fires on this vacation, and I didn't want to see another one, so I kept my eyes open. Insomnia was in the middle of nowhere, there was nothing else around it, and that made it the perfect place for a party. *Tell me everything about your dream*, Freud would say, and, lo and behold, these fools would tell him everything. Of course, they told him what he wanted to hear, so they told him their dirty secrets. Back then, no one could say no to him, but now, everyone says no, by not reading his books. Don't get me wrong, I still like to read a little Freud now and again, I mean, just for the laughs. But your mind can play tricks on you, it can fool you, lie to you, especially when you're thinking about the past. When you remember something, it's free association, so it's whatever you remember it to be. There is the real and there is the unreal, but what is between the two? Nothingness? Time? Space? I don't have a clue, do you? It's definitely something to think about, but I've said too much, I think, so I should stop now, before I get myself in trouble. In New York, it is all talk, talk, talk, you can't stop talking. But here, in Bulgaria, I didn't want to talk, I wanted to listen. I was on my vacation, I wanted to relax, I wanted to dance. In the city, it's a race to the finish line, and the marathon never ends. Even Alabaster was getting tired of the city; in the summer, he goes away to recharge his batteries, in the winter, he becomes a hermit that never leaves his apartment. *New York is an insane asylum,* Alabaster says, *filled with sick doctors.* Like most of us, he loves the city, but he doesn't like it. But he's in too deep, he can't escape it, and, just like me, he can't find a way out. He has too much invested in this business, so he can't stop the roller coaster ride. But he still had a few things up his sleeve, a few things to get off his chest, and he wasn't going anywhere. I had a couple of shows coming up, but I had to get out, so I let Alabaster deal with all that drama. The art business is just like a casino: you have *winners*, and you have *losers*. The art world is a broken pinball machine, it has too many balls in play, and there is no return lane. In this business, it's a reversal of fortune, so the poor losers have the money, and the sore winners have none. I have no axe to grind, I only have my palette knife, and a blank canvas, so they better watch out! But in this world of secret handshakes and anonymous donors, there is no fair play, there is only the deal to make. Yes, there is the seller, and there is the buyer, then there is the price. The painter or dealer is usually the seller, and the collector is always the buyer. This business model is a crapshoot, because nothing is promised, and everything is on loan, so you can't trust anyone. When one of my paintings is sold, I will always get a call from Alabaster. He will have good news or bad news to tell me, but it doesn't really matter, because the machine never stops. I'm just a cog in the wheel, Alabaster is the motor, and he makes this old thing run. A painter is only as good as his dealer, so I was in very good hands. But the city was a world away, and I didn't have to worry about anything, because Alabaster was holding down the fort. But here, on this beach, I was a complete nobody, I was a stranger in a strange land, and that made me feel humble. Yes, I was on the outside looking in, which was the best place to be, I thought, on a night like this. Have you ever read *The Stranger* by Albert Camus? Well, I have, and, let me tell you, that book is the devil! What can I say, it kills me every time I read it, I am murdered by it. Meursault, the main character in the book, is condemned for killing a man. He does not play the game, he is his own man, so he will do what he has to do, he says, to make his mark. When he pulls the trigger on his pistol, and shoots the man on the beach, he is indifferent, he does not know why he did it. He is repressed, truthful, and forgotten, which makes him a stranger in his own society. But tonight, I wasn't repressed, in truth, I didn't want to forget anything, I wanted to remember everything. But we were still in line, after all this time, we were still waiting to get in, so I wanted to kill someone. I could hear the music playing on the outside, but I couldn't see the people dancing to it on the inside. While the beat bounced up and down, the crowd screamed for more, as the music got louder and louder. It was German techno music, I think, it was slow and low, and it had a sneaky rhythm to it, plus a hard driving bassline. I was ready to dance, I couldn't wait any longer, so I started dancing in line. Everyone was dancing; Yanko, Iskra, even my wife was dancing to the music. It was unbelievable, the groove was so hot, when I closed my eyes, I got completely lost in it. I could feel my heart beating, it was ticking like a clock, as the beat slid in and out of the pocket. My body had taken over my mind, it was so easy, I just let the music move me. When I opened my eyes, my wife was still dancing in front of me, but Yanko and Iskra had disappeared. She looked like an angel, I swear, she had wings on, as she twirled in a circle, I was in pure bliss. I was loss in her glow, she blinded me with her light, she was shining like a diamond. *Where is Yanko and Iskra?* I asked my wife. She didn't know, and she didn't seem that concerned about them, so I wasn't. *Don't worry, they'll turn up sooner or later,* she said, *they always do!* I could see the sign flashing over door, we were almost in Insomnia. What took us so long? It felt like an eternity. We come from the earth, I thought, and we'll return to the earth. We all have a death certificate with our name written on it, so I didn't have that much time left, it was my destiny, it was time to dance. I can't deny it, I'm just like the earthworm, as I crawl through the dirt, I leave a trail of tears behind me. If I went back to the egg and sperm, I would still be *me*, and that made me want to dance. Old Sigmund Freud never got dirty, he was a clean freak, he was all talk and no action. His struggle between *eros* and *death* was his own private pickle, and not some universal problem, that needed to be fixed. Eros had already found me, and she was standing right in front of me, so I had nothing to worry about. Death was at my door, it would knock on it sooner or later, but tonight I was alive, and I was going to dance my ass off. I was free as a bird, so nothing was going to stop me from flying high. Freud had a bunch childhood hang-ups that he never got over, thus they turned into adult hang-ups. He was one of the sad and lazy *discontents* that he always talked about, but he didn't have a good enough sense of humor to laugh at himself. Freud was a real quack, he made his theories up on the spot, and most of his crazy ideas never panned out. His books are hogwash, I really hate them, but I still read them, because they make me laugh so much. But enough about Freud, I didn't want to think about him anymore, *Freud is dead to me!* I told myself. He was ruining my vacation, and I wasn't going to let him. No, I didn't want to think, I wanted to dance, so I had come to the right place. Club Insomnia looked like a fantasy, it was all dolled up, and it was waiting to kiss me. Danielle Steel would love this place, I thought, it was her kind of place, and it had all of the qualities that she held so dear. I was no fan of hers, but that didn't mean that I couldn't be a fan. Yes, from now on, only best sellers for me, I said, only the cream of the crop and the tippy top. I had to give her a chance, if I didn't, I would surely regret it. I'm sure she could teach me a thing or two about love, but she's a drama queen, and I didn't want any drama tonight. Steel was out of the question, so I didn't even want to think about her. But she has millions of fans that adore her, that buy her books, so I had to respect her. Can they all be wrong? I don't think so. Even my mother likes her books, and she dosn't like anyone. Steel is the real deal, she knows how to get people hooked on her stories, and she uses any means necessary. But I still couldn't wrap my head around why she was so damn popular. She's a fluke, a hack, she's a lucky son of a bitch! Flukes are a dime a dozen, they grow on trees, they fall from the sky, so you can't understand them. I need to come up with my own theory about flukes, I thought, that can explain them a little bit better. What is the nature of a fluke? I wish I knew. Is it an accident, chance, coincidence, a windfall, or just plain luck? Then, there is the question about love. Is love always a fluke? I don't know, is it? Yes, my theory will try to explain the impossible, it will lay out my manifesto in black and white, and it will tell you what I really think. Let me just shut up for now, I don't want to say anything stupid, there is plenty of time left for that. And if I show you my cards now, you will see my bluff, so let me stop talking about flukes. I should stick to paintings, I don't know about anything else; I'm a painter, I know paintings. Some of my paintings were flukes, but who cares, I like them just the same. They are what they are, and nothing is going to change them. Once I paint them, they become relics to the past, so I forget all about them. Let me tell you, painters are the best fakers in the world, we can fake just about anything on the canvas. It happens so fast, when I paint, I walk it like I talk it, if you know what I mean. A painting is beyond your control, you have no power over it, it has complete power over you. My wife is a fake fluke, she came straight from the stars, and she landed right on my lap. But she is as real as it gets, like a lightning strike, she came without warning, and she zapped me in the head. Yes, before I knew it, I was in love with a fluke, after I said *yes*, I was suddenly married! I don't think Freud ever mentioned flukes, it wasn't in his wheelhouse, so he didn't mess around with them. Yes, my fluke theory would be about love, it would be short and sweet, and funny as hell. Freud got too deep into his mind, so he lost control of his body. He was a dreamer, he had a huge imagination, and he used it to his advantage. He was just like Lewis Carroll, he made it all up as he went along. They're like Siamese twins; they share the same mind, and ponder the same questions. If I had to choose between the two, I would rather read a book by Lewis Carroll. Give me a reason to read *Alice's Adventures in Wonderland*, and I will read it. When I fall down the rabbit hole, I always laugh my ass off. Please don't make me read Freud, because I will throw up. His *Analysis of a Phobia in a Five-Year-Old-Boy* is rubbish, it's nothing but trash. What can I say, I'm more of a Mad Hatter than a mad chatter, so I was ready to dance my ass off. But I wasn't here for Sigmund Freud, no, I was here for Sir Freud, and I had to remind myself of that. Tonight, I didn't care about my mind, only my body mattered, so the music was my medicine. Above the entrance door, in pink neon, the words *Rabbit Hole* flashed on and off. I had to laugh at the sign, it was too funny, because my adventure was just about to begin. You can't escape your destiny, and I came face to face with mine, when a butterfly introduced herself to me. Of course, her name was *Alice*, and she was here to *help me* on my journey, she said. She had a wicker basket in her hand, that was filled with little pieces of white candy, and she had the cutest smile on her face. She was giving out candy to anybody who wanted some, and I couldn't say no, so she handed me two pieces of candy, then she said: *I'll see you on the other side!* I unwrapped one piece, I put it on my tongue, and I began to suck on it. Then I gave my wife the other piece, and she popped it into her mouth. It was bittersweet, and a little sour, it tasted just like a Life Saver. When I swallowed it, I shut my eyes for a moment, I wanted to cherish the flavor. When I opened my eyes again, my wife was gone, she had vanished! *Where is my wife?* I asked Alice. She didn't say a single word, she ignored me, like I wasn't even there. All of a sudden, I got goosebumps, my skin was tingling, I felt a chill go through my body, and my eyes began to well up with tears. I tried to stop crying, but I couldn't, I was crying like a baby and I didn't know why. I cried years of tears in minutes, but it wasn't enough, because they kept coming. When I finally stopped crying, I closed my eyes for a moment, then I gathered myself. As soon as I opened my eyes again, my wife was standing right there in front of me. I couldn't believe it, she was back, it was such a relief to see her, so I gave her a big kiss. *Why are you crying?* she said. I didn't know why, I didn't have a clue, and I told her that. I was a crying mess; I was cold, I was grinding my teeth, and my heart was racing. But my wife didn't seem to care how bad I felt, she just stood there and smiled at me. She was talking, but I couldn't understand what she was saying to me. Her lips were moving, and no words were coming out, so I got worried. For some reason, the people in line were dressed like animals, which seemed odd, because it wasn't a costume party. But I didn't care about the animals, I just wanted to get in, so I ignored them. Then they started making animal noises, they were croaking, oinking, quacking, roaring. I was sweating, my throat was beginning to burn, and my limbs felt very wobbly. When I looked up into the trees, there were birds everywhere, and they were all staring at me. They made me nervous, I tried to ignore them, but they kept chirping at me. To my left stood a tall white cat with a bushy mustache and a long beard; and to my right was a fat brown mouse, who looked bigger than a hippo. At first, I thought I was seeing things, but I wasn't, because the cat and mouse were playing games with me. When the cat licked his lips, the mouse did the same thing; they were doing their best *Tom and Jerry* routine, and they were killing! I couldn't stop laughing at them, they were full of jokes, they were cracking me up. I had never seen a cat and mouse duo like this before, they were hilarious, and they were having a great time. Then the cat surprised me, when it suddenly jumped into the air and did a back flip onto a tree branch. The birds looked scared, because this cat meant business, and it really wanted something to eat. The tree was vibrating, and the branches were dancing in unison, as the cat made its way up to the birds. When I took a closer look at the tree branches, I realized that they were not made out of wood, they were made out of snakes. Yes, real snakes, I swear, I saw them with my own eyes! As they slithered around the leaves, they changed colors; from green to blue, blue to yellow, yellow to red. They were like wiggling rainbows, I couldn't look away, the snakes were too beautiful. Then the line began to move, and I moved with it, which made me the happiest man on earth. My wife was standing right by my side, so I had nothing to worry about, it was only a matter of time, I thought, before we were both inside. When we finally got to the front entrance, the green lizard in the ticket booth winked at me, then he waved us in, so we walked right on through the door. I don't know why he let us in for free, but I was impressed by his hospitality, he really made us feel welcome. The lizard was dressed in a green leather suit and cowboy boots, which made him look like a pimp. His name was *Moola*, he said, and he was here to show us a good time. I didn't believe Moola, so I asked him if that was his real name. *Yes, that's my name, don't wear it out*, he said, then he slapped me across my face. I didn't know what to do, laugh at him or punch him, but I didn't do anything. When Moola handed me the two tickets, he told me to give them to the purple caterpillar, so that's what I did. *Madame Piggy* was a very purple, very large, and very mean caterpillar. Before we could enter the club, we had to be officially *chimed in*, she said, so she took out her metal gong and she banged it twice, then she yelled: *Nemo saltat sobrius!* Yes, she was right, *nobody dances sober*, when I heard that, I burst out laughing. I couldn't believe it, Madame Piggy spoke perfect Latin. Of course, my wife didn't say a word, she agreed with the caterpillar, so she wanted to find the bar. The vibe inside was very relaxed and very chill, it was my kind of place. Most of the people had tea cups in their hands, which seemed a bit weird for a dance club, but we were in Bulgaria, so I wasn't that surprised. *It's tea time*, I told my wife, but she was no longer my wife, she had turned into a pigeon. She nodded her feathered head yes, then she cooed at me and she flew away. My wife had turned into a pigeon, I didn't know what to do, so I just watched her fly away. While I stood there stunned, a white rabbit came up to me, and he asked me if I wanted milk and sugar in my tea. This is high quality service, I thought, this is a real classy place. *Yes, please, with extra sugar,* I said. Then the silly rabbit hopped away, and he disappeared into his hole. After a couple of seconds, a blue walrus appeared with my tea; he served it to me on a gold tray. But before I could drink my tea, the walrus had a riddle for me: *Why is the raven like a writing desk?* I was amused by his silly question, it sounded very familiar, but I didn't give him an answer. Some riddles deserve another riddle, so I gave him one of my own: *Why is the owl like a painter?* When I said it, he got mad, he looked pissed off, like I had offended him. He didn't give me his answer, so I gave him my answer: *Because an owl is a solitary and nocturnal creature.* The walrus seemed perplexed, like he didn't get the joke, so I waved him away. I took a sip of my tea, it tasted sweet and earthy, like mushrooms, but it was too hot, so I couldn't drink it. When the walrus came back, I put my cup back on his tray, which really upset him, and he started foaming at the mouth, as he huffed and puffed, he was singing: *I am the egg man, they are the egg men, I am the walrus!* I tried to ignore him, but I couldn't, he wouldn't stop singing. I needed to do something quick, it was time to dance, and I wasn't going to let a blue walrus ruin my night. When I took another sip of my tea, I spit it right back out; I couldn't help it, my mind wasn't right, the tea was too cold. The walrus didn't care, he kept on singing: *I am he as you are he as you are me, and we are all together!* Then he did something stupid, he threw an egg at me. When I turned my head, the egg was already in the air, but I saw it coming, so I ducked out of the way and it went right over my head. But as soon as I looked up, he threw another egg at me. This one missed me by a mile, his aim was shit, and I was too fast for him. To try to confuse him, I started dancing circles around him, which only made him more confused. When the walrus started dancing with me, I almost lost it, I couldn't stop laughing. After we did a bunch of circles together, he got tired, so he collapsed into my arms. He had fainted, he was out like a light, he was passed out. I didn't know what to do, but I needed to revive him, so I grabbed my cup again and I filled it up with tea. I had to do something, it was now or never, it was my time to shine. When I splashed his face with the tea, the walrus woke up! He looked surprised, but he was alive, and that was the good news. And, the bad news, well, he was really pissed off, so now I had to watch my back. As he jiggled away, he had a few choice words for me: *See how they run like pigs from a gun, see how they fly, I hope you die!* I was happy to see him go, it was a big relief, I was in no mood to fight, I wanted to dance. I went straight to the dance floor, then I found my spot, right by the speaker. The music was sent from heaven, it took over my body, I had no control over it. I was finally dancing, I couldn't stop my feet from moving, they were following the rhythm, as the groove lifted my spirit up. When I closed my eyes, I let the music take me, so it took me away. The dance floor was a real zoo; I was immediately surrounded by a flock of seagulls and a family of flamingos. The music had them in a frenzy, so they were dancing like there was no tomorrow. As I twisted with the flamingos, I rubbed shoulders with the seagulls, and I was covered in pink and white feathers. I couldn't see Sir Freud from the dance floor, but I could surely hear him, his music was loud and clear, so I was dancing my ass off. It was impossible to stop dancing, my mind was saying no, but my body was saying yes. Sir Freud already had me under his command, I was his slave and he was my master. Then I found the DJ booth, I could see Sir Freud now; well, I couldn't see his face, it was too dark, I could only see his two eyes. *Who are you?* I screamed at him. Sir Freud couldn't hear me over the music, so he didn't give me an answer, but I didn't care, because I knew who I was. I was a pink flamingo! Yes, the flamingos had taken me under their wings, and I was now one of them. I was pink and I was proud, so I was dancing my ass off. When I closed my eyes, I lost all control, I didn't resist, and I let Sir Freud lead the way. Dance music can do this to you, it can make you lose total control of your body and mind. I danced for hours, I never left the dance floor, and the pink flamingos never left my side. I was on it for the entire night, until the sun came up. When I got closer to the DJ booth, I finally saw Sir Freud up close. As soon as I got a glimpse of him, I burst out laughing, I couldn't believe what I saw: I saw a giant sea turtle! Yes, you heard me, he was a giant sea turtle. His shell was olive green, and his face was spotted with black and orange. As he spun his vinyl records with his tiny reptile feet, he bobbed his little head up and down to the beat. The crowd was going wild for him, and he felt it, so he was letting it all hang out. He was hilarious to watch, I couldn't take my eyes off him; I mean, come on, a giant sea turtle named Sir Freud is funny as hell. His music had taken over my body, I was in a dance rapture of some kind, I was in heaven. The crowd had inspired Sir Freud, so he was now breakdancing in the DJ booth. I saw him do a couple of flips, then he spun on his shell, and he ended with a sick headstand. Sir Freud was dancing his ass off, and that made the crowd go nuts. He was really getting into it, so I had to watch him. The flamingos got jealous, they were going crazy, flapping their wings, and doing a samba dance around me. Then the walrus reappeared with my tea, I was a bit surprised, I didn't expect to see him again. When I took a sip, I swallowed it with caution, because I didn't trust the walrus. But this time, my tea was at the perfect temperature, so it warmed my heart and soul.

When I finished my cup, I thanked the walrus, and I said: *Slave, thou hast slain me, villain, take my purse, if I ever bury my body!* He seemed happy to hear this verse, because he gave me a big kiss on the cheek. He looked very proud of himself, like he had done something special, he didn't say a word to me, he just kissed me. My wife was now circling the dance floor, trying to find a place to land. Well, I think it was my wife, because this pigeon looked just like her. I had never seen her fly like this before, she had so much grace, I couldn't take my eyes off her. Eventually, after a few loops around me, and a couple of narrow escapes, she came back down to the dance floor. When she landed, I lost sight of her, so she got lost in the crowd. I'll find her, *sooner or later*, I thought, when the time is right. Sir Freud's music was a blend of many styles, and his track selection was truly inspiring. I couldn't stop dancing, I was a dancing machine. When I finally found my wife, she was no longer a pigeon, now, she was a flamingo, just like me. I couldn't believe it, it was impossible, her pink evolution happened in seconds. She evolved right there before my eyes: one moment she was a pigeon, the next moment she was a flamingo. It was natural selection in action, it was the chicken before the egg, it was life after death. As I watched my wife's white feathers turn pink, I started to cry, I could barely control myself, because she looked so beautiful. She's a great dancer, well, she prances more than she dances, so she's a great prancer. She used to be a ballerina, she knows how to glide, he loves to slide, and that makes me high. As she spun on her tail feathers, she did a windmill kick over her head, then she did a pirouette. I could have watched her dance all night long, but a bunch of horny polar bears came between us. They were acting like freaks, sliding up and down on each other, and doing their very best to get noticed. I ignored them, and bears hate to be ignored, so they didn't stick around for very long.

The seals were acting silly, as usual, they were doing bellyflops on the dance floor. They were fun to watch, but they weren't great dancers, they kept bumping into me, so I was getting mad. Then I saw a dolphin getting down with an orca, it was awesome, they were acting like best friends. A giant lobster wanted to show me this new dance, so I let him. It was pretty easy to learn: first, you shake your hips around, and you swing your hands above your head, then you wave them in the air like you just don't care. The lobster was right, it was easy, so I danced like there was no tomorrow. My legs were on fire, they sizzled with each new step, I didn't what to do. But my legs weren't on fire, no, they were being electrocuted by an electric eel. It was wrapped around my ankles, I couldn't move my legs, I was in real pain. And this eel meant business, I could feel it burning inside, every few seconds it would shock me with a jolt of electricity. I tried to wrestle the eel, but the voltage was too high, so I had no chance of survival. But I got lucky, the eel got bored of me, he had had enough of my shit, and he finally let go of my legs. I was still in danger, though, because a tiger shark was now swimming around me; and every time it passed by, it would give me the evil eye. It was really creeping me out, it even brushed me a few times with its dorsal fin, just to show me who the boss was. The shark acted tough, like it wanted some trouble, but it was all a big bluff, because after a couple more brushes with death, it swam away like a sore loser. I was still kind of scared, so I got off the dance floor and I went to the bar. I was beyond thirsty, I was dehydrated, I had been dancing all night, and I needed some water. The bartender was also a bird, she was a beautiful raven, but she looked ravenous, so I avoided eye contact with her. When I ordered a water, she started singing a dreadful birdsong to me, it was a torturous tune that made my ears hurt. I wanted the pain to stop, so I asked her to stop singing, but she didn't listen to me, she kept on singing. I asked her for a bottle of water, but she gave me a bottle of beer, but I didn't care, I chugged it down. After two more bottles of beer, I went over to one of the speakers and I stood right in front of it. I couldn't believe it, my trick worked, I couldn't hear the raven's song anymore. I was happy to be back on the dance floor with the animals. Sir Freud's music had tamed us, he had freed us from our cages, and I could hear freedom ringing in my ears. When I saw a cobra playing with a mouse, I got worried, but they were dancing in harmony, so there was nothing to worry about. The vibe was great, until the vultures came, they all had two cocktails, and they wanted to party hard tonight, they said, *like they do in the Poland!* They were typical vultures, they let it all hang out, and they didn't think about tomorrow. I tried to talk to them but they ignored me, they were here to party and I was here to dance, so we had nothing in common. I was already dead to them, I was nice and warm, and they were waiting for their meat. When your destiny comes for you, you have to accept it, but I wasn't ready yet, I still needed a little more time. What I really needed was to get away from these vultures, so I came up with a plan, I bought them some more cocktails. And that did the trick, they were now drunk, and they couldn't stand up. I still wanted to dance, but I really needed to find my wife, I missed her, so I started looking for her. But I didn't have to find my wife, because she found me, and when she did, I was in ecstasy. When I breathed in, I closed my eyes, then I breathed out, I opened my eyes, and my wife was now dancing right there in front of me. *Where have you been?* I said. She stayed quiet, she didn't say anything, she just fell into my arms. Her skin was sweaty, her eyes were bloodshot, and her hands were ice-cold. It was a miracle that she had found me again, I almost didn't believe it, I was lucky. *Last night the DJ saved my life,* my wife told me. Those were the best words that I had heard all night, they were the perfect words, I thought, to describe last night. Most of it was a blur to me, my memory was shot, so I couldn't remember anything. But I do remember meeting a cat, yes, a black cat, and his name was *Chester.* Don't laugh, that was his real name, I swear, and he gave me some cheese from Cheshire. What can I say, a cat is a cat is a cat, but this cat was a *cheesy* cat. My wife had seen the same cat, she said, *singing a loony tune on the dance floor!* It had to be the same cat, because he was singing the same tune when I met him. Now, I have a surprise for you, are you ready? Chester came back! Yes, he reappeared right before my eyes, and he was holding a silver tray of desserts. He had cookies and tarts, he said, *and they're delicious!* I couldn't help but laugh at him, I mean, come on, a grinning cat with a tray of desserts is the definition of funny. *The cookies will make you smaller, and the tarts will make you taller!* Chester told us. I took a cookie and my wife took a tart, then we both ate them. It didn't take long, I felt the sugar rush right away, as soon as I swallowed it, I got smaller. My wife was still pink, but she got taller, and bigger, then she turned into an elephant. For some reason, Chester got scared, so he ran away like a scaredy-cat. When I kissed her long trunk, she flapped her ears and stomped her feet, then she gave me a kiss. If love is a dance, then it's a waltz that never ends, I thought, you have to learn the steps, if you don't, you will trip and fall. But you have to get right back up, if you want to keep on dancing. Yes, my mind was still here, but my body was gone; I had only the future to look forward to, my past was of no use to me. *Out of mind,* I told my wife, *out of sight!* I was still alive, and I still wanted to dance, but I couldn't move my body. The sun was just coming up over the horizon, the hills were blue and green, and the sky was pink and white. It was such a beautiful morning to be alive, a cool mist was in the air, the wind was blowing from the east, and I could smell lavender in the wind. When the sun hit my face, it tingled with pure vitamin D, it felt like a blessing from the god Helios. Luckily, my wife and I found a beach chair, so we could finally sit down. A bunch of ravens were staring at me, but I had no energy to scare them away, so I let them stare. I was dead tired, I had nothing left to say, I just sat there with the ravens. I have no idea how I got *here*, but I was here with my wife, and that was enough for me. Her hair smelled like lilac and vanilla, and her skin was as sticky as honey. The sky was blue, the sun was yellow, and the sea was green. I could still hear the music playing, but it was at a lower decibel level, so I could hear my wife breathing heavy. Her chest was going up and down, which was a good sign, and she still had a pulse, so there was nothing to worry about. I was in very bad shape, I could see and smell, but I couldn't feel my body. I wasn't in any pain, because I was completely numb, so I didn't feel anything. My mind was mush; last night had a story to tell, but I couldn't remember it. Well, I remember: waiting in line, eating a piece of candy, then seeing a bunch of animals. I had a wonderful night, I think, I had a ball, I had a blast! It was a night to remember, for sure, but I couldn't remember anything. But I didn't want to think, I was tired of thinking, so I turned my mind off. When my wife wakes up, she will tell me everything about last night, I told myself. But now, she was resting, her body was nice and warm, she was at peace, so I let her sleep. My mouth was dry, I had cotton-mouth, I really needed some water. My shoes and socks were nowhere to be seen, they were long gone–I must have lost them somewhere along the way, I thought. I couldn't feel my feet, but that didn't matter, because I couldn't feel me legs. For some reason, I had silver glitter all over me, and there was red lipstick smeared on my shirt. I was tired, so I closed my eyes, and I had a vision: A little bird was trapped in a net and it couldn't get out. Yes, it needed some help, I untangled the net and I freed the bird. This was just a vision, but I wanted to fly, so I became a bird. I couldn't believe it, I was in the air in no time, flying like a bird, I was free. I was miles above the beach, high in the sky, I was sailing through the atmosphere. Up here, I could see my body on the beach, I wasn't moving; and my wife's body was next to me, and she wasn't moving either. I had left my body behind, I was now flying solo, like an eagle in the sky, I didn't have a care in the world. In the thin air, I was aimless, so I got lost in the cirrus clouds. When I glanced down at the beach, Insomnia looked like the head of a pin, it was so tiny, it was almost invisible. My body was down there, but my mind was up here, and I was as free as a bird. Without the burden of the earth, I flew anywhere and everywhere, as I sailed through the ice crystals, gravity didn't exist, I was weightless, and I had nothing holding me back. But what goes up must come down, they say, so I came down like a comet! My time in the sky didn't last that long, before I knew it, I was free-falling back to earth. I was doing fine, until my altitude started to drop, then I got nervous. I was going too fast, the earth was getting bigger and bigger, I needed to slow down, but I couldn't. I had no fear, as I tumbled back to earth, I looked death straight in the eye. As I got closer and closer to the beach, I got more excited, I felt the sweet heat of speed and I loved it. I couldn't stop myself from falling, it was too late to stop, I had no control, it was out of my hands. As my whole life flashed before my eyes, my past became smaller and smaller, and my future became bigger and bigger. I wasn't scared, I was too high to be scared, I was laughing, I was smiling, I was falling. When I finally hit the ground, my body made a loud thump, I sounded like a piece of raw meat. As soon as I opened my eyes, I was back on the beach chair with my wife, and I was still alive. I was like Icarus, I had flown too close to the sun, and I got burnt, but I was still breathing. And my wife was still breathing, too, so I I could relax. A couple of people were still dancing in the sand, but they were barely moving their feet, they looked like snails, and they were the last ones standing. I took a peek at my watch, but the sun's glare was too bright, so I had no idea what time it was. I used to think that time was on my side, but now, here on this beach, I was almost sure of it. I felt timeless, but I didn't know why, it was just a feeling that I had inside. *What is time?* Well, time is the eternity of my next return, so I would have to wait for mine. *What is love?* Love is a forest fire, and my wife is the match. I'm lucky to be here, I've died and gone to heaven, I said to myself. When the music stopped, the speakers went silent. Sir Freud's set had finally come to an end, and it was time for the next DJ. *When the music stops*, they say, *is when the dancing stops*, so the snails stopped dancing. This beach in Bulgaria made me think about another beach; it reminded me of Picnic Island, a beach that I used to go to when I was a young boy. My family really loved this beach, so it was the only beach that we would go to. I don't know why it was called *Picnic Island*, because there were no picnic tables, and it wasn't even an island. This beach was hard to find, so most people got lost, which made it kind of a secret spot. My family loved this beach, but I hated it; it was dirty, smelly, and littered with trash. Of course, my family got lost every time, because my father would always make the wrong turn. It was an old hippie beach, clothing was optional, so it was *au naturel* all year round. My mother loved this beach, it was a sentimental place to her; my father had taken her there on their first date. She still talks about that night, just like it was yesterday, and she can tell you every last detail about that night. I don't remember that much about Picnic Island, but I do remember the crabs. Yes, the sand crabs were everywhere, they would take over the entire beach, which made it was unbearable. Back then, I was scared of crabs, I would have nightmares, and my mom would always have to come into my room and calm me down. One day at the Picnic Island really stands out: I fell asleep on the beach, when I woke up, the crabs were attacking me. I still have nightmares about that day, I will never forget it. When I woke up from my nap, hundreds of crabs were crawling all over my body. I can still remember their needle claws pinching me, as I screamed out in pain. Of course, my mother came and rescued me, when she grabbed a bucket of water and she drenched me with it. As soon as the water hit the crabs, they scattered back into their little holes. I was so happy, the crabs were all gone and there was no more pain. Well, at least, that's how I remember it, but I could be wrong, because I was only a boy. My mother might remember it differently, but that is her story to tell, not mine. I could be mistaken, maybe there were only a couple of crabs, and not hundreds of them. I don't remember, but it doesn't really matter, the past is the past, and it was so long ago. That was then, *this is now,* I said, as I closed my eyes. The present moment was all that I cared about; at this moment, on this beach, my mind was completely empty. Yes, I was mindless, at last, I had no thoughts in my head, only the facts. But I like to fudge the facts, tinker with the truth, and make shit up, so you can't always believe me. The details of a story always change, but the song remains the same. This story is factually true, the real names have been changed to protect the innocent, other than that, I swear, it's nothing but the truth! When I opened my eyes again, I saw my life blowing in the wind, I couldn't believe it, I was still *here.* I felt no pain, I was comfortably numb, it was heaven on earth. I could feel some object in my back pocket, it was nudging my behind; it wasn't that big, it felt flexible but firm. I couldn't tell what it was, but I was dead weight, so I couldn't move any part of my body. And the body and mind work against each other, they fight to the bitter end, until one surrenders. I couldn't feel my body, I was stuck with my mind, I had to find out what was in my pocket. I tried to lift my left arm, but it wouldn't move. Then I tried my right arm, and nothing happened. I needed to try harder, so with all of my will that was still left inside me, I jerked my right arm up onto my lap. I was surprised how heavy my arm was, it felt like a brick when it fell on my lap. I could only feel my thumb and forefinger, my other fingers were useless. I didn't know what to do next, so I just sat there in a fetal position. After a few minutes of baby talk, I got a little burst of energy, and I could move my hand. With a twist of my wrist, I guided my hand into my back pocket. My two good fingers slid easily into the hole, they had no resistance at all. When I lifted my arm, I freaked out, because I didn't move it, someone else did. I don't know who moved my arm, I didn't do it, but my arm moved, I swear it did! Who moved it? God? I don't know who in the hell moved it, but it wasn't God, I know that much. Was it one of the Greek gods? Was it Apollo? Dionysus? Poseidon? Well, it could have been any one of them, I mean, a god is a god is a god, if you know what I mean. But I had no time for God, or for any gods, I was already pass that point, I just wanted to know what was in my pocket. When I fingered the object, I pinched my two fingers together, then I slowly pulled it out. It was an easy operation, I was in and out in a jiffy, so I didn't have to wait to see the object. As soon as I saw the *it*, I burst out laughing! What can I say, the comedy gods were good to me: it was that old polaroid that I had stolen from my wife's grandparents apartment. Well, *stolen* is too harsh of a word, I *borrowed* it, that sounds much better. I don't know why I stole it, but I didn't feel guilty about it, it was just one picture, I thought. I was innocent until proven guilty, and nobody saw me take it, so I had nothing to worry about. If a picture is worth a thousand words, then this picture was worth a million, because it said everything that it needed to say. When I studied the photograph up close, I searched for a vanishing point, but I couldn't find one, so I gave up. My wife's grandparents looked truly in love, I could see it in their eyes, it was written all over their faces. I don't know where the photo was taken, but they were way overdressed, I thought, so they looked foolish in front of the old ruins. But the look of love always looks foolish, it's beautiful and ugly, and it's always ridiculous to look at. I really wanted to know where the picture had been taken, but it was almost impossible to know, because there was no defining landmarks. It could have been anywhere in the world, I mean, it could have taken almost anyplace on earth. As I looked closer at the photograph, I suddenly found a clue, at the bottom right corner, there appeared to be a stone pier. It looked very familiar, like I'd seen it before, but I couldn't place it. I should have noticed the pier before, but I didn't, I guess I was distracted. Then I looked even closer at the picture, and it started to jog my memory. If you look long and hard at something, sooner or later, it will reveal itself to you. When I looked at the polaroid, I saw my life flash in front of my eyes, then it came to me: the pier was from Perla Beach. Yes, without a doubt, the picture had been taken here in Primorsko. I couldn't tell the exact year, there was no way to know that, but it was surely taken in the Seventies. Their clothes and hairstyles gave it away, which only made me laugh even harder. This story is a little too kitsch for its own britches, but I don't care, because if Kundera can do it, then I can do it! I could barely hold the polaroid between my two fingers, so when a strong gust of wind came along, it went spinning down the beach, and the picture was gone with the wind. As I watched the picture of my wife's grandparents slowly disappear, I couldn't help but think about the two of us. We're just like them, I thought, we were on vacation, and we were way overdressed. But we were still alive, unlike them, so we still had a fighting chance. I still couldn't move my body, I was helpless to do anything, I was fading fast. When my wife finally opened her eyes, she had a peaceful look on her face, she didn't look scared, she looked at peace with herself. Then she said three last words: *Where am I?* I was surprised that she didn't know where she was, but it had been a long and crazy night, so I told her where. *You're in Insomnia,* I said, but she didn't seem to hear me, so I said it again. It was too late, she was already out like a light. She took a deep breath, sighed, then she closed her eyes. She really needed to rest, so I let her sleep. My body was still numb, but my mind was racing, and I needed to calm down. I didn't want my mind playing any more tricks on me, so closed my eyes. When the music started up again, my mind began to shut down. I was happy, because I didn't have to think anymore. But this time, it was house music, not techno music, it was all silky sax, milky horns, and rolling drums. Over a funky beat, the sultry singer sang her song: *The house, the house, the house is on fire!* I wanted to dance, so I opened my eyes again, but my body was useless. I was exhausted, finished, I had no more seconds on the clock, I was out of time, I was done! *How did I get here?* I said. I still didn't have a good answer, but I didn't care, because I was on my vacation. I wanted to sleep, but I couldn't, the music was now too loud. I saw the girl with the candy basket again, but she didn't see me this time, so she walked right on by us. One piece of candy had been enough, I didn't need another one, I was feeling just fine. When I looked at the Black Sea, it was bluer than ever, it was super blue, it was almost too blue. While the house beat bounced up and down, the bass bottomed out, then the bells began to chime, as she chanted her mantra: *The house, the house, the house is on fire!* The singer had a voice like an angel, I was hypnotized by her, as she slowly put me into a trance. I couldn't believe my ears, but I had to believe them, because the music was putting me to sleep. *The house, the house, the house is on fire!* My eyes wouldn't stay open any longer, I was drifting off, so I finally closed them. First, it got all black, then it got all white. I was a lost particle of dust, I was expanding into the cosmos, I was in the celestial void, I was infinite, and I was eternally grateful. I can't tell you where I *went*, I was here nor there, with no space and time, I was everywhere and nowhere, I was hydrogen and helium, I was an interstellar nobody, I was lost, I was *nada*, I guess, I was somewhere *in between*, if you know what I mean.